Francis Bond Head

The Horse and his Rider

Francis Bond Head

The Horse and his Rider

ISBN/EAN: 9783337389604

Hergestellt in Europa, USA, Kanada, Australien, Japan

Cover: Foto ©Andreas Hilbeck / pixelio.de

Weitere Bücher finden Sie auf **www.hansebooks.com**

THE HORSE AND HIS RIDER.

By SIR FRANCIS B. HEAD, Bart.

He grew unto his seat;
And to such wond'rous doing brought his horse,
As he had been incorps'd and demy-natur'd
With the brave beast.

Hamlet, Act iv. Scene 7.

SECOND EDITION.

LONDON:

JOHN MURRAY, ALBEMARLE STREET.

1861.

PREFACE.

THE writer of this little volume deems it only fair to forewarn his readers that he is not, and never has been, an inhabitant of that variegated region in creation commonly called " the sporting world."

He has never bred, raced, steeple-chased, nor betted sixpence on any colt, filly, horse, or mare. He has never seen, nor been seen by, the Jockey-Club. He has never been on the turf. He does not belong to " the ring."

Nevertheless, sometimes in the performance of public duties,—sometimes from private inclination,—sometimes for the benefit of his health,—sometimes for recreation, —sometimes for rumination,—sometimes to risk his life, —and more than once to save it, he has, throughout a long and chequered career, had to do an amount of rough-riding, a little larger than has fallen to the lot of many men.

. His observations and reflections on horses and horsemen he now ventures to submit to that portion only of the community who, like himself, preferring a long tether to a short one, take exercise on four legs, instead of on two.

A 2

CONTENTS.

MAN AND HIS RIDER.

MODE, IN NORTHERN PARTS OF SOUTH AMERICA, OF RIDING
OVER THE ANDES, ON A RED INDIAN.

QUERY, *which* IS "THE SAVAGE?"

To face page 7.

THE HORSE AND HIS RIDER.

THE HORSE.

IN almost every region of the globe, not only on its surface, but at different depths beneath it, the history of the horse is recorded.

"Fossil remains," says Colonel Hamilton Smith in the twelfth volume of the Naturalist's Library, " of the horse have been found in nearly every part of the world. His teeth lie in the Polar ice along with the bones of the Siberian mammoth; in the Himalaya mountains with lost, and but recently obtained, genera; in the caverns of Ireland; and, in one instance, from Barbary, completely fossilized. His bones, accompanied by those of the eléphant, rhinoceros, tiger, and hyæna, rest by thousands in the caves in Constadt; in Sevion at Argenteuil with those of the mastodon; in Val d'Arno and on the borders of the Rhine with colossal urus."

But what is most deserving of attention is that while all the other genera and species, found under the same conditions, have either ceased to exist, or have removed to higher temperatures, the horse alone has remained to the present time in the same regions, without, it would appear, any protracted interruption; fragments of his skeleton continuing to be traced upwards, in successive formations, to the present surface of the earth—the land we live in.

In like manner in history, sacred, profane, and modern, the horse is to be found omnipresent, sharing in the conquests, in the defeats, in the prosperity, in the adversity, in the joys, in the sorrows, in the occupations, and in the amusements of man.

In Genesis xlvii. 17, Moses records that the Egyptians (1729 years before Christ), at a time when the famine was sore in the land of Canaan, gave to Joseph their *horses* in exchange for bread.

Two hundred and thirty-eight years afterwards (1491 B.C.), six hundred chosen chariots for nobles and generals, all the war chariots of Egypt armed with iron to break the enemy's battalions, *the horsemen*, and all the host of Pharaoh, in their pursuit of the children of Israel, were overthrown in the midst of the Red Sea, so that there remained not so much as one of them—(Exodus, chap. xiv.)

" Then sang Moses and the children of Israel this song unto the Lord, and spake, saying, I will sing unto the Lord, for he has triumphed gloriously : *the horse and his rider* hath he thrown into the sea."—Exodus, chap. xv.

The Canaanites whom Joshua engaged at the waters of Merom had *cavalry,* and a multitude of chariots drawn by *horses.* Sisera, general of Jabin, King of Hazor, had 900 chariots of iron. Judah could not get possession of the lands because the ancient inhabitants of the country were strong in chariots of iron. The Philistines, in their war against Saul, had 30,000 chariots and 6000 *horsemen*. David having taken 1000 chariots of war from Hadadezer, King of Syria, hamstrung the *horses*, and burned 900 chariots. During the latter periods of the Jewish monarchy Palestine abounded in horses.

In 1 Kings, chap. iv., it is stated that Solomon had 40,000 stalls *of horses* for his chariots, and 12,000 *horsemen*.

Cyntacus, a King of Ethiopia, entered Egypt at the head of 100,000 cavalry; and from that period to Balaklava, and from it to the last battle in modern history, horses in greater or less numbers have shared in the dangers of war.

In many instances the history of an individual horse forms part and parcel of the history of his rider : accordingly we learn that Bucephalus (so called because his head resembled that of a bull, Βου κεφαλος), when thirty years old, saved the life of Alexander the Great, who, in remembrance, built a city which he called after his name.

We are, moreover, taught in our schools, that the Emperor C. Caligula, as an especial honour to his favourite horse, not only created him a high-priest and consul, but caused him to live in marble apartments, in which he stalked about adorned with the most valuable trappings and pearls the Roman empire could supply.

In statuary, ancient as well as modern, the horse lives with his rider.

On the frieze of the Temple of Minerva, in the Acropolis of Athens, at Nineveh, and numerous other localities, are to be seen sculptured or painted, more or less beautifully, ancient figures of men on horseback.

In all the great cities of Europe the horse and his rider, or rather the rider and his horse, are ornaments deemed worthy to occupy conspicuous positions in the most important thoroughfares. Accordingly in London, within a few hundred yards of each other, are to be seen equestrian statues of Kings Charles I., William III., George III., and George IV.

Mounted on one charger, the Duke of Wellington in his cocked hat and feathers, military cloak, sword, pistols and spurs, in all weathers, rides triumphantly on the summit of an arch at the western end of London, while, at the same moment, in pantaloons and shoes, without hat, stirrups, or spurs, mounted on another charger, he appears, as a sentinel, in front of the Bank of England, the commercial heart of the empire.

Among the great potentates of the earth, the coin that is most currently used, in proffers to each other of amity and friendship, is *a horse*. And accordingly, the

Beys of Tunis, of Algiers, and Egypt; every sovereign in Europe, including the Czar of Russia, and the Sultan of the Turks; the Emperor of Morocco, the Kings of Persia and Abyssinia, and other rulers of smaller name, have transmitted to the Queen of Great Britain, with due compliments, specimens of their finest *horses*.

In the Life of Bruce, the Abyssinian traveller, it is recorded that Fasil, after having assembled the leaders of the Galla tribes, said to the noble Briton, "Now, before all these men, ask me any thing you have at heart, and be it what it may, they know I cannot deny it to you!" Bruce, of course, asked to be conducted immediately to the head of the Nile. Fasil then turned to his seven chiefs, who got up. They all stood round in a circle and raised the palms of their hands, while he and the Galla with great apparent devotion repeated together a prayer, about a minute long. "Now," says Fasil, "go in peace: you are a Galla. This is a curse upon them and their children, their corn, grass, and cattle, if ever they lift their hand against you or yours, or do not defend you to the utmost, if attacked by others." Upon this, Bruce offered to kiss his hand, and they all went to the door of the tent, where there stood a very handsome grey horse. "Take this horse," said Fasil, "as a present from me. But do not mount it yourself. Drive it before you, saddled and bridled

as it is.   No man of Maitsha will touch you when he
sees *that horse*,"—which proved a magician that led him
towards his object—an Ægis that shielded him on his
way.

In like manner to the people of France, the '*Moniteur*'
has just officially made the two following announce-
ments :—

"Algiers, 19th September, 1860.

"The Emperor and Empress yesterday morning laid the first
stone of the fine boulevard which is to run along the shore.   An
immense concourse of persons, both French and native, were collected, eager to see their Majesties, and the ceremony displayed a
most picturesque character.   Under the skilful direction of General
Jusuf, contingents of the Kabyle infantry and cavalry of the three
provinces, with all the Aghas and Caids at their head, had been
assembled to come and pay homage to the Emperor.   After a sham
fight between the different tribes a grand fantasia took place by
from 9000 to 10,000 horsemen rushing forward at the swiftest
gallop, and discharging their firearms before their Majesties' tent ;
afterwards a magnificent charge was given by twelve squadrons of
Spahis, crossing the plain like a hurricane ; then followed tilting
matches, gazelle, ostrich, and falcon hunts ; a grand filing-off of
the Touaregs, with their faces veiled, and mounted on their
camels ; and of the Chambaas, those inhabitants of the depths of
the Desert, and the future carriers of French commerce into the
Soudan.   After, in short, one of the most splendid spectacles that
could be imagined, all the Goums, forming an immense line of
battle, advanced majestically, with banners displayed and muskets
held high in the air, towards the eminence on which the Emperor's
tent had been pitched.   The chiefs, clad in the richest burnous,
alighted from their steeds and came in a body to present *the horse
of homage*, caparisoned with gold, and thus perform an act of sub-
mission to the Sovereign of France.   At this moment, rendered

solemn by the beauty of the scene and the warlike appearance of the various tribes whose long resistance has given glory to the French arms, the Emperor could not prevent himself from giving way to visible emotion. The Bey of Tunis was present at this grand solemnity."

"Paris, 28th September, 1860.

"General Count Pierre Schouvaloff, Grand Master of Police at St. Petersburg, and his brother, Count Paul Schouvaloff, both aides-de-camp to the Emperor of Russia, were received the day before yesterday by the Emperor Napoleon, and had the honour of presenting to his Majesty four horses, sent as a present by the Emperor Alexander. These fine animals, which have been accompanied to Paris by a veterinary surgeon, four hussars, and a non-commissioned officer of the Imperial Guard, are of the celebrated Orloff race, and come from the Imperial breeding stud at Chrenovsky. They were selected from among a great number by the Czar himself; and during the two months that their journey from the very heart of Russia has occupied, they have been the objects of the greatest care. His Majesty greatly admired the beauty, strength, and symmetry of *the horses*, and expressed to the Counts Schouvaloff how gratified he felt at a mark of attention which showed the friendly relations existing between the two Sovereigns."

In war, the value of these noble animals to man is well described by Shakspeare's thrilling exclamation of King Richard—

"*A horse! a horse!* my kingdom for *a horse!*"

In like manner, in civil life, how often has the school-boy, who in his infancy had clutched with ecstasy his toy —a little spotted horse on wheels—felt that he would give his birthright for *a pony!*

On his arriving at Oxford or Cambridge, how often has the undergraduate, for the professed purposes of application and recreation, submitted to his parents or guardians a supplication for those three stereotyped wants of college life, "a little money, a private tutor, and *a horse!*" Afterwards, in his manhood, and even in his old age, how often has the Prime Minister of England, during a most important debate, risen from his seat in Parliament to propose to the legion of senators around him "that this House shall adjourn from Tuesday to Thursday," for the well known object (acknowledged by "loud and protracted cheering") of enabling *himself*, those who surround him, and everybody else, "to go to the Derby," to purchase "*Dorling's correct card of the names of the* HORSES, *and the colours of their* RIDERS !"

Among our leading statesmen, how many, as patrons of the turf, have purchased for several thousand guineas—*a horse!* How many, including Pitt, Fox, Lord Althorp, Lord Derby, Lord Palmerston, Sir Francis Burdett, &c., &c., have been ardent followers of hounds!

Her Majesty Queen Victoria and the Emperor Napoleon III. each keep a pack of stag-hounds ; the Prince Consort, a pack of harriers. During the Peninsular war, and again while commanding the army of occupation in France, the Duke of Wellington, besides fighting and writing,

maintained either a pack of fox-hounds or boar-hounds.*
George III. was strongly attached to hunting; his great
grandson, the Prince of Wales, " loves it better still."

In all our streets, in our fields, in our highways and
bye-ways, along the surface of merry England, and across
it; under ground in coal-mines; revolving in a mill;—
in short, in every direction, and wherever we go, we see
before us—sometimes as man's companion, sometimes as
his servant, sometimes as his slave, and occasionally as
his master—*the horse*, respecting which and his rider we
will now, without further preamble, venture to offer to
our readers the few following remarks.

---

* About 44 years ago a Frenchwoman, the proprietor of a small
farm, showed us, as a great curiosity, a "billet de logement"
which had been inflicted upon her, of which the following is a translated copy :—

"The widow —— will lodge for one night fifty-four dogs." [The Duke
of Wellington's hounds just arrived from England.]

"(Signed)   ——,

"Mayor."

"Imaginez-vous donc," exclaimed the poor old lady, uplifting
her eyes and the palms of both hands; "Imaginez-vous donc—
cinquante-quatre chiens ! !"

Mr. Rarey's Mode of Subduing Horses.

IT is a singular fact, that although England produces the finest horses in the world, and though the English people have always fancied they understood their management better than any other nation, yet, lately, not only have we all been astonished by the superior knowledge on this subject of a trans-Atlantic cousin, but what is still more surprising, our sporting men have rushed forwards to pay to Mr. Rarey no less a sum than about 15,000*l*. for exhibiting to them a system of horse-breaking, the philosophy of which is based upon a few simple facts, which, although unreflected on, have ever been lying close before our eyes.

Of all animals in creation, there is no one we should all of us be so very sorry to lose as the horse. In peace and in war, on burning sands under the equator, or on eternal snow in the frigid zone, for pleasure or for business, well fed or starving, he is always not only ready, but eager, to the utmost of his strength, to serve a master, but too often inconsiderate, ungrateful to him, and unjust. As soon as his courage is excited, no fall, bruise, blow, or wound, that does not paralyse the mechanism of his limbs, will stop him; indeed, with his upper and lower jaw shot away, and with the skin dangling in ribands, we have seen him cantering, apparently careless and unconscious of his state, alongside of the horse artillery gun from which he had just been cut adrift.

But although in the hunting-field, on the race-course, or in harness, a horse will generally, from sheer pluck, go till he drops, yet, whenever he encounters physical strength greater than his own, our hero all of a sudden acts like an arrant coward.

For instance, in the mail, it apparently matters not to the spirit of the horses whether there be one passenger or six—light bags or heavy ones; on the contrary, the greater the weight, the more eagerly do they strain to force it to follow them. The faster they are allowed to go, the harder do they pull, until, if the reins were to break, they would enjoy the opportunity by running away, not as in the days of Phaeton with the chariot of the sun, but with say a ton and a half, of they know not what, at their heels. And yet, if on the following day the same high-flying, high-spirited, high-mettled horses were to be hooked to a sturdy living oak tree, after two or three ineffectual snatches to move it, no amount of punishment would be sufficient to induce them to go to the end of their traces; in short, to use a well-known expression, they would all "*jib.*" Again, if a horse in harness, however resolutely he may be proceeding, slips upon pavement, and falls heavily on his side, after vainly making

B

three or four violent struggles to rise, he becomes all of a sudden so completely cowed, that not only without any resistance does he allow his harness piecemeal to be unbuckled, the carriage detached, and pushed away far behind him, but, when lying thus perfectly unfettered, it requires kicks, stripes, and a malediction or two, to induce him to make the little effort necessary to rise from his prostrate state.

Again, in the hunting-field, a noble, high-couraged horse, a rusher at any description of fence, the very sight of which seems to inflame his ardour, in most gallant style charges a brook, which when he is in the air he sees is too broad to be cleared. On his chest striking against the bank, and while his rider, delighted at feeling that he is not a bit hurt, is luxuriously rolling over and over on the green grass like a rabbit that at full speed has been shot dead, this gallant steed makes two, three, or four desperate efforts to get to him; and yet, simply because the mud at the bottom of the brook catches hold of his hind feet, and the sticky perpendicular clay bank grasps his fore ones, his courage suddenly fails him, and as nothing will then induce him to make another effort, it becomes necessary to send, often several miles, for cart-horses to drag this high-bred animal out by his neck.

But although this strange mixture of courage and cowardice appears to us at first to be inexplicable, yet on reflection we must perceive that it is in strict accordance with the beneficent decree that "man should have dominion over every beast of the field."

The weight and muscular strength of a horse multiplied into each other, form a momentum which, if his courage were as indomitable as that of man, would make him the master instead of the servant of the human race; and accordingly, although, for all the purposes for which man can require them, his energy and endurance are invincible, yet, to ensure his subjection, his courage has been so curiously constituted, that, as it were, by touching the small secret spring of a safety valve, the whole of it instantly evaporates; and although Mr. Rarey has not exactly explained this theory, he has, with extraordinary intelligence and success, reduced it to practice as follows :—

When a horse of a sensitive and sensible disposition is placed under the care of a man of weak nerves, he very soon finds out that, by the help of his body, teeth, and heels, that is to say by squeezing, crushing, biting, and kicking his groom, he is able to frighten him; and no sooner is this victory attained, than the tyrant begins to misbehave himself to everybody in every possible way, until, as in the case of *Cruiser*, it is declared dangerous to approach him, even with food ; that no man can ride him ;

B 2

in fact, that he is an animal beautiful to look at, but thoroughly useless to mankind.

Now, to cure this disorder, the wild beast, for such he is, with great precaution, by several guy-ropes, is led close to the wheel of a waggon, under which Mr. Rarey, putting his hands through the spokes, manages to lift up and gently strap up one fore-leg, and to affix a long strap to the fetlock of the other, which two simple operations at once ensure the victory he is about to attain.

As it gives a horse not the slightest pain or inconvenience to stand for a short time on one fore-leg, Cruiser, while "amazed he stares around," is scarcely aware that he is doing so; and as he is totally unconscious of the existence of the other strap, he is perfectly astounded to find that no sooner does he attempt to resent Mr. Rarey's bold approach and grasp, than, apparently by the irresistible power of man, he is suddenly deprived of the use of both his fore-legs.

The longer and the more violently he can be encouraged to resist, the more deathlike will be the trance in which he is about to lie. He struggles—struggles —struggles—until, as in the three instances we have described, his courage all at once evaporates, and with heaving flank, panting nostrils, palpitating heart, flabby muscles, and the perspiration bursting through every pore in the skin, he then allows his conqueror to sit on his ribs, to fiddle in his ears, drum to the gaping and gasping audience : in short, as the Duke of Wellington described Lord Ellenborough's proclamation about the gates of Sumnauth, to sing over his carcase "a song of triumph." And thus as Achilles was mortally wounded in the only vulnerable part of his body—the heel,—so does Cruiser find that in a heart which had never before failed him, and which had been the terror of all who approached him, there exists a weak point, discovered by Mr. Rarey, which has caused his complete subjection to man.

> "Is this the face that faced ten thousand men,
> And was at last out-faced by Bolingbroke ?"

In old times this conversion of the bully into the coward could only be effected, at great risk, by courage and physical force, as follows :—

Some years ago Captain ——, the well-known steeple-chase rider, bought at Tattersall's, for a very small sum, a magnificent horse that no stranger in the yard dared approach, and which therefore was "put up" and honestly sold as a "man-killer."

On these propensities being explained by the purchaser to his head groom, the resolute fellow bluntly replied that he would not at all object to take care of the beast provided he were allowed, "in self-defence, to kill or cure him ;" and accordingly, as soon as the homicide entered his stable, with a steady step, but avoiding looking into his eye, he walked up to him, and then, not waiting for a declaration of war, but with a short, heavy bludgeon, striking the inside of his knees, he knocked his fore legs from under him, and the instant he fell, belaboured his head and body until the savage proprietor of both became so completely terrified, that he ever afterwards seemed almost to quail whenever his conqueror walked up to him.

Now, on comparing the two opposite systems, humane and inhuman, scientific and unscientific, just described, it must be apparent to everybody, that while for the latter a powerful hero must be procured, all that is requisite for the former is calmness, gentleness, and two little straps which, in a lower stratum, physically fight a desperate battle, above which man morally and serenely presides ; the horse, nevertheless, all the while ascribing to him alone the whole credit of the victory eventually attained.

Under the ordinary process used by horse-breakers, it requires several weeks before a colt—often broken *down* as well as *in* by the operation—surrenders his own will to that of his rider, whereas Mr. Rarey has not only in public repeatedly demonstrated, but many who have followed his prescription have testified, that a young thorough-bred horse, perfectly unbroken, can, in the course of about half-an-hour, be so thoroughly conquered by the two straps which he conceives to be part and parcel of the irresistible strength of his master, that so soon as he is satisfied that his own powers of resistance are of no avail, he subserviently allows himself to be bridled, saddled, mounted, and ridden.

The principle of Mr. Rarey's system of domination is at this moment curiously exemplified in the little dairy farm-yard of Mr. Roff, residing on the Brighton road, near Croydon.

Some months ago, on approaching these premises, we observed a lot of children playing with a yearling colt, who, to our surprise, was allowing them to crawl between his legs and fondle him in various ways, just as if he were a dog. On riding into the yard to inquire by what magical means the little quadruped had been made so gentle and tame, we were informed by the old farmer who owned him that his wife, kind to all her beasts,—,

"She milk'd the dun cow that ne'er offer'd to stir:
    Though wicked to all, it was gentle to her,"—

had for many years been yearning to add to them a pet colt; that accordingly he had lately bought her one, and that she had tamed it: with uxorious pride he added "she could tame anything." As, however, we were perfectly convinced that his good wife, in spite of her comely,

honest face, could not fascinate a horse's heart quite as
easily as a husband's, we cross-questioned the latter for a
considerable time, until he at last mentioned (as if it had
nothing whatever to do with the subject) that when he
purchased the yearling (whose mother had just died), not
knowing how to bring it to his wife, with the assistance
of one or two men he strapped together all its four feet,
and then, lifting it into his cart, just as if it had been a
calf, he trotted away with it, jolting it and jumbling it
till he reached his home, where he uncarted it, and, in due
time, with his own hands, restored to it the use of its limbs.

Of course this was a much stronger dose of discipline
and subjection than Mr. Rarey has ever found necessary
to administer, even to Cruiser; and there can exist no
doubt it was this cooling medicine, this soothing mixture,
which had produced the strange and salutary effects that
had attracted us into the little yard.   And thus, in every
region of the globe, not only colts and horses, but all living
animals, man especially included, surrender at discretion
to any authority which, after a fruitless struggle—such
a one for instance as induced Napoleon I., on the 15th
of July, 1815, to seek for refuge on board H. M. ship
Bellerophon from the allied armies of Europe—they find
it to be utterly impossible to resist.

The differences between the character and conduct of

a wild horse and a tame one are, we believe, not very clearly understood. It is generally conceived that in the difficulty of adhering, technically termed sticking to the back of a horse, there exist three degrees of comparison, namely :—

1. That it is rather difficult to ride a horse that has been broken in.

2. That it is exceedingly difficult to ride one that has been petted, patted, bitted, lounged, but not mounted.

3. That it must be almost impossible to mount and ride a wild horse just caught, that has never been touched by a human hand.

We will, however, humbly venture to assert that, in certain instances, the three steps of this little ladder might be reversed.

1. In a state of nature the horse is such a zealous advocate of our popular principle of " self-government," he is so desirous to maintain his "independence," that although he will allow almost any quadruped, even wolves and lions, to approach within a certain distance, yet the moment he sees a man, though on horseback, he instinctively turns his tail towards him, and, when followed, gallops away.

If, consequently, by the triumph of reason over instinct he be caught, or rather by the lasso tumbled head over

heels, saddled, and if all of a sudden, to his vast astonishment, he finds sitting astride his back, with a cigar in his
mouth, the very human being he has always been avoiding, his first and almost only feeling is that of *fear ;* and
accordingly, if he be retained by the bridle, instantaneously, by a series of jumps on all four legs, he makes
impromptu his first hurried, untaught, unpractised effort
to dislocate a rider.   But if, instead of being as it were
invited to perform these unsophisticated antics, he be
allowed, or rather, by whip and severe spurs, be propelled
to do what he most ardently desires, namely, run away,
his power of resistance is over, and his subjection ine-
vitable.   For at the top of his speed, just as when swimming, a horse can neither rear, kick, nor plunge, and
therefore at his best pace he proceeds on his sure road
to ruin, until not only all his wind is pumped out of
him, but after that, until twisted hide-thong and sharp
iron have converted his terror of man into an ardent
desire to be obedient to his will.   In fact, like a small
nation that has unsuccessfully been contending against a
great one, he wishes to put an end to the horrors of war,
and to sue for the blessings of peace.

2. If a domestic horse that has been handled, fondled,
but never ridden, be suddenly saddled and mounted, the
rider has greater difficulties to encounter than those just
described : for the animal is not only gifted by nature

with all the propensities of the wild horse to reject man,
but, from being better fed, he has greater strength to
indulge in them; besides which he enjoys the immense
advantage of being in a civilized, or, in plainer terms, an
enclosed country. Accordingly, instead of being forced
to run away, his rider is particularly afraid lest he should
do so, simply because he knows that the remedy which
would cure the wild horse, would probably kill *him*. In
fact, the difference to the rider between an open and an
enclosed field of battle is exactly that which a naval officer
feels in scudding in a gale of wind out of sight of land,
and in being caught among sandbanks and rocks in a narrow
channel.

3. Of all descriptions of horses, wild and tame, by far
the most difficult to ride is that young British thorough-
bred colt of two or three years old that has been regularly
"broken in" *by himself*, without giving the slightest
warning, to jump away sideways, spin round, and at the
same moment kick off his rider. The feat is a beautiful
and well-arranged combination of nature and of art.
Like the pugilistic champion of England—Tom Sayers—
he is a professional performer, gifted with so much
strength and activity, and skilful in so many quick, artful
tricks and dodges, that any country practitioner who
comes to deal with him is no sooner up than down, to
rise from his mother earth with a vague, bewildered,

incoherent idea as to what had befallen him, or " how he got there."

If a horse of this description and a wild one were to be mounted simultaneously, each by an equally good rider, in an unenclosed, uncultivated region, both the quadrupeds probably at the same moment would be seen to run away: the Briton for ever, to gain his liberty; the other quadruped, just as surely, to lose it!

Having now sufficiently discussed the character and conduct of the horse, we will presume to offer, or rather to bequeath to our readers, a very few observations as regards his rider.

SEAT ON A HORSE.

The best position of a man on horseback is, of course, that which is most agreeable to both animals, and which, from its ease and flexibility, as they skim together over the surface of the earth, apparently combines them into one.

Like everything in Nature, the variety of seats is infinite. They may, however, generically be divided into two classes:

1. In the great plains of South America, in which it

may truly be stated that for every male inhabitant above five or six years of age Nature maintains at no cost, no tax, and at no trouble to him, a stud of horses whose number is legion, the rider sits almost perpendicularly, with the great toe of each foot resting very lightly on, and often merely touching its small triangular stirrup, his legs grasping the horse's sides slightly or tightly, as prosperous or adverse circumstances may require.

In this attitude, which may be said to be that of standing astride over rather than sitting upon the saddle, the pivot upon which the rider, gracefully bending his body with a ball and socket movement, turns—in throwing his lasso, in thrusting his lance forwards on either side, or in looking behind him—is what is termed by sporting men his " fork."

In the few instances where pistols are carried, they are affixed *behind* the right thigh, firstly, that in the common occurrence of the horse falling in his gallop, they may not prevent the rider from rolling clear away from him; and, secondly, because in that position the weapons are close to the rider's right hand, which, as he flies along, is to be seen always dangling just above the but ends, ready to grasp them the instant they are required.

This attitude is not only highly picturesque, but particularly easy to the rider, who, while partaking of the undulating motion of his horse, can rest his wearied body by slight imperceptible changes of position on the pivot or "fork," on which, like corn waving in the wind, it bends.

The British cavalry sit astride above their saddles very nearly in this attitude, which, as we have just explained, enables them with great facility to cut, or give point in front, right or left, at cavalry or at infantry; and if they were not embarrassed by their clothing, as well as by their accoutrements, and if, as in the region to which we have alluded, they were to use no pace but the gallop, each would soon become, or rather he could not help apparently becoming, part and parcel of his horse. But our gallant men, although they have been subjected to innumerable experimental changes of dress, &c., continue not only hampered and imperilled by a hard cloak, holsters, and carbine affixed in *front* of their thighs, and imprisoned, especially round their necks, within tight clothing, but their travelling pace, the trot (a jolting movement unknown and unheard of in the plains of South America), gives to their body and limbs a rigidity painful to look at, and in long journeys wearisome to man and horse. Indeed in the French cavalry, and occasionally in our own, the manner in which the soldier, in not a bad attitude, is seen hopping high into the air, on and off his saddle, as his horse, at apparently a different rate, trots beneath him, forms as ridiculous a caricature of *the art of riding* as the pencil of our Punch's " Leech " could possibly delineate.

2. Throughout the United Kingdom, civilians of all classes, gentlemen, farmers, and yeomen, especially those who occasionally follow the hounds, adopt what is commonly called " the hunting seat," in which, instead of " the fork," the *knees* form the pivot, or rather hinge, the legs beneath them the grasp, while the thighs, like the pastern of a horse, enable the body above to rise and fall as lightly as a carriage on its springs.

In this attitude the rider cannot turn his body to the right or left, or look behind him as easily as he could revolve upon his " fork."

For rough riding, however, of every description, the hunting seat, though infinitely less graceful, is superior to that of the cavalry of Europe, for the following reasons :—

One of the most usual devices by which a horse endeavours to, and but too often succeeds in dislodging his rider, is by giving to his back, by a sudden kick, a jerk upwards, which, of course, forces in the same direction towards the sky that nameless portion of humanity which was partly resting on it, and which in the cavalry cannot possibly get very far away from it.

But, in the hunting seat, the instant the rider expects such a kick, by merely rising in his stirrups he at once raises or abstracts from the saddle the point his enemy intends to attack, and accordingly the blow aimed at it fails to reach it.

Again, on approaching a large fence, by the same simple precaution, the rider entirely avoids the concussion of that sudden jerk or effort necessary to enable the horse to clear it. In a fall, the pommel of the saddle and the horse's neck and head are much easier cleared by short stirrup-leathers than by long ones. Lastly, in a common trot, the former soften the jolt, which the latter cannot easily avoid. In short, in a hunting seat, the rider, to his great comfort and relief, rests more or less on his saddle as long as he likes, and yet, the instant he anticipates a blow from it, leaves it, without metaphor . . . behind him.

Of horsemanship it may truly be said, that about four-fifths of the art depend on attaining a *just* seat, and one-fifth on possessing a pair of light hands.* But although the attainment of these advantages is not incompatible with an easy, erect position on horseback,

---

* Beckford says, "First attribute of a good huntsman is courage. Next, hands and seat."

the generality of riders are but too apt to sit on their horses in the bent attitude of the last paroxysm or exertion which helped them into the saddle. Now, when a man in this toad-like position rides along—say a macadamized road—he travels always ready, at a moment's notice, to proceed by himself in the direction in which he is pointing, in case the progress of his horse should be suddenly stopped by his falling down. Indeed, when a horse, without falling down, recovers by a violent struggle from a bad trip, a heavy rider in this attitude (called by Sir Bellingham Graham "a wash-ball seat") is very liable to shoot forwards over his head in a parabolic curve, ending in a concussion of his brain or in the dislocation of his neck,—the horse standing by his motionless body perfectly uninjured.

On the other hand, when a man sits upright, justly balanced on his saddle, any sudden jerk or movement forwards throws his shoulders backwards. If therefore, while proceeding in that position, the horse thinks proper to fall, the animal in the first instance is the sole sufferer. He cuts his forehead, hurts his nose, breaks his knees, bruises his chest, while his head, neck, forelegs, and the forepart of his body, forced into each other like the joints of a telescope, form a buffer, preventing the concussion the horse has received, from injuring, in the smallest degree, the rider, or even the watch in his pocket, which, without being ejected from the saddle, goes ticking, ticking, ticking on, just as merrily as if nothing had happened. If he only trips, a rider poised justly in his saddle can easily recover him.

A horse will not only refrain from treading upon any creature lying on the ground, but in hunting he will make the utmost possible effort to avoid putting a foot upon his master whenever

"On the bare earth exposed he lies."

If, however, his owner, from a bad seat or from false precaution, has suddenly thrown himself from his back, it is often impossible for the animal, while struggling to recover from a desperate trip, to avoid either trampling upon or violently striking him.

For this reason a rider should never abandon his saddle so long as his horse beneath it has a leg, or an infinitesimal part of one, to stand on. But so soon as his downfall is announced by that heavy, thundering concussion against the ground, the meaning of which it is impossible to mistake, the partnership should instantaneously be dissolved by the horseman rolling, if possible, out of harm's way.

But it occasionally happens not only that the horse rolls too, but that the larger roller overtakes the smaller one, the two lying prostrate, with the legs in boots under the body whose limbs wear only shoes.

If the rider happens fortunately to have the saddle between him and the horse, his legs merely sustain a heavy weight, from which they are harmlessly extricated the instant the animal rises.

Should he happen *un*fortunately to have the girths between him and the horse, he lies, like Ariel in the cloven pine, " painfully imprisoned," in a predicament of which it is impossible for any one to foretell the results.

As the quadruped is always more or less cowed by his fall, he remains usually for about a minute or two as still as if he were dead.

All of a sudden, however, just as if a bayonet had been run into him, he struggles to rise.

To do so it is necessary that all his feet should take hold of the ground. This they are prevented from doing by the rider's boots, which, operating as a handspike under the body, keep it in a horizontal position, thereby causing the four legs, like two pairs of blacksmith's sledge-hammers, to continue to strike heavily towards each other.

Between them lies, acting in this little tragedy the part of Anvil, the poor rider, who can only avoid the hard blows of two fore iron shoes, by wincing from them to within the reach of two hind ones.

This violent struggle eventually ends by the horse rising, leaving on the field of battle, slightly, seriously, or desperately wounded, his master, whom he never intended to hurt.

In the hunting field, the bent position in the saddle produces equally unpleasant results. On man and horse coming cheerily to a fence, with what mathematicians call "an unknown quantity" on the other side, if the rider sits justly on his saddle, it is the horse and not he that receives the concussion of any fall that may ensue, simply because the spring of his animal in taking the leap had thrown his shoulders backwards, and consequently his head out of danger; whereas the nose of the gentleman who had been riding alongside of him in the bent attitude of a note of interrogation, is seen to plough into its mother earth the instant the muzzle of his horse impinges upon it.

For exactly the same reasons, in every description of fall (and no volume would be large enough to contain them all), similar results occur; and yet there is no predicament in which "Toady" appears to greater disadvantage, and so keenly feels it, than when, in following the hounds, he has to descend a very precipitous and rather slippery grass hill.

If a horse be but properly dealt with, he can gallop down a turf hill with nearly as much rapidity as along a racecourse. A tea-table would stand ill at ease on the declivity, because its limbs are immoveable; but a quadruped, by throwing all his legs forwards and his body backwards, has the power to adjust himself, with mathematical precision, to almost any descent.

To insure his safety, however, it is essential that he should be encouraged, by a loose rein, to carry his head as low as possible, to enable him to take care of his feet, and in case of treading on a rolling-stone to recover his balance by throwing it up. Now, when in this position, if the rider, following the instinct and the example of the horse, throws his weight backwards—in fact, if from the saddle the backs of the two animals are separated from each other by only a very small angle, both can descend the hill together at considerable speed without the smallest danger. The only embarrassment the rider has to contend against is an over-caution on the part of the horse, amounting to fear, which induces him to try to take the slope diagonally, very likely to result in the poor animal slipping up on his side. In keeping his head straight, however, care must be taken not to induce him to raise it *up;* and when this little difficulty is overcome, no other of any sort or kind remains to impede a safe and rapid descent.

Seated on his saddle, in the attitude we have described, that admirable rider Jack Shirley, whipper-in to the Tedworth hunt, with a large open clasp-knife in his mouth, was one day observed fixing a piece of whipcord to his lash, while following his hounds at a slapping pace, down hill, his reins lying nearly loose on old "Gadsby's" neck.

On the other hand when a gentleman, however fearless he may be, sitting at an angle of 45°, like a 13-inch mortar on its bed, attempts to ride down the steep declivity described, the afflictions that befall him are really piteous, for the instant his horse's fore legs sink considerably lower than the hind ones, he feels that unless he holds on very tightly, he must inevitably pitch over the bows of the vessel that is carrying him. To maintain his equilibrium he therefore pulls a little at his curb-bit, which not only raises his horse's head till it nearly touches his nose, but throws the animal and the weight he carries into such a false position, that it becomes difficult and dangerous to advance. The restrained quadruped, impatient to follow the horses before him, yet altogether out of gear, on every little twitch at his bridle keeps chucking up his head, until the rider, who a moment ago expected to fall over his ears, now feels that he is going to glide backwards over his tail, which is nearly touching the hill. In short, the poor horse is resting on his hocks instead of his hoofs, with his fore feet barely touching the ground.

When a lot of riders find themselves in this hopeless attitude, they generally, according to their amount of activity, crawl, jump, or vault from their saddles to descend on foot, which they soon find very little improves their case, for the heels of their boots not being, like horse-shoes, concave, take insufficient hold of the turf; and thus while they are slipping, sliding, and tottering in the descent, each linked to a quadruped that is bothering him to death, if, feeling a little alarmed, they resolve to stop for a moment or two, their impatient horses, unable to advance and unwilling to stand still, often compromise the matter by running round their masters, with the chance of rolling them, like ninepins, down the hill.

In galloping for many hours, and especially for many days, as soon as the muscles of the rider, by getting tired, lose their obstinacy, it becomes impossible for him, if he sits upright, to prevent his body undulating, to the infinite relief of both parties, with every movement of the horse; whereas, if, like an English jockey, whose seat is well adapted for galloping at the utmost speed for a few minutes, he rides like a frog on a shovel, he inflicts upon his whole frame, as well as upon the poor animal that carries him, an amount of unnecessary fatigue which prematurely tires both.

For the foregoing reasons if gentlemen sportsmen who occupy on the road and the hunting-field this false position, would but allow Mr. Calcraft, in his peculiar way,

to lift them about half a dozen times a few inches into the
air, and then, as a tallow-chandler dips his candles, lower
them gently, easily, and perpendicularly to their saddles,
they would find themselves promoted in the world to a seat
on horseback which they would never wish to abandon.

As, however, our readers, we fear, must have become
very tired of the saddle, we will now relieve them from
hogskin, to submit to them a very few practical observations on the management of the bridle, the ordinary
uses of which, as everybody knows, are twofold, namely,
first to guide a horse, and secondly to restrain, or, when
requisite, to stop him.

As it is the disposition of a horse, when mounted, to
go fast, and as it is the disposition of a man to pull at any
thing in this world as little as possible, curb-bits and
curb-chains (as their names truly denote) have been invented, by which the animal in all his movements on
parade or on the road is slightly thrown on his haunches,
with his head raised more or less above its natural level.
In this position his eyes are of course proportionally
elevated, and as there exists no obstruction on the macadamized roads, &c., on which he travels, he soon ceases to
look downwards; and although, if he then happens to
pass over a little hole, he may put a foot into it, or may
slightly blunder over half a shovelfull of loose stones which

had escaped his observation, yet, if he has good action, and a tolerable rider, he earns the character of being a " capital hack."

Now to metamorphose "a hack" into "a hunter" is principally effected by the bridle, and yet the great difficulty of the art is to learn not how much, but how little to use it; in short, a considerable portion of what the bridle has done has to be undone. Accordingly, instead of being encouraged to travel on his haunches with his fore legs lightly touching the ground, the latter must be required to bear the greater portion of the burden, which it is the duty of the hind legs to propel. The head has to be brought down to its proper level; and to induce or rather to oblige the horse to make his eyes the lantern of his feet, to study geology instead of astronomy, he should be slowly ridden, with a loose rein, over every little hole, grip, or heap that would be likely to throw a hack down. Whenever he can be made to stumble (if the rider feels that he will not actually fall), the reins should instantly be dropped. In like manner he should be walked for several days over the roughest ground that can be found, particularly land that has been excavated to obtain the substratum and left in holes. With a perfectly loose rein he should be gently trotted, gently cantered, and gently galloped over a surface of this description, the rider always dropping the rein when he blunders. Vegetius, in describing the horsemanship of the Parthians in the time of Xerxes, states that in order to make their horses sure-footed over rough, broken ground, they placed on a space of level ground a number of wooden troughs of different heights, filled with earth, over which in galloping they had many falls.

Under similar treatment, the strength, activity, intelligence, and eyesight of the animal will, as in a wild state, cordially be combined by him to protect himself from the degradation as well as punishment of falling; and so ample and sufficient are these powers, that the rider will soon find, that instead of having to hold his horse up, it has become out of his power to throw him down. In fact, under the guidance of nature, rather than of man, "the hack" in a very short period, and without going over a fence of any sort or kind, may thus be made competent to follow hounds across any country in the United Kingdom; while, on the other hand, the nag that had only been taught in a riding-school or in a dealer's yard to jump neatly over bars, gates, and hurdles, would, most particularly to the neck of his rider, prove to be infinitely worse than useless.

Of course a horse is not a perfect hunter until he has had a small amount (for he does not require much) of experience in leaping; but as, with the exception of water, every horse is able, willing, and eager to jump, generally speaking, more than is desired, his rider has merely to teach the noble animal beneath him to add to his valour just enough discretion to induce him to look, not *before*, but *while* he leaps.

A hunter when following hounds is so excited, that if, in addition to his own eagerness, he be hurried at his fences, he rushes more and more recklessly at them, until he gets into needless trouble. On the other hand, just as he approaches every fence, if he be always patted on the neck, and gently restrained, he feels satisfied that he is to be allowed to do the job; and accordingly, curtailing his stride as he approaches, he does it not only cleverly, but without any waste of exertion, which, to use a common hunting-field expression, " he may want before the day's over."

When a horse is enabled, like a soldier whose stiff stock has just been unbuckled, to drop his head to its natural position, he not only goes safely, but, without risk of cutting his fetlocks, he can gallop over ground deeply covered with loose impediments of any description; and, accordingly, in Surrey it has long been a hunting axiom that it is the curb bridles which by throwing hunters on their haunches in a false position cause them to cut their back sinews with those sharp flints which, in a snaffle bit, they can clatter over without injury. A good Northamptonshire rider, in lately taking a fence, jumped over it into a stone quarry. Now, if he had been in the bent attitude we have described, he must inevitably have pitched on, and have fractured his skull. From, however, sitting correctly on his saddle, his ankles, and not his head, suffered.

In like manner when Mehemet Ali, under the pretence of investing his son, Toossoon Pacha, with the command of an army, by a treacherous invitation inveigled the Mamelukes into the summit of the citadel of El Kahira (the Victorious), commonly called Cairo, and then suddenly dropping the portcullis, directed upon them from barred windows on three sides a murderous fire, Amyn Bey, rather than submit to such a death, spurring his Arab charger over his writhing comrades, and across the low crenated wall, jumped over a precipice of about fifty feet; and yet, although of the horse it may truly be said that

"Headlong from the mountain's height
He plunged to endless night,"

for, on reaching the hard rock, he was smashed to death, the rider, who, no doubt, had expected the same fate, was enabled, with only a broken ankle, to crawl away, recover, and for nearly thirty years enjoy, with health and wealth, the well-earned appellation of "the last of the Mamelukes;" in short

"The man recovered from the blow, the *horse* it was that died."

In further evidence, however, of the theory that when a man sits properly in his saddle, it is the horse, and not he, who suffers by a tumble, we submit to our readers the following extraordinary narration by a young General officer of high character, who has kindly permitted us to publish it, briefly describing a fall on horseback to a depth equal to 40 feet more than the height of the weather-cock on the steeple of St. Martin's church, in London, or to double the height of the Duke of York's monument at the bottom of Regent Street.

"United Service Club, 18th March, 1860.

"In June, 1848, at the island of Dominica, in the West Indies, I fell over a precipice of 237 feet perpendicular height, upon the rocks by the sea-side. This occurred about a quarter past 7 o'clock P.M., then quite dark, as no twilight exists in the tropics. Every bone of my horse was broken, and I conceive my escape from instant death the most miraculous that ever occurred. Three men, at various periods, had previously been dashed to atoms at the same spot, and one man twelve months after me, when the Legislative Assembly passed a resolution to secure the road; but if twenty thousand men were to fall there, I think nothing short of a miracle could save one of them. My recovery from the shock I sustained was also as miraculous as my escape with life. I sent out an artist to take a drawing on the spot, and also had the place surveyed by an engineer. I have often thought of putting down all the circumstances of that extraordinary accident, but the dread of being taken for a Baron Munchausen has restrained me. I do not expect that any one will believe it, although there are many living witnesses. Nor do I expect any sympathy, for, as soon as I could hold a pen, I detailed the catastrophe to my mother to account for my long silence. I received, in reply, in due course, a long letter detailing family news, without any allusion to my unfortunate case, except in a postscript, in which she merely said, ' *Oh! William, I wish you would give up riding after dinner.*' *

"WM. YORKE MOORE, Major-Gen.

"P.S. During the fall I stuck to my horse."

The details of this astonishing accident are very shortly as follows :—

Colonel Moore, while commanding the troops in Dominica, lost his way one evening after sunset.

As, in utter darkness, he was endeavouring to get home, he came to several little imperceptible objects which he forced his horse to cross. Shortly afterwards the animal stopped at one which he seemed particularly afraid of.

The soldier, unwilling to halt between two opinions, but, on the contrary, determined to proceed as he thought straight towards his home, at almost full speed rode at the unknown impediment several times in vain, until the animal, surrendering his instinctive fears, and possibly knowledge, to the spurs that were propelling him, with a violent jump into the air cleared the little low hedge, for such it proved to be, bounding that awful precipice which, like a wall, connected the upper story or table-land of the island with the ocean which in solemn darkness reigned beneath it.

Colonel Moore states that during his passage on horse-

* The accident occurred *before* dinner.

back through the air, almost every event of his life, large as well as small, at about the rate of the electric telegraph, which transmits its ideas one hundred and eighty thousand miles in a second, flashed across his mind as distinctly and as vividly as if they were recurring.

By a sort of clairvoyance, of which in medical annals there exist recorded several similar instances, he saw all that in his lifetime he had done or left undone, and was thinking, seriatim, of almost every friend and relative, when, in an instant, all these bright fiery thoughts on the past, present, or future tenses of his existence became extinguished by a concussion which, depriving him of his senses, left him with his legs in the sea and his body on the rocks, apparently dead.

While lying, corpse-like, in this lonely state, whose beneficent hand was it that all of a sudden dashed upon his face the cool, fresh soft water that recovered him? Whose voice was it that, almost at the same moment, explained to him, not only the accident which had befallen him, but the time that had elapsed since it occurred?

The hand that restored to him his senses was that which had already graciously placed his head in safety upon the rock above the ocean that would have drowned him, but in which his feet had been harmlessly floating. It was the hand that had just created the tropical shower which, as if administered to him by an angel, awakened him from his swoon.

It was the hand that, "in the beginning," when the earth was without form and void, and darkness was upon the face of the deep, had created that "lesser light to rule the night," which, just before he fell, he had observed rising from the horizon, but which now, shining above his head, upon four upturned glittering horse-shoes (all he could see of his mangled beast), made known to him, at a glance, that what had evidently befallen him, according to the illuminated clock in the heavens, must have occurred many hours ago.

With cool presence of mind, Colonel Moore, after making several experimental movements, ascertained that he was severely cut about the body and head ; that his right ankle was dislocated, and that his back was benumbed or paralysed by the concussion of his fall. As soon, however, as the long wished-for sun rose, it shone upon his bare, bleeding head with such excruciating force, that, as a protection from its rays, he transferred his cotton neckerchief to his scalp and forehead, leaving sticking up above them the two ends, which, like the remainder, were stained with his red blood.

After remaining in extreme pain for several hours, to his great joy he saw a boat full of sable natives rowing towards the spot on which, in the head-dress just described, he was reclining. As soon as they came near to him, in a faint tone he hailed them. On hearing his voice, for a few moments they looked eagerly around in all directions, until they espied him, when, instantly, just as if they had seen and were pursued by an evil spirit, away they rowed at their utmost speed.

After a considerable interval another black man came clambering over the rocks, intent only on catching fish.

As soon, however, as his eyes caught a glimpse of the poor sufferer's bloody head and head-gear, the fisherman was evidently seized with the same impression, and, accordingly, in a paroxysm of fear, chucking his rod and line upwards to fall into the sea, as fast as his hands and feet could carry him, he also, in his way, scrambled out of sight.

After a long, painful interval, Colonel Moore's servant, who, alarmed by his master not having returned, had for many hours been in search of him, at last tracked his horse's feet to the edge of the precipice, and on looking over it, seeing about half way down a pockethandkerchief sticking in the boughs of a small projecting tree, he returned to the barracks, gave the alarm, and accordingly, as soon as a boat could be procured, the soldiers, who rushed forward to man it, proceeded round the rocks, until Colonel Moore (who knew nothing of his servant's discovery) joyfully saw them

D

pulling, as hard as they could lay to their oars, towards him.

It need scarcely be added that, regardless of the overwhelming heat of the sun, the gallant fellows succeeded in conveying their commanding officer on their shoulders to the barracks, where he lay for some months in great pain and danger.

However, in due time, the paralysed muscles of his back recovered their tone, and eventually, without even being lame, he became completely restored to the health, activity, and energy that had always characterised him.

For a considerable time portions of his saddle, strips of the hide and the broken bones of his horse, which, lacerated by the branches of the trees through which the poor animal had fallen, was literally smashed to atoms, were collected by people, who amassed a considerable amount of money by exhibiting and selling them as relics in evidence of one of the most extraordinary accidents that, under the superintending direction of Divine Providence, has ever been survived by man.

Mode of riding at Timber.

In getting rapidly across a difficult country there are two sorts of fences, each of which has to be jumped in a manner the very opposite of that required by the other. A young hunter will leap almost any ordinary fence, particularly if it be broad, as well, and, from his impetuosity, often better than an old one. But there is one description of barrier, called by hunting men " timber" (that is to say stiles, gates, and rails, that cannot be broken), which requires, in both rider and horse, a great deal more discretion than valour : indeed of " timber" it may truly be said that it is the most dangerous and, on the other hand, the safest fence a man can ride at.

If a young horse, highly excited, be ridden fast for the first time in his life at a gate, it is very likely he will clear it; on the other hand, it is quite certain that if, despising bars through which he can see daylight, he resolves to break the top one, the penalty attached to his mistake will be a very heavy one : indeed nothing can be more disagreeable to a rider and frightful to look at than the result. Now, of course, the obvious way of preventing this catastrophe is simply to teach a horse —firstly, that he cannot break timber,—and secondly, that he will have to suffer acute pain if he attempts to do so. Accordingly, away from hounds and under no excitement, he should be slowly ridden over two or three low rails that will not break, with an unexpected little twitch at his rein sufficient to make them severely strike his hind legs. The moment this is effected the rider should jump off, to allay anything like excitement, and to allow the animal, who will probably stand lifting up the injured leg, to feel, appreciate, and reflect on the whole amount of the pain he has incurred. As soon as it has subsided, he should be again quietly ridden two or three times over the offending rails, which, it will then be found, nothing can induce him to touch;. and having thus, at a small cost, purchased for himself very valuable experience, he may afterwards in the hunting-field be carefully made to jump any ordinary amount of timber.

A sportsman can hardly ride too slowly at high timber; for as height and width (that is to say to jump upwards or forwards) require different efforts, it is a waste of the poor animal's powers to make him do both when one only is required. In slowly trotting up to timber of any height or description, the rider should carefully abstain from attempting, by the bridle, to give his horse the smallest assistance. On the contrary, the moment the animal begins to rise, his reins should be loosened, to be drawn up and tightened only as he descends. With the single exception we shall soon notice, this principle of self-management applies to jumps of all sorts and sizes; for although, by a firm management of his bridle, a hunter ought to be made to feel as he approaches a fence that it is utterly impossible for him to swerve from it, yet the instant he is on the brink of taking it, his reins, as if by paralysis, should suddenly cease to afford him the smallest help, or to interfere with the mode in which (with only half a second to think) he may determine to deal with it. If he expects assistance, it may arrive a little sooner or a little later than his patience or impatience approves of, and thus between two stools (his own will and that of his rider) both come to the ground; whereas, if he knows that he has nothing to rely on but himself, he rises at his timber in the best and safest possible manner—namely, *in his own way.*

If we should have succeeded in satisfying our readers that they cannot ride too slowly at timber, we trust they will pardon us if we now endeavour to enforce upon them as an equally immutable axiom, that it is impossible for them to ride too fast at water.

WATER JUMPING.

Throughout England, and especially in Leicestershire and Northamptonshire, there are two descriptions of brooks. In one the water is about a foot or two below the level of the green fields through which it peacefully meanders. In the other, though deep enough to drown a man, it flows and occasionally rushes ten or twelve feet below the surface, between two loamy banks as perpendicular as the wall of a house. If a red, brown, or black coat, attended by a pair of leather, kersey, or corduroy breeches, ending in boots, plunge together into the first, they simply go in dry and come out wet. But, if a horse fails to clear the chasm, he is liable not only to fall backwards upon these articles of apparel, but afterwards, quite unintentionally, to strike their owner during the awkward struggles of both animals to swim.

Now, although to some of our readers it may possibly appear that the act of riding over "a bit of water" of the latter description has no legal claim to be included in the schedule headed "the pleasures and amusements of man," yet it may most truly be said that in a good run, or even in a bad one, there exists nothing that gives an ordinary rider more intense pleasure than the sight, say a quarter of a mile before him, of those well-known willows that indicate to him the line of beauty of the brook he is shortly to have the enjoyment of encountering—provided always that he knows his horse to be, what is justly called, "*good at water.*" On the other hand, it would be quite impossible to describe into how very small a compass the same man's heart would gradually collapse, as it approached the very same brook, on what is just as truly termed "*a brute at water.*" In any other description of fence the rider, if he has not ruined his horse's courage by vacillation of hand or heart, may confidently rely that he will accomplish it for him if he can, and if it cannot be accomplished, that he will try to jump through or over it, or, generally speaking, a good deal more than humanity dares to ride at.

If the bull-finch be too strong, the hunter may stick in it, or forcing through it into the ditch on the other side, may leave his owner hanging like a bird's-nest in its branches. An ox-fence—composed of two ditches, a bank, a pair of hedges, and a stiff, low, oak rail—may altogether prove too broad to be cleared. Timber also may be too high to be topped; yet, in all these cases, if the rider be but willing, the noble horse is always ready, ay, eager, to do his very best, and many a broken back and prostrate carcase, divested of its saddle and bridle, has been the melancholy result; and yet, with all this superabundance of high courage, almost every horse instinctively dislikes to jump water, an element which (until by a good rider it has been unbewitched) he appears to conceive to be forbidden to him to cross. For this reason, before a sportsman can ride with confidence at a brook, he requires not only a stout horse, but to know what sort of a heart lived beneath the waistcoat of the man by whom the animal was last hunted, for however badly bred he may be, he may have been made bold at water; while, on the other hand, however high-bred and handsome he may appear, however splendidly and cleverly he may throughout the run have been crossing single and double fences of every variety, yet, by an irresolute pair of hands, he may have been spoiled at water. Accordingly, when a gallant fox, followed after a short interval by a pack of hounds and a large scattered body of men and horses, passing like the shadows of summer clouds over the beautiful green sward of Northamptonshire, glide rapidly towards a brook, there occasionally appears among several of them a sudden transmigration of hearts and bodies, which to a foreigner, who did not understand the reason, would appear to be utterly inexplicable.

Although ten or twelve horses, gallantly taking it in their stride, have proved the jump to be an easy one, two or three of the foremost riders are seen to pull up, apparently afraid. In like manner, as horses and horsemen who had been riding boldly approach, it becomes evident to the meanest capacity, that the peg that holds in their steam is getting—sometimes in the biped, sometimes in the quadruped, and sometimes in both—looser and looser as they advance. The gallop is observed gradually to faint into a canter, which, as they approach the water, gets slower and slower, until souse! souse! souse! they one after the other blunder into it.

While a horse here is swimming, and there is struggling, and while a human head with handsome aristocratic features and black lank hair looking like that of Don Quixote when drenched with curds and whey, is seen rising in agony from below, two little thick-set, short-thighed men in scarlet, who throughout the run had been shirking many a small fence, cross the brook with terrific courage. That thoroughbred-mare, which has been clearing everything, swerves, while the ugly brute in her wake bucks over what she had refused as if he enjoyed the fun, which he really does. See! at what a tremendous pace this splendid-looking bay horse is galloping towards his doom. Both spurs are in his sides; the slight waving movement of the arms and shoulders of his fearless rider, and the firm grip of his hands, as he draws upon first one side of the bit and then the other, appear altogether to insure success. As soon, however, as the well-known rogue gets sight of the glare of the water, though his head is in such a vice that it is out of his power to swerve, and though his pace is such that it is utterly impossible for him to stop, yet, as if all his four legs were suddenly paralysed by fear, the high-bred sinner, all of a sudden, refuses to lift them, and accordingly, for thirty or forty feet, leaving behind a track like that of a railway, they slide along the wet, rich, loamy turf, until horse, and gallant, glorious Charlie * dive together, head-foremost, into the brook! In a few minutes, men in coats of all colours, trotting up one after another, walk their horses cautiously to the edge of the chasm, crane over as if to gaze at the frightened frogs that inhabit it, and after thus losing more or less of time they can never live to recover, canter or gallop in different directions in quest either of a bridge or a ford.

Now, while this serio-comic picture is before the eyes of our readers, that very small portion of them who have never been actors in such a scene will no doubt be not a little astonished to learn that of all fences on the surface of the globe there is no one that is so easy for a horse to jump as water.

If the footmarks of a good horse that has galloped over turf be measured, it will be found that in every stride his four feet have covered a space of twenty-two feet. If, in cool blood, he be very gently cantered at a common sheep-hurdle, without any ditch on one side of it or the other, it will be found that he has cleared, or rather has not been able to help clearing, from ten to twelve feet. In Egypt, an antelope chased by hounds on coming suddenly to a little crack or crevice in the ground caused

* The Honourable C. C.

by the heat of the sun, has been observed at a bound to clear thirty feet, and yet, on approaching a high wall, the same animal slackens his pace, stops for a second, and then pops over it. Almost any horse, particularly a young one, if cantered at a small prickly furze-hedge, would probably with a little skip rather than a jump clear at least fourteen feet, which in water would form a " brook " that would stop more than half of the large field of riders who in Northamptonshire and Leicestershire follow the Pytchley, Quorn, and Cottesmore hounds. Indeed, it not unfrequently happens that a ditch of glittering water, not seven feet broad, over which every hound has hopped hardly looking at it, will not only stop a number of horses and riders, but in a few minutes will, to the utter disgust and astonishment of the latter, *contain* several of them.

To prevent, however, this unnecessary and apparently discreditable botheration, all that is necessary is for the rider to overcome and overrule the instinctive aversion which his horse, and possibly he himself, have to jump water.

If, during a run with hounds, a young horse, that has never seen a brook, going a good pace, without receiving from the hands of his rider any tremulous check, arrives at, say a low hedge, on the other side of which he suddenly sees a wide expanse of water, he is quite sure to clear it ; and having thus broken the spell, if he be afterwards only fairly ridden, he will probably require no other instruction. If, however, as but too often is the case, on arriving at water that can be jumped favourably at a particular place, a young horse is obliged to wait for his turn, and during that awful pause sees some hunters refuse, and others splash in and flounder, he naturally combines together theory and practice, and accordingly, when called upon, refuses to do what he has always instinctively considered to be wrong; and as, generally speaking, it is impossible at that moment to force him, the run is lost.

Under this state of the case, the master of the culprit on some fine non-hunting day, armed with spurs and a cut-whip, should conduct him to any ugly-looking little ditch, not above half a dozen feet broad (for it is the quality and not the quantity of the shining element that creates his fear), and then, carefully abstaining to excite his courage, ride him at it very slowly and timidly, on purpose to ensure his refusing it, which, of course, he is quite certain to do. After once again leading him into this trap, a duel, perfectly harmless to the biped, must be fought. It may last ten minutes, a quarter, half an hour, or possibly two hours; but, sooner or later, the little misunderstanding is certain to end in the rebel all of a sudden doing willingly, and then repeating five or six times, what, after all, was nothing at all for him

to do; and from that moment, if he be only fairly
"handled," he will remember, whenever he sees water,
the lesson which taught him that it was made on purpose
to be crossed.

To maintain and encourage this doctrine, on coming
in sight of a brook, his courage, by very gentle touches
of the spur, should be excited, while, by pulling harder
and harder at the bridle, his speed inversely should be
slightly diminished, until he arrives within about eighty
yards, when, gradually relaxing the reins, and yet grasping them so firmly that it is impossible for him to swerve,
his pace should *always* be made to freshen as he proceeds, until on arriving at the brink it has attained its
maximum. In short, in riding at a brook, a horse should
be taught to feel that no choice will be given to him *to*
go in or over, but that over he *must* go, for want of time
to jump in.

By this simple management a horse will very soon
learn not only to rush at water, but to enjoy the very
sight of it; and as his rider can then trust implicitly
to his honour, we end as we almost began, by stating
that, although there exists no obstruction in a run that
creates so many sorrows as water, there is no fence that
is so easy for a horse to jump, if he will but try; in fact
on coming to it at the top of his speed, if he will only
hop upwards a few feet, his momentum cannot fail to

carry him across; whereas, if in approaching it he slackens his speed, nine times out of ten he may safely be booked to be "*in*."

MODES OF SWIMMING A HORSE.

In England, a hunting man, in deference to the thermometer and for the love of his clothes, usually avoids forcing his horse to swim. In a warm climate, however, the operation is attended with no danger or inconvenience whatever. In riding gradually into deep water the animal, just before he floats, appears to step rather uneasily, as if on legs of different lengths; but the instant his feet take leave of the ground, or if at once he plunges out of his depth from a bank, as soon as his head comes up he proceeds as free from jolts of any sort as a balloon in the air, grunting and groaning, nevertheless, heavily, at the injustice of having a man's weight superadded to his own, the specific gravity of which but little exceeds that of the element into which he is striving not to sink. Instinctively, however, adjusting himself to the most favourable position, which throws the hind part of his body about a foot under water, he makes the best of a bad bargain, and then all the rider has to do is not to destroy the poor animal's equilibrium by pulling even an ounce at his bridle. Indeed, in crossing a broad stream, the most effectual way to prevent over-balancing him, and also to stop his grunting, is either to slip sideways from his back, and then, half-swimming, to be dragged alongside him by a lock of his mane firmly entwined among the fingers of the right hand, or, as is invariably practised by the red Indians, to be towed by his tail, in which case the man floating on the surface of the water is quite safe from the heels of the horse struggling many feet below him. By this plan, of course, the water, instead of the horse, sustains the weight of the man.

JUDICIOUS RIDING.

In a closely-enclosed country, with slow hounds, a cold scent, and a fat huntsman, a good jumping nag is what is mainly required. But to follow fleet hounds across large grass fields, however excellent may be a horse's jumping, however clever at doubles, safe at timber, bold at water ; and though to all of these accomplishments be added every qualification of hand, heel, head, and heart, which an experienced rider can possibly possess, "the tottle of the whole" must inevitably amount to "disappointment," unless the animal be able to maintain the requisite pace. And yet in a run it does not at all follow that the leading horse is the fastest, that the hindmost is the slowest, that a heaving flank is an indication of impaired lungs, or a still one of good wind. On the contrary, it is often but too true that the first ought to have been the last, and the last the first; so much depends on the manner in which the different horses have been ridden.

When a man, pursued by a detachment of cavalry, is riding to save his own life, or when, at the risk of his life, he is trying to take away that of a poor little fox, success in either case depends of course on the pace at which he can proceed. Now it is a very common mistake in both the instances we have named to endeavour to attain the desired object by maintaining, like the seconds-hand of a clock, an equable rate, whereas, just as a ship spreads out and unreefs all her canvas when the wind is light, and before a hurricane scuds away under bare poles, so should the pace which a rider exacts from his horse depend on the state or character of the ground he has to traverse; that is to say, he should hold him together and save him through deep-ploughed land,—race him across light, dry turf,—grasping the mane, go slowly up the last half of an ordinary hill,—spin him very fast indeed down every declivity,—and in jumping fences endeavour, by tranquillizing rather than exciting, to induce him to take as little out of himself at each, as is possible.

With considerate treatment of this sort, a warrior or a sportsman may go from a given point to another in a given time without distressing his horse, while the hot-faced man who, in attempting to follow him, has been straining through heavy ground, rushing up steep accli-vities, restraining in going down hills, and galloping at every fence, large or small, has not only blown his poor horse, but as he sits astride his panting body and bleeding sides, fancies he has done so *by going fast;* and accord-ingly, when he sees afar off the fellow who, on an inferior animal, has outstripped him, he contemptuously wonders to himself how such a tortoise could possibly have beaten such a hare!

USE AND ABUSE OF SPURS.

Buxtorff, in describing the horses, chariots, and riders of the ancient Egyptians, says that the word "*Parash,*" or rider, is derived from the Hebrew root to prick, or spur.

In horsemanship there is no subject so worthy of consi-deration, most especially by any one wearing the name of

E

a gentleman, as the use and the abuse of spurs. In riding horses that since their birth have been roaming in a state of nature, that have never tasted corn, and that have never been excited by men to race against each other, it would be impossible to induce them to exhaust in man's service the *whole* of their strength except by punishment; for, as they have never obeyed any other will than their own, so soon as they become tired, they attempt not only to diminish their speed, but to stop altogether, and as their bodies have no value whatever, and as their riders have spurs with rowels an inch long, and no mercy, it might be supposed that, under such circumstances, an uncivilized human being would be very apt to inflict unnecessary punishment on the poor subdued animal beneath him. But it is mercifully ordained that it is the interest as well as the duty of man to husband the powers of the animals that serve him, and accordingly the wild rider, when carefully observed, is found to be infinitely more lenient in the use of his spurs than the comrade who calls himself civilized, simply because the former by his own and his hereditary experience has learned that the spur should be the *last*, and not the *first* resource of any rider who desires to be carried a given distance in the smallest possible amount of time. Accordingly, to attain this object, the animal on starting, without any punishment, is restrained by his bridle, and encouraged, so long as it is possible to do so, in his zeal to advance : when that begins to flag, by working the bit in his mouth he is induced to proceed ; when this fails, a very slight touch of one spur becomes necessary, to be increased only as required. When excitation on that side is found to have lost its effect, it is tried very gently on the other ; and thus does the wild rider proceed, until he ends the distance by coming in violently spurring with both heels at every step of a gallop, that, from sheer faintness, has dwindled down to a rate of hardly six miles an hour.

Now a civilized traveller almost invariably commits not only the unnecessary cruelty but the error of using his spurs the moment his horse, as he fancies, *requires* them ; by which means he for a very short time encourages, and then so completely discourages his poor weak animal that he often fails altogether to get to the end of the distance which his wild comrade, without the slightest desire to be merciful, has rapidly and scientifically accomplished.

In the management, however, of horses in England, the conditions of the case are totally different. Tied to mangers, in which they feast on dry oats, beans, and hay, no sooner do they leave their stables than the very sight of creation animates them ; every carriage that trots by, and every rider that passes, excites them. When brought into condition, and then encouraged to compete against each other, their physical strength, though artificially raised to the maximum, remains far behind their instinctive courage and disposition to go till they die, in almost any service in which they may be employed.

Under these circumstances, the *use* of the spur is to enable man to maintain his supremacy, and, whenever necessary, promptly and efficiently to suppress mutiny in whatever form it may break out. If a restiff horse objects to pass a particular post, he must be forced to do so. If he refuses to jump water, he must, as we have described, be conquered. But in every case of this nature a combination of cool determination, plenty of time, and a little punishment, invariably form a more permanent cure than a prescription composed only of the last ingredient; for as anger, in a horse as in a man, is a short madness, an animal under its influence is not in so good a state to learn and remember the lesson of obedience which man is entitled to impart, as when he has time given to him to observe that the just sentence to which he is sternly required to submit, is tempered with mercy.

But if the *uses* of the spur are few, its *abuses* are many. On the race-course, the eagerness and impetuosity of thorough bred horses to contend against each other are so great, that for a considerable time it is difficult to prevent them, especially young ones, from starting before the signal is given. As soon as they are " off," it becomes all that the best riders in the world can do merely to guide them : to stop them would be impossible. Occasionally their very limbs "break down" in their endeavours to win ; and yet, while they are exerting their utmost powers and strength,— to the shame of their owners and to the disgrace of the nation, the riders are allowed, as a sort of show off, to end the contest by whipping and spurring, which, nine times out of ten, has the effect of making the noblest quadruped in creation do what is technically called " SHUT UP," which means that the ungenerous and ungrateful punishment and degradation that have been unjustly inflicted upon him have cowed his gallant spirit, and have broken an honest heart !

But the ignorance as well as the brutality of unnecessarily spurring a hunter is even worse than that just portrayed. When a young horse that has never seen a hound, is ridden up, for the first time in his life, *not* to a meet, at which the whole pack are to be seen, but merely to the side of a covert, which, hidden from view, they are drawing, it might reasonably be conceived that under such circumstances he could not have an idea of their past, present, or future proceedings—we mean, where they had come from, what they were doing, or what they were going to do. However, no sooner does a hound, from laziness, or possibly from feeling that he has been sufficiently pricked by thorns, briars, and gorse, creep out for a few seconds before him, than—" Angels and ministers of grace defend us!"—the young horse pricks up his ears, stares intently at him, holds his breath, and, with a heart beating so hard that it may be not only heard but felt by the rider, he breaks out into a perspiration, which, on the appearance of a few more hounds, turns into foam as white as soap-suds. On an old hound—by a single deep tone, instantaneously certified by the sharp, shrill, resolute voice of the huntsman—announcing to creation that the one little animal which so many bigger ones have been so good as to visit, is " at home," the young horse paws the ground; if restrained, evinces a slight disposition to rear; until, by the time the whole pack—encouraged by the cheery cry, " *Have at him!* "—in full chorus have struck up their band of music, he appears to have become almost ungovernable, and is evidently outrageously anxious to do—he knows not what; and accordingly, when a sudden shriek, scream, or, as the Irish term it, " screech," rather than a holla, from the opposite side of the covert, briefly announces, as by a telegram, the joyous little word " AWAY!" suiting his action to it, " *away* " the young horse often bolts with his rider, just as likely " away " from the hounds as with them. If he follows them, infuriated by ardour, which neither he nor his rider have power to control, he looks at nothing, thinks of nothing, until at full speed coming to say a stiff fence he disdains to rise at, a lesson is offered to him, which, however, he is a great deal too much excited to learn by heart; and so, before his rider has had time enough to uncoil himself from his roll, the "young 'un," without a thought or disposition to wait for the old gentleman, leaves him on the ground to think about the hounds; while with dangling stirrups, reins hanging loose on his neck, and outstretched neck and tail, he is once again "up and at 'em!"

Although, however, a horse, when his blood is hot, does not appear to notice a fall, he thinks a good deal about it in the stable; and, accordingly, the next time he comes out, instead of being infuriated, he only evinces a superabundance of eagerness and excitement to follow the hounds, which his rider can gradually and often rapidly succeed in allaying, until the animal may be honestly warranted as "steady with hounds," which means that, although he will follow them over anything till he drops, he has lived to learn that to enable him to do so he had better not unnecessarily maim his legs or tumble himself head over heels. With this mixture of high courage and discretion he does his best; and, as affecting evidence of this truth, although, after having been ten or twelve hours out of his stable, with apparent cheerfulness, he brings his rider home, yet it is the latter only that then proves to be "as hungry as a hunter," while the exhausted stomach of the "vrai Amphitryon" —the real hunter, remains for many hours, and sometimes days, without the smallest appetite for corn or beans.

If this plain statement be correct, leaving humanity entirely out of the question, how ignorant and contemptible is that man who is seen during a run not only to be spurring his horse with both heels whenever he comes to deep ploughed ground or to the bottom of a steep hill, but who, just as if he were singing to himself a little song, or, "for want of thought," whistling to himself a favourite tune, throughout the run, continues, as a sort of idle accompaniment to his music, to dangle more or less severely the rowel of one spur into the side of a singed hunter, who all the time is a great deal more anxious to live with the hounds than he is! But, as dishonesty is always the worst policy, so does this discreditable conduct produce results opposite to those expected to be attained; for instead of spurring a poor horse throughout a run hastening his speed, it has very often put a fatal end to it.

In riding to hounds it occasionally happens that a resolute, experienced hunter, knowing what he can break through, what he must clear, and who has learned to

be cunning enough never to jump farther than is necessary, approaches a fence on the other side of which a
horse and rider have been just observed to disappear in
a brook that has received them. Now, if throughout the
run the rider has never once touched his faithful horse
with spurs, and if on reaching this fence both rowels
suddenly are made to prick him, in an instant he under-
stands the friendly hint, and accordingly, by exerting
much greater powers than he had intended, he saves
himself and his benefactor from a bad fall. In a few
cases of this nature the use of spurs to a sportsman is
not only excusable, but invaluable. On no account,
however, should they be used to propel a hunter to
the end of a run, but, on the contrary, whenever the
noble animal tells his rider honestly that he is distressed, he should gratefully be patted on the neck,
pulled up, and walked carefully to the nearest habitation,
where he can rest and obtain a few gulps of warm gruel.
Humanity will not disapprove of this course; but we also
recommend young sportsmen to adopt it, to maintain
their pleasures and to save their own purses. To ride
a distressed horse at a strong fence, is very likely to
break a collar-bone, that will require a surgeon and half
the hunting season to mend. To ride him to death,
entails extortion from the breeches-pocket of a sum of
money—usually of three figures—to replace him.

How to treat a Hunter in the Field.

Of the Ten Commandments which man is ordered to obey, it may truly be said that there is no one which it is not alike his interest as well as his duty to fulfil. In every station in life in which it may have pleased God to call him, he rises by being honest—sinks by being dishonest; gains more by forgiving an injury than by avenging it; creates friends by kindness—enemies by unkindness; causes even bad servants to be faithful by making them happy; and thus, while he is apparently serving others, in reality he is materially benefiting himself.

By a similar dispensation of Providence, it is the interest as well as the duty of man to be merciful to the animals created for his use.

The better they are fed, and the more carefully they are attended to, the more valuable they become. If by any accident they be either maimed or lamed, money is gained by giving them rest, lost by forcing them to continue to move; in short, while sickness is costly so long as it remains uncured, any neglect which causes a diseased animal to die, inflicts upon the owner thereof a fine exactly equal to what would have been gained had he been saved.

This humane regulation of Nature, which may justly

be entitled "a law for the protection of animals from cruelty," applies to every hunting stable, large as well as small, not only in the United Kingdom, but throughout the world. Indeed if it be lucrative to a man to take care of the sheep, oxen, and other animals he is rearing merely to eat, it is most especially his interest by every attention in his power to enable his hunter to carry him safely; and yet, on this vital subject, for such it is, there usually exists in the horseman a want of consideration which, to any one who will reflect on the subject, must appear highly reprehensible.

It may readily be admitted that hunting men, generally speaking, make great efforts first to obtain horses sufficiently strong to carry them, and secondly, to increase their strength by administering to them plenty of the very best food, with every thing that science can add, to improve what is called their condition. But, strange to say, after having thus made every possible exertion to create or constitute a power sufficient to carry them, after having at great expense and infinite trouble amassed it, they unscientifically exhaust it; and accordingly at the end of a long day it continually happens that a rider dislocates a bone, cracks a limb, or loses his life, from having as it were; like an improvident spendthrift, simply from want of consideration, expended funds necessary for his existence.

When Alexander the Great pompously asked Diogenes what he could do to serve him, the cynic curtly replied, "*Get out of my sunshine.*" In like manner if a heavy man, patting his hunter on the neck, were to ask "What can I do to please you?" the dumb animal, if he could but speak, would just as bluntly reply, "*Get off my back;*" and yet men, especially heavy ones, will throughout a long day sit smiling in their saddles, without reflecting that by doing so they are every minute and every hour wearying muscles which, after having carried them brilliantly in one run, are, if a second fox can be found, to be required to carry them through another.

A deal board of the length of a horse's back, with its ends resting on the bottoms of two chairs, would break, a stout pole would snap, and a rod of iron would bend, under the feet of a heavy man jumping upon them only for a few minutes; and yet the same heavy man who in the same short period would become dead tired of carrying even his only child, neglects to consider the mechanical effects caused by the mere pressure (to say nothing of the concussion produced by jumping) for seven or eight hours of fourteen, sixteen, or eighteen stone on a horse's back, which is not a solid bone, but one scotched or sawn by Nature into a decreasing series of twenty-nine vertebræ (namely, dorsal, 18; lumbar, 6;

sacral, 5), averaging less than two inches in length and breadth.

The wearying effects which the infliction of weight produces on the muscular powers of a horse may be practically demonstrated as follows:

In crossing a particular region in the plains of South America, in which there are literally no inhabitants to assist in catching the horses, it is necessary for the attendant on the traveller to select and drive a troop of them, which continue to gallop before him in high spirits, while the animal beneath him, unaccustomed to extra weight, becomes weaker and fainter, until with bleeding sides, drooping head, and panting flanks, he is left standing by himself on the plain completely exhausted.

No less than five times is the traveller obliged to repeat the operation of remounting what is called, what is considered, and what really is "a fresh horse," which in his turn, solely by his rider's *weight*, becomes tired, without metaphor, almost "to death," in the presence of the unmounted horses, who, with nothing to carry but their own carcases, are still showing no signs whatever of distress.*

Now although a horse highly fed and in good wind

---

* The ancient Greeks practised riding two or three horses tied together: the horseman vaulting from the tired to the fresh one.

and condition has greater muscular power than those in
the state of nature just described, it is undeniable that
the difference between carrying weight and no weight
must produce in each of them similar results; that is
to say, those muscles which are oppressed suffer by the
amount of weight inflicted upon them, multiplied by the
time they are subjected to it, and again negatively enjoy
the periods of rest, be they ever so short, during which
they are relieved from it.

And yet, although every body learns by daily experience that the imposition of weight tires his own muscles,
that the abstraction of weight instantly relieves them;
and although it is a known fact that when two thorough-
bred horses are racing together, an addition of only
seven pounds weight will cause the bearer of it to be
" distanced," yet men of rank, intelligence, wealth, and
generous feelings, are, at the outside of a covert which
the hounds are drawing, to be constantly seen late in the
day with cigars in their mouths, conversing and occasionally even extolling to each other the qualifications of the noble animals on whose backs they have
been thoughtlessly sitting for six or eight hours, as
hard as a hen upon a nest full of eggs just about to
hatch.

In the army when a soldier who has committed an
offence is sentenced to crawl for several hours up and

down a parade "in heavy marching order," it is justly called "*punishment drill.*"

In like manner, if an unruly horse were to be sentenced merely to stand in his stable for ten hours with a sack of heavy oats, weighing (at forty-two pounds the bushel) exactly twelve stone, the punishment or pain his muscles would undergo in bearing such a weight for so long a time would be so severe that by almost everybody it would be termed "cruel." But if, instead of being quiescent, the sack of oats could by mechanical contrivances be continually lifted up, and then by a series of heavy blows dropped down upon vertebræ which have nothing but muscles to support them, the punishment would be condemned as excruciating; and yet this excruciating punishment is quite unnecessarily inflicted upon hunters by a lot of good-humoured heavy men, simply from neglecting to reflect that if they would, only even for a minute or two, occasionally unload their saddles, to walk a little, stand still a little, or, while the hounds are drawing, sit placidly upon the stile or gate that is often close beside them, they would not only perform an act of mercy, but they would impart or rather restore strength, tone, and activity to muscles which, if vigorous, can carry them safely, but which, if exhausted, must inevitably fail when tested by a severe run.

In deference and in reference to this law of Nature, it may truly be added that the proprietor of a valuable stud of horses would gain a great deal of money as well as ensure safety if he would select and set apart, say two of them for his groom to ride to covert, leading by his side, with an empty saddle, the horse that is to *hunt;* by which arrangement the cheap hack, which from the covert-side has only to return to his stable, would carry, and the costly hunter which is to endure the toil of a long day would for two, three, and occasionally four hours be relieved from the weight of about a sack of oats, to say nothing of but too often a pair of hard and heavy hands; and thus the wealthy rider, on descending from the box of his four-in-hand drag, would, at a saving rather than an expenditure of money, have secured for himself the benefit of mounting a fresh hunter, instead of one more or less tired by what in our statistical returns are designated "*preventible causes.*"

How to bring a Hunter home.

Of the long list of hunters annually killed by what is called "a severe day," about one-third may be said to have died from bad riding, and two-thirds by improper treatment after the run was over.

Supposing, as is often the case, that the majority of the horses that are "in at the death" have been out of their stables from seven to eight hours, that they have been conspicuous in two or three runs, and that, with the lower edge of the sun nearly touching the horizon, they have to travel from fifteen to twenty miles to their stables, a question of vital importance has to be determined, namely, whether they are to perform that exertion in the way most agreeable to their riders, or most advantageous to themselves.

In the settlement of this problem the poor horses have, of course, neither voice nor vote.   On their behalf, therefore, we will endeavour to contrast the attentions that ought to be bestowed upon them, with the inconsiderate treatment to which they are usually subjected.

In a severe day's work a hunter suffers from a combination of three causes: violent muscular exertion, an overexcitement of the circulation of the blood, and debility of his whole system caused by abstinence from food.

Of these causes, the latter produces by far the worst results ; for although to the muscles may be given rest, and to the circulation repose, the stomach of a horse is so small and, in comparison to his noble spirit, so delicate, that on becoming empty and exhausted it is in an unfit state to digest food, and accordingly is beneficently deprived by Nature of appetite to receive it.

F

Now, under all these circumstances, it is evident that the most humane, and, taking the money value of the poor animal into consideration, the most economical course which the rider can pursue is as follows :

As soon as the day's sport is over, the hunter should be led, or ridden, at a walk for about a mile to some stable—it little matters whether it be good, bad, or indifferent—or strawyard, where he can stand for a minute or two.

When the object for which he has been taken there has been accomplished, about a third of a pail of gruel, or lukewarm water, with a mouthful or two of hay, should be given to him. To prevent his being chilled, the instant he has swallowed it he should be mounted ; and whatever be the distance he has to accomplish, he should then be ridden homewards at a constant steady pace of about seven miles an hour.

After a staghunt in which the hunter may have been galloping principally on roads, soft ground (if it be not deep) should be selected ; but when, as is usually the case in fox hunting, the muscles have, during the greater part of the day, been struggling in heavy soil, he should be permitted to travel, as he invariably tries to do, on the hard road.

As they proceed together, if the rider will dismount for a few minutes to lead his horse down or up any very steep hill, both animals will be greatly relieved. With this exception, however, there should be no alteration of pace or stoppage of any sort or kind.

If, at the quiet rate described, the hunter begins to blunder, it will be proper that he should be what is termed "wakened" by a word of remonstrance, or, if that prove insufficient, by a slight touch of the spur. But if, as is usual, the noble animal travels safely, the duller he is encouraged to go, the greater will be the relief to that overexcitement of the circulation of his blood, and that violent palpitation of his heart, from which he has suffered.

By this treatment a hunter in good condition can, in the shortest possible time, be brought home not only cool in body and tranquil in mind, but with limbs *less* wearied than when they took leave of the hounds.

On entering his stable, in the manger of which he should find, ready to welcome him, a handful or two of picked sweet hay, his bridle should be taken off, his girths unloosened, and then, before his body is touched, all his four legs, after being cleared only of rough dirt, should, without a moment's delay, be swathed from the knees and hocks to the hoofs by rough bandages of coarse common drugget, which maintain in the extremities that healthy circulation which, from the minuteness of their veins, is prone, after great exhaustion, to stagnate, producing (especially when caused by the ignorant custom of washing the legs) disorganisation and disease throughout the whole system, as the following fact will exemplify.

Several seasons ago almost every hunter in Leicestershire and Northamptonshire was afflicted by a combination of lumps, bumps, swelled legs, and cracked heels, caused by the extraordinary wetness of the ground, and the consequent ablutions of the legs. After the veterinary surgeons had in vain nearly exhausted their pharmacopœia, the oldest and most experienced among them directed that on no account should horses' legs, after hunting, be washed; and wherever this plain, sensible prescription was followed, all the symptoms just described rapidly subsided.

If the hunter, as is now-a-days almost invariably the case, has been singed, the less he is excited and tormented by cleaning (the main object of which, with many strappers, seems to be to make the poor animal crouch his back, bite his manger, and violently work all his legs as if they were on a tread-mill) the better.

At the expiration of about an hour white flannel bandages should, however, be substituted for the coarse ones, under which the dirt will then be found to crumble away like warm sand.

If his ears (the opposite extremities or antipodes of

his legs) have become cold, circulation therein should be restored by the groom quietly rubbing them with a cloth; and as soon as they are dry, and the animal what is called "comfortable," a pailful of warm gruel given to him at intervals, a bran mash, a rackful of hay, a clean stall, some chilled water, and a fresh bed, will do all that is possible to procure for him a night's rest, free from fever; and this vital object having been accomplished, *the next day* he may receive without injury, and indeed with great benefit, his usual allow ance of the best oats and beans.

Now, in contrast to the mode of treatment just described, we will endeavour to offer to our readers a similar sketch of that which, especially by what are termed "fast men" (possibly because "lucus à non lucendo" they make it a rule never to "fast" or abstain from any thing they desire to do), is usually adopted.

After the run is over, while one sturdy hound that all the rest seem to be afraid of is stealing straight away with the poor fox's head, and while another at his utmost speed, chased by several, is meandering through the pack with a lump of unsavoury, very dirty fur in his mouth, groups of riders, some sitting astride, some like pretty ladies with a right leg hanging over the saddle's pommel, some with cambric handkerchiefs mopping moist heads and red faces, and some adjusting

mustachios, are to be seen reciting to each other incidents aqueous, terrestrial, and amphibious, of the run.
Here and there, one of the most handsome, as he talks,
leans forward for a moment to pat the neck of his
thorough bred animal in grateful acknowledgment of
the particular feat he is describing.

In what is considered by all to be hardly a quarter of
an hour, (for when men sit conversing about themselves,
they little know how fast old father Time gallops), this
joyous *conversazione* ends by the talkers, after giving to
each other here and there a farewell nod, radiating in
masses along roads, or across a fence or two, to gain the
road that leads to their respective homes; but as, by
this time, in almost every mouth a newly-lighted cigar
happens to be gleaming, they resume their talk as they
walk towards an object described at the back of the head
of almost every one, in the humane words "gruel for
my horse," to be obtained, not exactly at the first farm,
but at the first great town, be it even half a dozen or so,
miles off.

On reaching the best hotel, at which there is seldom
hot water enough ready for all the cavalcade, the horses
are handed over to that lot of idle attendants who,
some out of the stable and some from the bar, greedily
rush forward to grasp their bridles. "GRUEL" is most
kindly ordered for them all; but as it is voted that

there is no great necessity to see them drink it, the landlord's smiling invitation is accepted, and in a few minutes, by one of those extraordinary contingencies that nobody could have anticipated, each gentleman rider is to be seen, in high glee and good-humour, sipping from a tumbler (which for some quaint reason or other happens to contain a silver spoon) something that is evidently very wet and very *warm*. Alas! little thinking that his poor faithful horse, whose perform- ances he had so lately been describing, with cold clammy ears is shivering, chilled by having just drank too freely of "a summut," without a spoon in it, that was wet and *cold*.

On mounting, and clattering out of the paved yard of the hotel, most of the riders fancy they are all the better —many of their horses feel that they are all the worse for the half hour's rest and "gruelling" that was ordered for them. But although the quadrupeds leave behind them the fatal pail, the silver spoon has apparently accompanied the bipeds, who, like the favoured children of Fortune, are, externally as well as internally, under the influence of ardent spirits.

All thoroughly happy, they think neither of their horses nor their homes; but, according to the subject of their conversation, and the state of their cigars, they walk, trot, sometimes very slow, and sometimes very

fast, until, on coming to a portion of the road bounded
by grass, although their poor horses have had an over-
dose of both excitement and of heavy ground, they touch
them with their spurs, to re-enjoy, for a short distance,
a hand-gallop.

In short, travelling at what may either be described
as "every pace," or "no pace at all," they unnecessarily
excite and fatigue their horses; and yet, after all, though
undoubtedly "fast men," they are often considerably
more than an hour longer in getting home than if they
had proceeded at a *slow*, quiet, steady, but unceasing
rate.

On reaching this goal the poor horse who, from eight
o'clock in the morning, has been working on an empty
stomach, is led by his bridle to his stable.   The rich
man prepares himself for his dinner.   Since he break-
fasted, at a quarter before nine in the morning, he has, at
a low average, enjoyed the slight intoxication of very
nearly a cigar per hour, besides certain refreshments
which he brought out with him, and the few crumbs of
comfort at the hotel at which he stopped to give "gruel"
to his horse.

Nevertheless, on the principle that "by-gones are
by-gones," after his ablutions, exactly as if he had been
fasting, he sits down to a capital meal, joyous conversation, luscious wine.   In due time he "joins the ladies,"

and as, with rosy cheeks, and with a cup of fragrant coffee in his hand, he stands in patent-leather boots, whispering soft nonsense, the butler, white in waistcoat and in tie, most respectfully interrupts it to inform his Lordship that "Mr. Willo'thewhisp" has just sent up a strapper from the stable to say that "Harkaway" "has took to shaking, and seems very queer indeed all over!" and accordingly, on the evening of the next day, the poor high-bred animal, with protruding tongue, glacy eyes dishonoured by a few particles of dust, hollow flank, and outstretched limbs, lies in his stall, stiff and stark, a victim to the unintentional maltreatment and thoughtless mismanagement of his noble master.

How to dress for Hunting.

As in our Nursery Rhymes it is truly stated that—

" Whatever brawls disturb the streets, there should be peace at home,"

so it might be expected that, however violently men may differ among each other as to the shape, cut, or fashion of their clothes, they would at all events, like a brood of chickens nestling under their parent hen, concur together in selecting that description of warmth which is congenial, and in avoiding every substance uncongenial to their nature. And yet how true and how strange it is to say that of the best educated, most scientific, most intelligent, and wealthiest classes in England, more than three-quarters live and suffer, wither and decay, in clothing as uncongenial to their nature as a covering of slate, in substitution of their mother, would be to a nest of young birds!

In a cold, wet, variable climate like England, where, especially in winter, extra clothing to that granted to man by nature is absolutely required, the sensible and self evident course for the Lord of Creation to pursue would be to select from the living creatures around him, and appropriate, the fur, feathers, wool, or hair that warm *them*.

And yet, instead of thus cherishing blood by what has especially been created by Nature to warm blood, we repair to the cold ground for succour! From its produce we pick cotton and hemp, nourished by a circulation of *sap ;* in short, from a mixture of perversity and ignorance which appear to be as inexcusable as they are unaccountable, we run for protection to the wrong kingdom, to commit the unnatural error of clothing ourselves as vegetables instead of as animals !

If a man has had nothing to do in this world but, with a crown on his head and with his knees closed, to sit very still on a throne,—with a coronet balanced on his head, to walk very gently from one carpeted room to another,—or in very tight boots to stand gaping at his fellow creatures as, at different rates, they pass in procession before his club window, he may live, die, and be screwed up in his coffin without ever discovering the mistake he has committed; but, on the other hand, if he has only for a few years been exposed to hard work, and even without severe labour to the vicissitudes of climate, he very soon finds out that he is suffering from the uncongenial clothing in which he has been existing. Indeed, our soldiers and sailors on active service, whether within the tropics or the polar regions; our labourers, especially those who work underground in mines; in fact all classes of people, sooner or later, are not only by medical men admonished, but by the aches and pains of Caliban, with all the ills which flesh is heir to when it has been suddenly chilled, are forced to discard vegetable covering, in order to nestle, for the remainder of their lives, in woollen clothing next to their skin; and when a man has lived to make this important discovery, he keenly feels that although his friend and neighbour would be grievously out of fashion were he to walk about the world with his cotton drawers over his woollen trousers, and with his Irish-linen shirt outside his coat, yet that it would be less insane and infinitely more reasonable for him to do so than to exist, as is still the general custom of the community, in vegetable garments, covered on the outside with woollen clothing. In fact, it is undeniable that a sinner doing penance in a hair shirt enjoys better health than a saint in a lawn one.

For ordinary work only ordinary protection may be required; but as in hunting the rider is exposed to every variety of weather, good, bad, and indifferent,—to sunshine, cold, wind, rain, sleet, and snow,—to a heating gallop, with a plunge into a brook, ending by a chilling detention at every fresh covert which the hounds are drawing, it must be obvious that to fortify himself against all these alternations, he requires not merely the dress superficially prescribed, namely, a scarlet coat, leather breeches, top boots, and a hat or a hunting cap, but beneath this gaudy surface the most wholesome description of underclothing that science can devise.

Now in the hunting field, experience, after a desperate struggle, has at last demonstrated the advantages of wool; and, accordingly, for some years it has been, and is, the habit and the fashion of most men, especially "the fast ones," entirely to discard linen, and in lieu thereof to ride in flannel shirts—pink, red, crimson, or many coloured —and in drawers drawn either from the back of a lamb or a sheep. The coats are lined throughout backs and sleeves with flannel; and as the waistcoats have also

sleeves of the same material, the rider of the present day
is not only wholesomely warmed, but his clothing, from
being divided into many layers, is capable of keeping
out a moderate shower of several hours' duration.

To provide, however, against a soaking day, it is usual
to put on woollen drawers of extra thickness; but as it
is impossible to foretell how long it will rain—for when
it pours early in the morning, it not unusually becomes
bright at eleven, and vice versâ—this precaution often
proves not only unnecessary, but throughout the whole day
a very unpleasant incumbrance, which, after all, fortifies a
great deal more of the propria persona than is required.

A better plan, or "dodge," therefore, when the morning
threatens to turn into a drenching day, is to place over
the thin drawers on the surface only of each thigh,
(which, from its position in riding, and from the dripping
from the brim of the hat, invariably becomes wet, while
all the rest of the drawers remain dry), a piece of stout
serge or saddler's flannel, which will keep out the rain
for a long time; which, when wet, can in a moment be
drawn out, dried at any little inn, farm, or cottage fire,
and then replaced; and which, if, from the cessation of
the rain, it be not needed, instead of heating the owner,
can be rolled up and transferred into one of his coat
pockets, to remain there like a letter addressed Poste
restante, "till called for."

Of boots there are just two sorts: those that do protect the mechanism of the knee, and those that don't protect it. Of these, the latter are the most fashionable. However, leaving the rider to make his choice, it need only be observed that if the soles are broad, the feet within them will be warm; and, if narrow, cold; simply from the circulation of the blood having, by pressure, become impeded.

Chilblains are often the result, though more usually caused by the mistaken luxury, as it is called, of putting the feet when chilled by hunting into warm instead of into cold water, the temperature of which, if possible, should be lowered in proportion to the coldness of the feet: indeed, whenever flesh is frost-bitten, the well-known practical remedy is snow; while on the other hand an approach to fire instantly produces mortification.

And now for a very few words respecting the upper, or garret-story of the rider.

In Leicestershire, many years ago, it was, and in Surrey it still is, the fashion for "fast men" to ride in the hunting caps worn by all huntsmen and whippers in.

They were invented to protect the head, whereas they have very properly been discarded in the shires because they have proved to be its enemy, or rather the enemy of the rider's neck, which is liable, on a very slight fall, as was lately the case with poor Lord Waterford, to be broken, literally on account of the protection given to the head by the cap, which, instead of collapsing like the buffer of a railway carriage, as a hat does when it is crushed by a fall, transfers to the neck the whole concussion of the blow.

In all hunting hats a small hole should be made, either in the crown or sides, to admit fresh air, and to allow the steam from a hot head to escape, instead of heating the brain and injuring the hair.

As regards the latter, for the sake not only of our masculine, but of our feminine readers (one of whose innumerable natural ornaments is their hair), we will venture to point out another mistake which is generally committed by our seeking assistance from the inanimate instead of the animate portion of creation.

We all know that throughout our country, and indeed throughout the world, there are exposed for sale two descriptions of oil; and as one of them is compressed from vegetables, and the other obtained from animals, without reflecting for a moment, it ought surely, at once, to occur to everybody, that as all things were created good, "according to their kind," vegetable oil would not prove to be "good" for animal substances; and accordingly, every coachman and stable-man concur in testifying, on their practical experience, that while animal oil mollifies and preserves all descriptions of bridles and harness, vegetable oil burns and destroys any leather it is applied to, disfiguring as well as impairing it by deep cracks, crossing each other like network (declared in Johnson's Dictionary to mean "anything reticulated or decussated at equal distances, with interstices between the intersections ").

But just as the texture of linen is infinitely finer and more beautiful than that of broadcloth or flannel, so is vegetable oil clearer and more inodorous than animal oil, for which reasons the former, instead of the latter, is almost invariably used by perfumers in concocting what is sold by them as " hair oil," which, when extracted from almonds, olives, or any other vegetable substance, is, although highly scented, exactly as injurious to hair as it would be to harness; and thus it is lamentable to observe young people blooming around us in all directions becoming prematurely bald-headed, and older ones more or less rheumatic, dyspeptic, &c., from having by their own acts and deeds, namely, by rubbing their heads and clothing their bodies with the wrong substances, foolishly deserted the animal kingdom to which they belong, to go over to an alien, that, for the purposes for which they seek its protection, is really their enemy.

HOW TO EAT AND DRINK FOR HUNTING.

When a young man "too tall for school," that is to say, who has just concluded his studies, is on the point of what is called embarking in life, it would be well for him if he would but pause for a few moments, on the brink of his earthly career, to determine, not how he can avoid, but on the contrary, which, out of the many alluring pleasures standing in array before him, will afford him, when selected, the greatest and most enduring enjoyments.

Now these pleasures, sensual, literary, and religious, may be compared to the different qualifications in a large stud of horses, which, as we all know, may be divided into three classes, namely—

1. Those that will carry their rider brilliantly for a short time, and then, gradually failing, bring him early in the day to what, in the hunting field, is termed "grief."

2. Those that will carry him well through three quarters of a good run, and then give in.

3. Those which will not only carry him through any run, however severe it may be, but end a happy day by bringing him gloriously to his long home.

G

If this classification of the pleasures of this world be correct, there can exist no doubt that it is the interest of every young person to select from them those which, in intensity, increase instead of diminish the longer they are enjoyed, and which in duration are eternal, instead of being shorter than life.

Yet, supposing this wise selection to be made, it does not follow, because one set of pleasures rank infinitely higher than others, that the former should be exclusively pursued, and the latter wholly abandoned.

On the contrary, as rest restores the strength of the body after hard labour, so do pleasures of a lower order, if judiciously administered, recruit the exhaustion caused by mental exertion.

Now, of all sensual pleasures, those of eating and drinking produce, as we either use or abuse them, the most opposite results.

When a young man commences his career, the engine which is to propel him throughout his life, is, his stomach.

If he preserves it, it will in return render him good service. If he inconsiderately wears it out, whatever abilities he may possess become to him of no avail. Indeed the Spanish proverb truly says that in man's progress in the army, navy, law, church, or state, in short in every profession, " it is the belly that lifts the feet."

But the same remark is applicable, not only to every profession, but to all our amusements and recreations. A young horseman, therefore, who wishes to enjoy the greatest possible amount of hunting, should ensure it by taking the greatest possible care, not of his neck—not even of his life, for, as has been shown, the less he interferes with his horse in jumping, the safer he will go—but of his stomach, or in other words, of his *health*. To attain this object he has no penance whatever to perform, for, as he is undergoing strong exercise, his system requires, is entitled to, and ought to be allowed ample support, say a capital breakfast; a crust of sweet bread in the middle of the day; and after hunting is over, a glass of pure cold water to bring him home to a good, wholesome dinner, with three or four glasses of super-excellent wine. Now if a young rider were to resolve to rough it on, or as many of his companions would call it, to "stint himself" to, the diet above described, he would sit down to every meal with an appetite that nothing but healthy hunger can create; and thus, even from the sensual gratification of eating and drinking, he would derive the maximum of enjoyment, which would not only on the following day exhilarate his spirits, and strengthen his body, but which, by invigorating his nerves as well as his stomach, would maintain for him, to old age, the best possible recreation to his intellectual occupations, the manly exercise of hunting.

Instead, however, of subsisting on the healthy diet just described, the ordinary practice of many hunting men is to add to what may be called "Nature's prescription for the enjoyment of good health" the following ingredients :—

1. After breakfast, before mounting the spiry covert hack—a cigar.

2. On arriving at a hand-gallop at the meet; again on reaching the covert—a cigar.

3. At two o'clock some cold grouse, a long suck from a flat flask full of sherry, or brandy and water, and—a cigar.

4. After the run, another suck at the flat flask—a cigar. Refreshment at the nearest inn, for man and horse, and—a cigar.

5. While riding home, per hour—a cigar.

6. On reaching home, a heavy dinner, a superstratum of wine, an astronomical peep at the new moon, and—a cigar.

For a short time, a stout system is exhilarated, and a strong stomach may be invigorated, by a series of gifts so munificently bestowed upon them by the right hand of their lord and master.

But as Death eventually levels all distinctions, so do a constant slight intoxication produced by tobacco, vinous and spirituous liquors, with a superabundance of rich food, sooner or later first weaken the stomach, and then gradually debilitate the system, of the strong man as well as of the puny one.

The first symptom of premature decay is announced by the nerves, which, to the astonishment of the young rider, sometimes fail so rapidly, that while the whole of the rest of his system appears to him and to everybody to be as blooming and as vigorous as ever, he is compelled, under the best excuse he can invent, to sell his stud, and abandon for the rest of his life the favourite recreation he has himself destroyed.

Again, although the delicate network of the nervous system may continue uninjured, the stomach, from being continually over-excited, overwhelmed, and over-burdened by a heavy, conglomerated mixture which it has not power to digest, begins to become unable to execute, not its natural functions, but the unnatural amount of work it is called upon to perform.   The blood becomes impure, secretions are vitiated, the liver gets disordered, the oppressed lungs are ready for inflammation, the brain is heated, the pulse irregular; in fact, the whole mechanism

of the system becomes so deranged that the rider
eventually experiences, to his vast regret, that he enjoys
rest more than exercise, and accordingly in due, or
rather in undue time, he retires from his saddle to an
elbow chair.

But he is hardly seated therein when the sudden
change in his habits, from an active to a sedentary life,
rapidly produces the usual effects. Did his big toe, unknown to him, receive yesterday any little blow? Can
he have sprained it in his sleep? What can possibly
have swelled it so? How shiny and scarlet it looks!
How burning hot it is getting! Gracious heavens, what
a twitch that was!! something must be *in* it. That
something, oh! seems to be a red-hot file in the hands
of a demon who is rasping a hole in the bone. Ah!
Ai! o o o OH!!

But this little mischievous demon is only one of a
legion; for besides the eating complaint, commonly called
gout, diseases, all more or less painful, produced by in-
temperate habits, or, in other words, by giving to the
poor willing stomach more food and liquor than it could
digest, are so innumerable, that it would require, and
does require, a library of books to describe them, with
regiments of medicine-men to prescribe for them—in
vain.

"India, my boy," said an Irishman to a friend on his

arrival at Calcutta, "is jist the finest climate under the sun.   But a lot of young fellows come out here, and they dhrink and they ate, and they ate and they dhrink, and they die.   And thin, they write home to their friends a pack o' lies, and say, it's *the climate* as has killed 'em!"

But to return to the saddle.   Instead of preaching from it abstinence to hunting-men, they ought, on the contrary, to be urged to enjoy the greatest amount of gratification that can possibly be derived from eating and drinking, not for a single day, week, month, or year, but throughout their whole lives.

To enable themselves, however, to ascertain this amount, it is necessary for them to put into a pair of scales, to be accurately weighed against each other, the enjoyments of temperance, and the sorrows and anguish of intemperance.   If, on doing so, they ascertain that the balance is in favour of eating, drinking, and tobacco-smoking *ad libitum*, they will act wisely in indulging in all three to the utmost possible extent.   If, on the contrary, they ascertain that some of these pleasures last only for a few seconds, some for a few minutes, and none for more than one or two hours, while, on the other hand, the afflictions caused by intemperance endure for months and years;—that "felo-de-se" they put an end to hunting, spoil cricket, stop shooting, and last, but

not least,· ruin not only bodily but intellectual enjoyments, they will act wisely by resolving to befriend
themselves as they befriend their horses, namely, by
prescribing for all and each an ample quantity of food of
the very best description, and, if more be required by a
greedy stomach—*the muzzle.*

DIFFERENCE BETWEEN LEICESTERSHIRE AND SURREY HUNTING.

When a stranger comes to hunt in "the shires" he is
surprised, and is usually a little alarmed, at the size of
the fences, until he learns, by experience, how very easily
they are crossed; for although almost all non-hunting
people, especially ladies, fancy that it must be dangerous
to encounter a large fence, and easy to pass over a small
one, yet in practice the reverse, within moderate bounds,
may be said to be the truth: indeed, it is notorious that
of the bad accidents that happen in the hunting-field, at
least three-fourths occur either at small impediments or
at no impediment at all. For instance, perhaps the very
worst fall a rider can get is by his horse, at full speed,
stepping on the edge of a little rabbit-hole; next comes
that occasioned by one of his fore feet in his gallop
dropping into a deep drain about six inches broad; next

to that by his coming to a ditch too narrow to attract his observation, or to a stiff hedge so low that he disdains to rise at it; and at this rate danger diminishes, until the rider arrives at what may be termed the point of greatest safety, namely, a moderately high fence through which (as in the county first mentioned) a horse can at a glimpse see on the other side a broad and deep ditch or small brook.

A hunter coming fast and cheerfully at a fence of this description, no sooner is observed to prick his ears, than in self-defence he is *sure* to try, and if he tries he is not only sure, but by his momentum he *cannot help* to clear it.

The great ease with which large fences can be crossed produces the following rather curious result, namely, that although the horses ridden after hounds in Leicestershire, Northamptonshire, and Lincolnshire are infinitely superior to those ridden in Surrey, yet the small, blind, cramped, awkward, and consequently *difficult*, fences of the latter county require, and therefore create, better horsemen than those who, in " the shires," as joyously as swallows in summer, are to be seen in leafless November skimming together across grass fields separated by broad fences.

And it is for this reason, that while a horseman from the small, difficult fences, if well mounted, has always been found able to go and clear the broad, easier ones, the very best riders from the region of the latter, whenever for the first time they try to get across the former, must, until they have been sufficiently educated, either submit to follow experienced leaders or—break their necks.

But although of valour discretion has been declared to be the better part, yet in hunting a constant necessity to "look before you leap" is a virtue so exceedingly painful to practise, that on the principle that "where ignorance is bliss 'tis folly to be wise," the imperfect rider, in a good country, may rest well satisfied that he has infinitely more enjoyment than is allotted to the superior horseman in a bad one.

THE STABLE.

A comparison between the true Briton's love for his home, and that of a horse for his stable, elicits conflicting facts which are very remarkable; for although in theory and in law the house of the former is said to be "his castle," and although the latter is confined to his stable by head-collars, pillar-reins, rack-chains, halter-ropes, yet the hard, honest fact is, that the owner of the castle often seizes every possible opportunity to escape from it, while the inhabitant of the stable, if left to his own accord, would never leave it.

It sounds very beautiful for the Englishman to sing—

> " Be it ever so humble, there 's no place like home ;"

for the Scotch poet to write—

> " Oh Caledonia stern and wild,
> Meet nurse for a poetic child ;"

and for his brother Paddy to exclaim—

> " Sweetest isle of the ocean,
> Erin mavourneen, Erin go Bragh :"

yet it is impossible to deny that the song, the poetry, and the exclamation are not in unison with the fact that the songster, the poet, and the exclaimer are constantly caught in the fact of having stolen away from the very "home," the very "nurse," and the very " isle " they so ardently profess to love : indeed, in proof of the alibi, every region of the globe, healthy or unhealthy, and especially every town, city, and bathing-place in Europe, could not only declare on affidavit that its localities, high-roads, bye-roads, paths, and streets, are, especially in summer time or flea-season, to be seen crawling alive with deserters from British homes, but to the questions, Who is waving that flag in the balloon high above our heads?—Who is standing in solitary triumph on the summit of that white capped mountain ? —Who is it that has just descended from human sight to the bottom of the sea in a diving-bell? nine times out of ten it might truly be answered "*A Briton*," who, in apparent desperation, has sought refuge in the clouds, in the region of eternal snow, or in the briny deep, in order to get away from his "dulce domum," and from "the right little, tight little island" that contains it.

In almost every instance the home he has deserted is, comparatively speaking, replete with luxury and comfort; and yet, from stuffed sofas, easy chairs, feather beds, soft mattresses, warm fires, good carpets, a well-stocked library, cellar, larder, and dairy, flower and fruit gardens, carriages on buoyant springs, a stud of horses, faithful servants, and friendly neighbours, he has fled, with, in one pocket, a purse which, wherever he stops, by everybody is to be plundered; and in the other a passport, not to happiness, but to every description of what he has been educated to consider as a discomfort, simply because, instead of being homesick, he has become sick, almost unto death, of his "*home*."

Now, with these facts before us, which nobody can deny, it is strange to reflect that while man, from all parts of the United Kingdom, is to be seen centrifugally flying from his domicile, the horse's love for his stable is a flame which brightens as it burns, and which nothing but death can extinguish.

Those who have not studied or even observed the propensities of a horse, fancy that when, like a galley slave chained to his oar, he stands tied to his manger, he is in a prison, from which it would be an act of humanity to liberate him; and accordingly, if the animal has faithfully served them for many years, they feel disposed to reward him, as the great Duke of Wellington rewarded his gallant war-horse Copenhagen, by *"turning him out for the rest of his life."*

These notions, however, are perfectly erroneous. A horse not only loves his stable, he not only never wishes to leave it, but whenever he is taken out of it, although he may have been confined in it for many months, he no sooner gets out of the door than he evinces a desire to re-enter it. Every horseman, every coachman knows and feels that the difference between riding or driving, especially a thoroughbred horse from or towards his stable is so great, that while in the one case it is often necessary to spur or flog him *from* his home, the animal invariably pulls hard, and on any trifling occurrence will start or kick with joy, all the time he is returning to it; and his neighs, responded to by his comrades within, express, in horse language, how pleased he is to get back to them, and how glad they are to recover him.

A horse loves his stable for the same reasons that ought to induce his master to love his home—namely, because, in society that pleases him, he lives well clothed, well fed, and well housed; and therefore (however well intended it may be) nothing can be more cruel to a faithful animal that has all his life been accustomed to such artificial luxuries, than to turn or ostracise him into a park so soon as his age and infirmities require for him if possible still greater comforts.

It would be thought harsh, ungenerous, and unjust, were a nobleman to *reward* his old worn out butler, and bent, decrepit, toothless housekeeper, by consigning them both for the winter of their lives to the parish workhouse, where, at no cost to themselves, they would receive lodging, firing, food, and raiment; but if, without a shilling in their pockets, and without a rag on their backs, his Lordship were to turn the poor old couple adrift in the back-woods of North America, he would confer upon them, in return for their services, exactly the same sort of reward which is conferred upon an old worn out horse when, suddenly deprived of the oats, beans, hay, bed, clothing, warm stable, and companions he has been accustomed to, he is all of a sudden, as a reward in full for all the work he has performed, "turned out for the rest of his life."

The extraordinary attachment of a horse to his stable, especially if it contains many comrades, may be exemplified by the following anecdote :—

Some years ago a brown thorough-bred mare became gradually afflicted by a spavin on each hind leg, which, on due consultation, were declared to be incurable except by firing.

To undergo this painful prescription she was led from a stable where she had been residing by herself to the cavalry barracks at Hounslow, about a mile off, where she was placed in a stable full of horses for a day or two to undergo a preparatory dose of physic.

By men and ropes she was then cast, fired, and in the course of two or three days, as soon as she could bear moving, she was slowly led back to her master, who, with kind intentions, turned her into a small field of nice, cool, luxuriant grass, about one hundred yards beyond his house.

After eating a few mouthfuls the poor animal raised her head, snorted, looked first on one side, then on the other, snorted again, stretched out her tail, trotted up to a stiff post and rail fence, which she cleared, and then passing unnoticed the loose box in which for many months she had lived, forgetting and forgiving all the sufferings that had been inflicted upon her, with raw, bleeding legs, she galloped along the hard macadamised road to the cavalry stable, to re-enjoy the society of the dozen horses which only for a few days she had had the happiness of associating with.

In constructing a stable the main object should be to secure to the lungs of the horse pure air, and to prevent the hay in the loft above him from being impaired by foul air.*

By a simple shaft or chimney, and by other well-known modes of ventilation, both these advantages can be obtained; and yet they are, comparatively speaking, of no avail, if beneath the straw bed on which the horse lies there exists a substratum generating and emitting gases of a highly deleterious composition.

A stable may be well ventilated and well drained, the forage may be of the best description, and yet all may be impaired by an atmosphere unfit for respiration; for if foul litter beneath be only covered, as is often, and in many stables is usually the case, by a layer of white straw, (like a dirty shirt under a suit of fine new clothing), distemper and disease must be the result.

Although therefore it should be the secondary duty of a good groom to clean his *horse*, his primary duty is to clean *his stable*; for as, in a fast and long run across a deep country, it is undeniable that the healthiest lungs must triumph, it follows that a clean horse out of a dirty stable cannot live with a dirty one of exactly the same character and cast out of a clean stable.

But as it is always easier to preach wisdom than to practise it, so is it infinitely easier to prescribe clean

* Youatt, in his valuable work entitled "THE HORSE," truly says that changes from cold to heated foul air are as dangerous to the animal as from heat to cold.

litter than to maintain it. Indeed, it is almost impossible to keep straw under a horse perfectly pure; and accordingly, throughout the United States of America, and even in New York, horses are often made to lie on bare boards, on which they appear to sleep just as soundly as in a state of nature they would sleep on ground baked hard by the sun.

On this fact being privately whispered by us to the authorities at the Horse Guards, it was at once repudiated by the assertion that it would ruin English cavalry horses were they to be made to sleep without litter on hard boards; and yet all the soldiers of Europe, cavalry as well as infantry, in their guard rooms sleep and snore on wooden beds, probably a good deal sounder than do their respective sovereigns on bedding composed of wool, hair, down, feathers, fine linen, blankets, and counterpanes.

> " Canst thou, O partial Sleep ! give thy repose
> To the wet sea-boy in an hour so rude ;
> And, in the calmest and most stillest night,
> With all appliances and means to boot,
> Deny it to a king ?"—*Henry IV.*

Another disadvantage of straw-litter is that horses with a voracious appetite are sometimes prone to eat it, whether it be clean or dirty. To prevent them from thus distending as well as injuring their stomachs, it is usual to inflict upon them a muzzle, which, by impeding respiration, is more or less injurious to the lungs.

H

A better and indeed an effectual mode of prevention is to substitute for straw, wooden shavings, which form a cheap, wholesome, clean, and comfortable bed.

ON SHOEING.

As a railway carriage is constructed on springs to soften all ordinary jolts, and with buffers to alleviate any violent concussion;—as the human mind is gifted with a buoyancy which enables it cheerfully to meet any trifling vexation, and with sentiments of religion which maintain its serenity under the severest afflictions, so do the pastern above a horse's foot and the frog beneath it protect the body of the animal from the continual slight concussions and occasional severe ones to which, in ordinary and extraordinary exertions, it is liable to be subjected.

The pastern, like the instep of those Spanish women whose heels in walking scarcely touch the ground, gives grace and elasticity to every step; indeed, in the walk, trot, canter, and gallop of a horse we clearly see the spring of his pasterns softening the movements of their own creation.

But while the career of the body is thus rendered

safe and delightful, the interior mechanism of the foot is protected by one of those simple, beautiful, mechanical arrangements which in every direction demonstrate to us the superintending providence of an Almighty Power.

If the sole, front, sides, and back of a hunter's foot had been created as solid and as inelastic as the gold or silver case of what is called a hunting watch, the interior of the former, like that of the latter, would receive material damage from a heavy blow against the ground.

The coating, however, of hard horn or armour which shields the front and sides of the sensitive foot from any obstacle in its course, does not equally extend to that portion of it in the rear, out of harm's way, called the heels, beneath which we find on examination a triangular cushion of an Indiarubber-like composition, which, on concussion, or even by compression, acting as a wedge, forces the heels that contain it, outwards.

By this beautiful arrangement, when a hunter with his front legs extended, jumping over a broad fence, lands on a hard macadamised road upon his two fore-feet, the heels which receive the greater portion of the concussion are expanded by it in exact proportion to the weight of the bodies of the horse and rider, and the violence of the blow being thus alleviated, the sensitive mechanism of the foot is shielded from injury.

And yet, strange to say, simply by the act of shoeing, this merciful protection in every country in the world is, generally speaking, destroyed!

If a mischievous or ignorant clown were to drive a nail through a chronometer, he would only destroy an insensible and inanimate work of art; but when a man of wealth, intelligence, and science—the proprietor of a valuable horse, on whose safe going his comfort, and occasionally his life depends—deliberately nails to the poor creature's living, expansible feet four obdurate, inexpansible iron shoes, he is really guilty of an act of barbarity and barbarism which would scarcely be expected from a savage, for besides instantly impeding the expansive apparatus of the foot, he effectually stops its growth.

Under this treatment the young horse, by day and by night, not only lives in shoes which, though they may not hurt him very much in the stable, always pinch him "in his utmost need," or rather speed; but, like a Chinese lady, he outgrows his own feet, until, on attaining his full size, it is discovered that his body, which, like that of Dives, his master, has always worn fine clothing, and has fared sumptuously every day, has nothing but a set of colt's feet with contracted heels to carry it!

To prevent, or at least to alleviate the sufferings acute and chronic just described, Mr. Turner, of Regent Street, introduced the unilateral system of what he called "half-nailing," which consists in affixing the shoe by nails on the outside and round the toe only, leaving the inner side totally unsecured.

By theorists it was, of course, asserted that this arrangement would prove to be defective and inefficient. In practice, however, not only is the contrary the result, but, on nearly thirty years' experience, we are enabled to maintain the apparent paradox that in riding along or across any and every description of country, a shoe, when *half*-nailed, is more secure than when *wholly* nailed; in fact, that it is insecure almost in proportion as it is tightly nailed, and secure in proportion as it is loosely nailed.

The reasons are obvious.

When a horse is standing still, or lying fast asleep in his stable, his shoes are, of course, firmer when wholly than when only half-nailed. So soon, however, as, mounted by say a heavy man, he begins to move, there commences, out of sight of every human eye, a desperate, and in deep ground a subterranean struggle between the works of Nature and of Vulcan the blacksmith, or, in plainer words, between the expansive efforts of the frog and hoof and the arbitrary metallic shoe that is restraining them.

At each step the contest is renewed; and while, by

an acceleration of pace, its violence is increased, the domination of the tyrant at every stride is infinitesimally diminished in consequence of the nails, which have to bear the whole brunt of the battle, becoming looser and looser, until, by a jump on hard ground, or some other violent concussion, the expansive power of the foot bursts the impaired fetters that have been restraining it, and the poor animal, thus suddenly emancipated from his shoe, leaves it either buried in mud, or, with every nail in its socket, glittering on the grass behind him.

Now, under the system of *half*-nailing, the battle we have just very faintly described does not take place. The foot can't struggle against nails which don't exist; and accordingly, just as the pliant reed remains erect after the storm that in its immediate neighbourhood has torn up by its roots the sturdy oak, so does the half-nailed shoe, by allowing the horse's foot to expand, perform by gentleness what violence has failed to effect; and therefore it remains, throughout a severe run, hard and fast, where Vulcan placed it.

The Greeks and Romans did not shoe their horses, but, for long journeys, were in the habit of protecting, by leathern sandals, strengthened by iron, and ornamented with silver or gold, their feet, to the substance and shape of which they paid great attention.

"The first thing," wrote Xenophon more than 2200 years ago,

"that ought to be looked to in a horse is his foot. For as a house would be of no use, though all the upper parts of it were beautiful, if the lower parts of it had not a proper foundation, so a horse would not be of any use in war if he had tender feet, even though he should have all other good qualities, for his good qualities could not be made of any available use."

In many parts of the world the horse, though severely worked, has never yet been shod. Indeed, in some of the towns in South America it would still cost more money to shoe a horse than was paid to purchase him.

On Roughing Horses.

Although of all axioms no one is more trite and true than that "there is a right and a wrong way of doing everything," yet our readers will hardly be prepared to learn that the Anglo-Saxon on one side of the Atlantic roughs his horse in the right way, and on the other side in the wrong way!

In the United States, and especially in Canada, the surface of which for half a dozen months in every year, white as a bridal plum-cake, is composed of snow or ice, the *toe* as well as the two heels of each shoe are roughed; and as, in consequence thereof, the horse on every foot stands upon a tripod, his sinews and muscles not only remain in their proper position all the time he is in a stable, but while crossing a level country the sole of each foot when it presses the ground is parallel to its surface.

In ascending a hill the front cog, in descending a hill the two hind cogs, and in traversing a plain the three cogs, of each shoe catch firm hold of the ground; and accordingly the horse, whether in ascent, descent, or on level ground, works in so true a position, and is so efficiently roughed, that out of deep snow he can, at any gradient, gallop suddenly upon what is called "glare ice," almost as hard as iron, without the slightest danger to himself or his rider.

Now, in England, generally speaking, horses are most unscientifically roughed on their heels *solely*, which not only at once, even in the stable, especially when the outside cogs are unequally turned up, throws the mechanism of their feet and fetlocks out of gear—it not only forces them while travelling on a dead level into a false position, but, after all this maltreatment, the poor animal finds out that he is very inefficiently roughed.

For instance, in descending a hill, only the cog or cogs of the heels of each foot, which can never be placed parallel to the ground, take hold of it. In ascending, his case is infinitely worse; for, as it becomes necessary, especially when he is drawing a very heavy load, that he should raise his heels off the road in order to stick into it his toes, he then discovers that while the hind portion of his shoe which he abstains from using has been roughed for him, the *front* part, which, for the ascent, especially requires to be roughed, has been left untouched. Even to gallop a horse, shod in the English fashion, over level ice, is exceedingly dangerous; for although, so long as by a powerful bit he is forced on his haunches, the two cogs at the back of each shoe take hold, yet, if the poor animal be allowed to drop his head in order to propel himself at his utmost speed by his unroughed toes, they immediately slip from under him, and he thus experiences a defect, which it is astonishing should have been so long perpetrated by a nation who, at an enormous expenditure of time, intelligence, and money, have succeeded in rearing a breed of horses, the finest in the world, coveted by every foreigner, but which they persist in rudely roughing in the wrong way!

SADDLES.

If a saddle does not come down upon the withers and back-bone of a horse, the closer it approaches them the firmer it fits; and as, in the matrimonial alliance which exists between the quadruped and the biped, whatever is agreeable to the one is usually so to the other, a roomy saddle, on which the rider can sit with ease and comfort, is also beneficial to the horse, because it spreads the weight he has to carry over a large surface, and the pressure per square inch being thereby diminished, a sore back is less likely to be created, and per contra, for the very same reason, the human skin is less likely to be rubbed.

Less than a century ago it was deemed necessary by hunting men to tie their saddle to their horse's tail by a crupper, which, at every jump, must have compressed the vertebræ of the poor animal, like the joints of a telescope when slightly closed by a jerk. The object of this barbarous apparatus was to prevent the saddle slipping *forwards*, whereas, by the opposite apparatus of the present day, a breast-plate has been substituted, to prevent the saddle from slipping *backwards*. The difference between these two conflicting precautions has been caused by the difference in the breeding, and consequently in the size of the horse's belly, which, in the time of our ancestors, was lusty, instead of being—as in the present day, when many hunters are racers, and all in high condition—fine and slim.

When a horse is exceedingly light in the carcase, or as it is technically termed " tucked up," it is usual among grooms and riders to girth the poor creature as tightly as they can, in order, as much as is possible, to relieve the breast-plate; but instead of assisting it, the grievous mistake first paralyses its action, and then, if it be weak, breaks it, for the following simple reasons.

If a horse, with a belly tapering like a cone, be tightly girthed, his saddle, whenever it slips backwards (which it must do in ascending a steep hill or bank), remains. hard and fast on the part of the back to which it has retired, straining against the breast-plate, whose straps have not power to make it re-ascend the cone: whereas if, on the contrary, the saddle of a light-carcased horse be unusually loosely girthed, although in ascending an acclivity the saddle slips backwards until it is retained by the breast-plate, yet, the instant the horse either descends a hill, or gallops upon level ground, his own action, combined with the power of the breast-plate straps affixed to the saddle and girths, put an end to all strain upon the latter, by drawing the loosely-girthed saddle forwards into its proper position. And it is for this reason that horses of all shapes ought to be girthed less tightly when they carry breast-plates than when they are without them, and always two holes looser when they are light-carcased than when they are lusty.

Formerly it was the usual custom in the hunting-field,

as it still is on the road, to secure the saddle by two narrow girths, each buckled on either side to one strap. This arrangement has lately been superseded by what are called Fitzwilliam girths, composed of one of double breadth with two buckles at each end, and of a narrow one encircling and secured to the broad one by two loops, through which it passes.

By this admirable alteration perfect safety is obtained; for, as the broad girth is secured to four straps, if, say one on each side burst at a leap, the other two remain efficient; and even if all break, those of the narrow girth retain the broad one in its place; while, on the other hand, if the straps of the broad girth hold, the narrow one is prevented by the loops above described from dangling, in case either of its two buckles should give way.

Whereas, by the old arrangement, if out of four straps any one burst at a leap, its girth instantly dangled, leaving the safety, and possibly the life of the rider, to depend on only two straps, by the rupture of either one of which he would suddenly, without his knowledge, be riding, possibly at a large fence, without any girths at all.

But, although hunting men have gained a step or stride by this new fashioned girth, they have lately, as if to balance the account, retrograded to the wisdom of their ancestors by discarding the modern stuffed saddle-flap in favour of that ancient hard one which for many years has been used only by postilions.

For ordinary riding, and especially for ordinary riders, a quantity of stuffing in the form of a sausage, in front of their shins, no doubt retains them in their seat.

In hunting, however, this retention has for many years been producing strains of the large muscles of the thigh, which, although of common occurrence, none of the sufferers could very clearly account for. On reflection, the cause is obvious.

In riding over a large fence, or in any sudden blunder the horse may commit, the rider, without losing his seat, is liable to be thrown, body and bones, forward two or three inches, and accordingly on the plain flat hard flap he glides onwards without inconvenience or injury to the exact extent required.

But when, instead of being able to do so, his knees and shins are suddenly arrested by the stuffing immediately in front of them, the momentum of his body causes it to bend forwards on the pivot formed by his knees, on the same principle as a cart-load of earth propelled along a new railway embankment is chucked over its extremity on being suddenly stopped by a log of timber placed there transversely for that very object; and accordingly, the great muscles of the thigh which have to sustain this conflict between the moveable and immoveable parts of one frame are often so severely strained, that they require, for many months, to be bandaged by a leathern strap.

The plain flap is considerably lighter than the stuffed one. It is a sovereign cheaper; in case it gets into a brook it dries easier; and after all, it is infinitely more agreeable to ride on. For all these good reasons, in Leicestershire, Northamptonshire, and Lincolnshire, which may be termed the region in England of large fences, it has been generally adopted. However, as Peter in his 'Letters to his Kinsfolk' truly observed that although the mail ran from London to Edinburgh in forty-eight hours, it required always six months for fashions in dress to travel from the former metropolis to the latter, so throughout almost all the other counties hunting men continue to sit behind that costly, ugly, thigh-straining sausage stuffing which the riders to the Pytchley, Quorn, and Cottesmore hounds have so properly discarded.

BRIDLES.

Arrian states that the Persians, in battle, had no bridles, but governed and guided their horses by nose bands, covering sharp pieces of iron, brass, or ivory.

The curb bit, though used in the time of the Roman emperors (in an ancient sculpture Theodosius is represented riding with one of extraordinary leverage), was not adopted by the English until Charles I. in the third year of his reign issued a proclamation, commanding that no person serving in the cavalry should use the snaffle, but in lieu thereof the curb only.

On the frieze of the Temple of Minerva, in the Acropolis of Athens, the horses are represented as ridden (as in the races through the Strada Reale in Malta they are still ridden) without bridles or saddles.

The best bridle for a horse is, of course, that which is best adapted to the particular work he is required to perform.

For racing over turf, where he is required to extend himself like a greyhound, the snaffle-bit only is almost invariably selected.

For cavalry purposes, where he is required suddenly to throw himself on his haunches, wheel to either side, or right about, the curb-bit is added; while by the Turks and those Asiatics who practise their horses to approach a wall at full speed, stop, turn round, and then gallop back again, a curb-bit only is used.

For hunting, both bits are necessary; for while across turf, light soil, and over fences of almost every description, the snaffle is a safer guide than the curb-bit, yet

in going through deep ground the latter is absolutely
necessary to enable the rider, by holding his horse together,
not only to prevent him from extending himself—in which
attitude his hind feet would overreach his fore ones before
they could be extricated from the sub-soil—but to stop
him quickly, for instance to pop through a gap on either
side, which he would otherwise override for a considerable
distance.

To leap over the hedge of a plantation full of trees
on a hot horse, with only a snaffle-bit in his mouth,
would be dangerous, and often impracticable; whereas
it might easily be effected with a curb-bit, by which
the animal could moreover be made to ascend a steep
narrow bank, creep along it, and then jump off it,
over perhaps the only practicable point in the fence
beyond it.

The shape, make, and leverage of bits of all descriptions of course depend on the mouth and disposition of
the particular animal for which they are required.

It may, however, be generally stated that for all horses
a plain snaffle is better than a twisted one; and that of
curb-bits, those are the best which give to the rider the
maximum of mechanical power, with, to the noble animal
beneath him, the minimum of pain.

To a war horse, as well as to his rider, it may be
immaterial whether he be infuriated by spurs pricking

his sides, or from the laceration of his mouth by a harsh bit, purposely constructed to hurt him.

As regards a hunter, however, the case is quite different; for while on the one hand his becoming infuriated is dangerous to his master as well as himself, a total absence of pain induces him to give calm attention to the difficult work he has to perform.

Although, therefore, according to the animal's disposition a sufficient amount of leverage is required, the smoother the bit is made the more willing will he be to submit to it, and the less will he be disposed to quarrel with it; indeed this principle has more than once been exemplified by the fact of a runaway horse, over which his rider had apparently no control, stopping gradually of his own accord, in consequence of the rupture of the curb chain, which, having infuriated him by the agony it had inflicted on his lower jaw, nad actually caused the very danger it had been created to prevent. And it is for this reason that a leathern strap ought almost invariably to be placed under the hard twisted curb chain, by which simple addition acute pain is removed, without any diminution of strength of the chain or of the leverage of the curb-bit.

Intrinsic Value of a Horse.

Although it is a common axiom that "the value of a thing is exactly what it will fetch," yet in the hunting-field the price at which a horse has been sold is very rarely a criterion of his real worth, the reason being that his performances are made up of three items, of which he himself forms only one, the other two being stable management and good riding, for neither of which is the quadruped entitled to claim the smallest amount of credit; and yet, on the principle that "handsome is that handsome does," it is a usual error, especially among young sportsmen, to estimate that a horse which goes brilliantly must be a good one, and vice versâ; whereas an ordinary description of animal, in splendid condition, and judiciously ridden, cannot fail to leave far behind him a superior one injudiciously ridden, made up of flesh instead of muscle, of impure instead of pure blood, and of bloated, unpractised, instead of healthy, well-exercised lungs. For these reasons it continually happens that a horse that has been observed to go what is called "brilliantly" throughout a run, is, at its conclusion, sold for a considerable sum, in addition to another horse, on which the purchaser, in a few weeks, leaves behind him the animal he had sold, whose owner now to his cost discovers that

> " The lovely toy so keenly sought
> Has lost its charms by being caught "

by *him*.

But the price of a hunter is materially affected by the quality as well as the qualifications of his rider, whose position in the world often confers upon his horses a fictitious value; and accordingly the hunting stud of the late Sir Richard Sutton—sold by public auction shortly after his death—realised sums exceeding by at least 40 per cent. what subsequently proved to be their current value when transferred to the stables of people of less renown.

Again, a respectable, first-rate horse dealer succeeds in his profession, not so much by his superior knowledge of the animals he *buys*, but by the quantity and quality of the eloquence he exerts in *selling* them. Every hunter, therefore, that is purchased from a great man of this description is necessarily composed of, 1st, his intrinsic value; and 2nd, of the anecdotes, smiles, compliments, and praises, which, although when duly mixed up with an evident carelessness about selling him, captivated the listener to purchase him, like a bottle of uncorked ardent spirits evaporate, or, like a swarm of bees, fly away, almost as soon as the transaction is concluded, leaving behind them nothing but the animal's intrinsic value.

On Shying.

It often happens that a horse brimfull of qualifications of the very best description is most reluctantly sold by his master " because he shies so dreadfully," a frolic which, to a good rider, is perfectly harmless, and which, if he deems it worth the trouble, he is almost certain to cure.

A timid horseman, however, not only believes that his horse is frightened at the little heap of stones at which he shies, but for this very reason he becomes frightened at it himself; whereas the truth is that the animal's sensations in passing it are usually compounded as follows :—

$$\text{Of fear of} \begin{cases} \text{the little heap} & \cdot \cdot \ \frac{1}{10}. \\ \text{whip and spur} & \cdot \cdot \ \frac{9}{10}. \end{cases}$$

Now, if this be the case, which no one of experience will deny, it is evident that the simple remedy to be adopted is, first, at once to remove the great cause of the evil complained of, by ceasing to apply either whip or spur; and, secondly, gradually to remove the lesser cause by a little patient management which shall briefly be explained.

When a horse has been overloaded with a heavy charge of oats and beans, which may be termed jumping powder, and primed by a very short allowance of work, his spirits, like the hair trigger of a rifle, are prepared on the smallest touch to cause a very violent explosion. In fact, without metaphor, on the slightest occurrence he is not only ready, but exceedingly desirous, to jump for joy.

The *casus belli* which the animal would perhaps most enjoy would be to meet a temperance run-away awning-covered waggon full of stout, healthy young women in hysterics, all screaming; or to have a house fall down just as he was passing it. However, as a great conqueror, if he cannot discover a large excuse for invading the territory of his neighbour, is sure to pick out a very little one, so does the high mettled horse who has nothing to start at, proceed under his rider with his eyes searching in all directions for something which he may pretend to be afraid of. Influenced by these explosive propensities he cocks his ears at a large leaf which the air had gently roused from its sleep, as if it were a crouching tiger; and shortly afterwards a fore leg drops under him as suddenly as if it had been carried away by a cannon shot, because in the hedge beside him a wren has just hopped from one twig to another nearly an inch.

Now, of course, the effective cure for all these symptoms of exuberant, pent up spirits is a long, steady hand-gallop up and down hill across rather deep ground. Before, however, this opportunity offers, man can offer to the brute beneath him a more reasonable remedy.

The instant that a horse at a walk sees at a short dis-

tance before him, say a heap of stones, at which he pre-
tends to be or really is afraid, instead of forcing him on,
he should be allowed or, if it be necessary, forced to
stop, not only till he has ceased to fear it, but until, dead
tired of looking at it, he averts his eyes elsewhere.

While advancing towards it, so often as his fear,
or pretended fear, breaks out, by instantly bringing
him to a stand-still it should in like manner be over-
appeased.

In slowly passing any object which a horse appears to
be afraid of, the error which is almost invariably committed is to turn his head towards it, in which case, revolving upon his bit as on a pivot, the animal turns his
hind-quarters from it, and in that position with great
ease shies more or less away from it; whereas, if the rein
opposite to it be pulled firmly, he not only instantly
ascertains that his rider's desire is in opposition to, instead
of in favour of forcing him towards the object of his fear,
but when his head is drawn away from it, although he is
able to rush forwards, it is out of his power to shy *late-
rally*.

Now, instead of endeavouring thus to triumph ovei
instinct by reason, instead of allowing a horse more time
even than he requires to appease his own apprehensions,
be they real or pretended, the course which a gentleman's groom usually adopts is, like giving fuel to fire,

to add to the animal's fear of the object he is unwilling to approach, his infinitely greater fear of a pair of plated spurs.

The oftener and the stronger this ignorant prescription is applied, the more violent becomes the disease it undertakes to alleviate, until, on its being declared to be incurable, the poor frightened animal is sold for a fault almost entirely created by human hands and inhuman heels.

The extent to which a timid animal can be appeased by kindness is, at the present moment, beautifully exemplified by a deer, which has been so divested of its fears by Tom Hill, the huntsman of the Surrey foxhounds, that the animal not only accompanies the hounds when taken out for exercise, but eats biscuit, and actually sleeps with them in the kennel.

If, during their meal, two of the hounds fight, by a pat with his fore feet he tries to separate them. If, at exercise, anything alarms him, with a bound or two he vaults for safety into the middle of the pack. And yet, when in this citadel, if any strange dog approaches them, with malice prepense he rushes out at him, as if determined to kill him. In short, by kind superintendence the deer has become as fond of blood-thirsty hounds as they of him.

SINGEING.

As it is incumbent on all civilized communities to be kind to every living being,—as our laws profess to maintain this Christian axiom,—and as there exists among us a Society self-constituted for the especial purpose of " the Prevention of Cruelty to Animals," it would be very difficult satisfactorily to explain, at least to *them*, why, in violation of so benign a theory, we deliberately practise the following fashions :—

1. Of cutting off all our sheep's tails.

2. Of dittoing the tails of all dogs that take care of sheep.

3. Of dittoing the ears of terriers.

4. Of dittoing a portion of the tails, and occasionally of the ears, of our horses.

5. Of piercing with a sharp awl the ears of all our daughters, in order to insert therein golden rings, which, by equalizing all, can confer no possible benefit on any one: that is to say, provided Euclid is correct in declaring that " when equals are added to equals, their sums are equal."

If any person among us defaces a statue, he is liable to punishment and to the execration of the public; and yet there can be no doubt that in every sense of the word it is more barbarous to mutilate the living original of an Almighty Creator than a cold stone or marble copy thereof, chiselled more or less imperfectly by human hands.

About forty years ago it was the general custom to dock the tails of all hunters, covert-hacks, and waggon-horses, so close, that nothing remained of this picturesque, beautiful ornament of Nature but an ugly, stiff stump, very little longer than the human thumb, which, especially in summer time, was seen continually wagging to the right or left, in impotent attempts to brush off a hungry fly, biting the skin more than a yard off. At about the same period an officer in our army took to the Cape of Good Hope a gentle, beautiful, thoroughbred mare, which, to his astonishment, the natives appeared exceedingly unwilling to approach. The reason was, that her ears had been cropped; and as among themselves that punishment was inflicted for crimes, they were induced to infer that the handsome mutilated animal had suffered from a similar cause—in fact, that she was *vicious*.

From the same premises, and by the same reasoning faculties, they might as erroneously have conceived that the holes bored through most of the English ladies' ears denoted the existence of a uniform speck of some sort or other in their characters.

Having briefly enumerated only a few of the mutila-
tions which, in different regions of the earth, man inflicts,
not only upon the animals around him, but upon himself,
we will proceed to notice a prescription of modern date
which has produced very astonishing results.

As in crime there exists an essential difference between
cutting off a man's head, and cutting off only his hair, so
in cruelty does there exist a similar difference between
the fashion which mutilates the body of an animal, and
that which deprives him only of its covering: still, however, the practice of clipping, shaving, and singeing horses
must, to every person, at first sight appear so incomprehensible that a slight notice of the subject may possibly be
deemed worthy of a few minutes' consideration.

To a wild horse, roaming in a state of perfect freedom,
Nature grants an allowance very similar to that which
every inhabitant of Grosvenor Square gives to each of
his tall powdered footmen: namely, board, lodging, and
two suits of clothing per annum; with this important
difference, however, that while the poor pampered, gaudy
menial is ignorantly dressed throughout the whole year
in cloth and plush of the same thickness, the animal is
beneficently provided with two different descriptions of
clothing, namely, a light thin silky coat for summer
wear, and a thick fur one to keep him warm and comfortable throughout the winter months.

Now it might be expected that if man undertook to interfere with this provision, he would, in accordance with the spirit and meaning of the act by which it had been decreed, extend its principle by relieving the horse of a portion of his covering during the excessive heat of summer, and by bestowing upon him a little extra warmth in winter; whereas, by the operation about to be described, he makes the animal's cold weather coat infinitely less able to resist cold tha that purposely created for sunshine only.

About fifty years ago, during the Peninsular war, it was observed that the Spanish muleteers gave to the animals they had charge of great apparent relief by rudely shearing off the hair that covered their bodies ; and on the idea being imported into England, our hunting men, principally at Melton, commenced the practice by "clipping," at a cost at first of about five guineas, their hunters.

This operation, which, in its infancy, occupied four or five days, was succeeded by the practice of shaving, which, in about as many hours, left the animal as bare as the hide of a pig that had just been killed, scalded, and scraped.

This latter operation, however, was found to be attended with two opposite disadvantages : for, if perpetrated too soon, it required to be repeated, or rather to be succeeded by clipping; and if delayed till the growth of the thick coat had subsided, the horse remained throughout the winter naked like an elephant.

In order therefore to shorten the coat exactly in proportion to its uncertain growth, it was determined gradually and repeatedly to burn it by fire to the minimum length prescribed, that is, leaving only sufficient to conceal the bare skin.

When the animal has thus been denuded of his coat, so long as he remains in his hot stable it is restored to him with compound interest, by two, and occasionally by three suits of warm clothing, which he might expect would, like that worn by his lord and master, be increased as soon as he should be led from his covered domicile into the open air. But the contrary operation takes place; for while his owner is swathing himself in his extra flannel hunting clothing, the singed quadruped at the same moment, in order to be taken to the meet, at one haul is denuded of the whole of his indoor clothing, a bridle is put into his mouth, a saddle on his bare back, and in this state, literally, without metaphor, more naked than he was born, he is suddenly led or ridden ten or fifteen miles through perhaps wind, rain, sleet, or snow, to be exposed throughout the whole day to sudden sweats and sudden chills, in temperatures and at elevations of the most trying description.

Now, of course, in theory, nothing can be more un-natural, and it might be added more barbarous, than this treatment; and yet, strange to say, by acclamation it would be declared by every horse-owner who has⌐ tried it that, in practice, it produces to the animal not only beneficial, but unexpected, results.

The lungs appear to become stouter.

Hot swelled legs suddenly get cool and fine.

The appetite grows stronger.

The flesh increases.

The muscles thicken.

In consequence of greatly diminished perspiration the amount of food necessary to recruit the body may be reduced, at least, one feed per day.

After hunting, the skin, instead of breaking out from internal debility and exhaustion, remains dry.

Lastly, as mud and dirt cannot take hold of a singed coat, and consequently as little or no grooming is re-quired, the animal, on reaching his stable, soon enjoys rest, instead of being for an hour or two teased, excited, and irritated, by being tied up, hissed at, and cleaned.

But, against all these advantages, it is only fair to weigh the amount of suffering which it is supposed by us a horse endures by being stripped of his coat and clothing, and in that naked state being suddenly plunged, during winter, into the external air.

In ascertaining this amount of suffering, however, we must not commit the error of estimating a horse's sensation by what, under similar circumstances, we imagine would be our own, for the cases are quite different.

Throughout the frame or fabric of man, his blood, however proud it may be, circulates so feebly, that on being subjected to a low temperature it actually, like fluid in a pipe, freezes in his veins; whereas throughout the body of a horse it is propelled with such violence, that, like the deep water in the Canada lakes, it is beyond the power of cold, however intense, to stop it; and accordingly, when everything else around stands frozen, it triumphantly continues its fluent course. In fact, the relative power of the two animals to resist cold is fully proportionate to the difference between their muscular strength; and as the human being, notwithstanding its weakness, is strong enough to endure the sudden transition from a hot bath to a cold one, or, as is the custom in Russia, to a roll on the snow, so, à fortiori, is a hunter gifted by Nature with a circulation of blood powerful enough to enable him, without injury or suffering, to bear an apparently unnatural mode of treatment, which, although it makes *us* almost shiver to think of, is productive to his stouter frame of beneficial results, of inestimable value.

MEET OF THE PYTCHLEY HOUNDS AT ARTHING-WORTH.

Among hunting men there is nothing so unpopular as what is called by the rest of the world a most beautiful, clear, bright day.   The gaudy thing is disagreeable to eyes because it is dangerous to the bodies to which they respectively belong; for when every twig glitters in the sunshine, and every drop of dew that hangs upon them looks like a diamond, the fences so dazzle the eyes of riders, and especially of horses, that a number of extra falls are very commonly the result.   Soft ground, dull weather, an easterly wind, and a cloudy sky, form the compound that is most approved of.   On such a day, and under such circumstances, we beg leave to invite our readers to sit with us patiently for a very few minutes in a balloon, as, like a hawk hovering above a partridge, it hangs over the quiet little village of Arthingworth, in Northamptonshire.   Those hounds, headed by that whipper-in riding so lightly and neatly on his horse, and surrounding their huntsman Charles Payne, jogging along, seated in his saddle as if he had grown there, are on that portion of the Queen's highway which connects Northampton with Market Harborough.   They are the Pytchley hounds, the hereditary property, not of the pre-

sent master, but of the hunt. They are on their way from
their kennel at Brixworth to a park at Arthingworth to
draw " Waterloo Gorse," which means that every man
who intends to come (and their name is legion) will send
there, not his best-looking, but, what is infinitely better,
that which he knows to be " his best horse," simply
because the covert of Waterloo not only usually holds a
good fox, but because it is encircled by very large grass-
fields, enlivened in every direction by the severest fences
in Northamptonshire. See how quietly along every high-
road, bye-road, and footpath, horses and riders, of various
sizes and sorts, walking, jogging, or gently trotting, are
converging towards a central point! Schoolboys are
coming to see the start on ponies; farmers on clever
nags; others on young horses of great price; neatly-
dressed grooms, some heavy and some light, are riding, or
riding and leading, horses magnificent in shape and breeding, in the most beautiful condition, all as clean and well-
appointed as if they had been prepared to do miserable
penance in Rotten Row. And are all these noble and
ignoble animals beneath us going to the hunt? Yes,
and many more that we cannot see. Look at those
straight streams of white steam that through green fields
are concentrating from north, south, east, and west upon
Market Harborough, from Leicester, from Northampton,
from Stamford, and from Rugby—denoting trains that,

at the rate of thirty or forty miles an hour, are hurrying boxes all containing hunters for the meet.

On the huntsman and hounds slowly entering and taking up their positions in the small park at Arthingworth, excepting two or three farmers, no one is there to receive or notice them. However, in a few minutes, through large gates and through smaller ones, grooms on and with their horses walk steadily in ; while Charles Payne, occasionally chucking from his coat-pocket a few crumbs of bread to his hounds, most of whom are looking upwards at him, leaning over his horse, is holding confidential conversation with a keeper. "*It's too bad !*" whispers an old farmer, who had just been entrusted with the secret that another fox had last night been shot by poachers; "*and, what's more, it's been a-going on* IN MANY WAYS *a long time.*" "*Yes !*" replies Charles Payne, looking as calmly and philosophically as Hamlet when he was moralising over Yorick's skull; "*you may rely upon it that, what with greyhounds,—and poachers, —and traps,—and poison,—there are very few foxes now-a-days that die a natural death*"—meaning that they were not eaten up alive by the Pytchley hounds.

But during all this precious time where are all the scarlet coats? Oh! here they come, trotting, riding, and galloping to the meet from every point of the compass, and apparently from every region of the habitable globe,

K

some of the young ones—diverging as usual from their
path of rectitude—to lark over a fence or two. Along
the turnpike and country roads, drags' with four horses,
light dog-carts with two, post-chaises and gigs, each laden
with men muffled up in heavy clothing, showing no pink,
save a little bit peeping out at the collar, are all hurrying
onwards to the same goal; and as these living bundles,
with cigars in their mouths, are rapidly landing in the
park, it will be advisable that we also should descend
there to observe them.

By about a quarter before eleven the grass in front of
the hospitable hunting-box of one of the late masters
of the Pytchley—who, take him all in all, is one of the
very best riders in the hunt—becomes as crowded as a fair
with sportsmen of all classes, from the highest rank in the
peerage down to—not exactly those who rent a 6l. house,
—but who can afford money and time enough to " hoont,"
as they call it. While two or three well-appointed servants in livery are very quietly, from a large barrel,
handing glasses of bright-looking ale to any farmer or
groom who, after his long ride, may happen to feel a
little thirsty, and while others from white wicker-baskets
are distributing bits of bread and lumps of cheese to any
man who may feel that beneath his waistcoat there is
house-room to receive them, the honourable and gallant
proprietor of the brown barrel and white baskets, lounging

in his red coat, &c., on his exalted lawn, with sundry
small scratches (from bull-finches) on his face, with something now and then smoking a little from his mouth,
and with that placid and easy manner which in every
situation of life distinguishes him, says to any friend in
pink that happens to pass him, " *Won't ye go* IN *for a
moment ?*"   But, without invitation, most of the aristo-
crats, leaving their horses with their grooms, to ascend
a flight of ladder steps which raises them to the lawn, walk
slowly and majestically across it, adjusting their hair,
" just to make their bow."   When that compliment has
been paid, they pause for a second or two in the hall,
and then recross the lawn, indolently munching, and
with perfumed handkerchiefs carefully wiping lips or
mustachios (as the case may be), which, if they were
very closely approached, might possibly smell *partly* of
cherries, to proceed to their respective grooms, and mount
their horses.

" *Move-*ON,-*Sir ?*" says Charles Payne, in his sharp,
quick tone, touching his cap to the master, who slightly
nods to him.   " *Now-then,-gentlemen !*" he adds, " *ware*
HOUNDS, *if you please !*" and accordingly, surrounded by
them, onwards he, his two whips, and about two hundred
horsemen, proceed at a walk to cross for nearly half a
mile magnificent fields of grass of from eighty to a hundred acres.   As the Pytchley and Quorn men are, for the

reasons we have explained, each mounted on the very best of their stud, it need hardly be stated that the lot of horses before us are an accumulation of the finest specimens in the world; and yet with the highest breeding, courage, and condition, with magnificent figures, and with bone and substance sufficient to carry, through deep ground, from twelve to eighteen stone, there is a calm, unassuming demeanour in their walk, which it seems almost impossible sufficiently to admire. In like manner, among the riders, nobody appears to have the smallest disposition to talk about what he is going to do, or apparently even to think of where he is proceeding. A man from Warwickshire will perhaps describe the run he had there on Thursday; while another will fashionably say to a Leicestershire friend—"Did you *do* anything on Friday?"—but most of the field are conversing as they ride along, not at all about foxes, but about Lords Palmerston, Derby, Italy, the Pope, &c.

On arriving close to Waterloo Gorse, Charles Payne pulls up to remain stationary for a couple of minutes, surrounded by his hounds, who, instead of gazing at his face, are all looking most eagerly at the covert, until the two whips, getting round it, have each taken up a position on the other side. "Now-then-*little-bitches!*" says Charles, as, with a twitch corresponding with his voice, he waves forwards his right hand, in which is grasped the silver horn presented to him by the farmers. Without taking the smallest offence at the appellation (which after all is a just one, for, as they are the fastest of his two packs, Charles does not object to bringing them to "Waterloo"), in they dash; and in a second Charles and his horse are over the low flight of rails, to gallop along a briary path which conducts them to a small open space in the centre of the covert. The greater portion of the field, in coats of many colours, congregate on its right.

But "quanto sono insensibili questi Inglesi!" Instead of evincing the smallest degree of anxiety, the conversations we have described are renewed; and though certainly nobody seems to care the hundred-thousandth part of a farthing about what his lips are saying, and though the countenance of every man appears to acknowledge that, on the whole, he is well enough satisfied with this world, yet men and horses remain perfectly cool, and occasionally cold, until it might be fancied by any old soldier standing a mile off that a shell had suddenly burst in the middle of them. "PRAY, *don't holla!*" exclaims an old sportsman in a loud whisper. "BY JOVE, HE'S AWAY!" screams a very young one in pink, pointing to a shepherd who, grasping a struggling dog with one hand, is holding up his hat with the other. Half a dozen loud, slow, decisive, monotonous blasts from

Charles Payne's horn are instantly heard, while his hounds, tumbling over each other, jump almost together over a small hedge and ditch out of the covert, with their beautiful heads all pointing towards Leicestershire. As they and reynard take the opposite side of the large grass field in which the riders had assembled, the start of the latter is very nearly as sudden as that of the former. Packed together almost as closely as the wild young creatures that on Epsom course run for the Derby, the best men and the best horses belonging to the Pytchley, Quorn, Cottesmore, and Warwickshire hounds start together over turf down a gentle declivity, at the bottom of which runs an insignificant stream. Steady horsemanship in every rider is necessary to prevent treading on those immediately before, or jostling those on each side. Many a horse, by shaking his head, clearly enough shows how unwelcome to him is the restraint. From this conglomeration nearly a dozen men extricate themselves by the superior speed and management of their horses. Before them * is a well-known broad and strong fence, which, without competing against each other, they most gallantly charge, "magnâ comitante catervâ," followed by the great ruck. One,—two,—three,—four,—five,— six men and horses take it almost together in their stride, and, to the astonishment of the remainder, all disappear! Every horse had well cleared the broad ditch

* This scene we happened to witness.

on the other side, but all nearly simultaneously had landed in an artificial bog beyond it, made for draining purposes only a few days before, and in which the six men and the six horses, each perfectly unhurt, are now as prostrate and as " comfortable " as if they had, to use the old nurse's expression, "just been put to bed." The Hon. Fred. Villiers and Harry Everard are the first over and down. As they lie together in the mud, looking upwards, they see coming over the stakes of the hedge the Fitzwilliam girths of the horses of Henry Forrester and Thomas Atkinson (*Vive L'Empereur!*), followed almost instantly by two strangers. However, nearly as quickly as they all fell, they severally arise, mount their horses, and gallantly regain the hounds. The field of riders, unable to comprehend what has happened, and moreover unable as well as unwilling to stop their horses, as it were by word of command, all gracefully swerve together in a curve to the right to take two stiff fences instead of one. About half a dozen, on perfect timber-jumpers, cross a ditch overhung by a stout ash rail, firmly fixed between two trees; the remainder break their way through a bull-finch, and then, throwing their right shoulders forward, at a very honest pace, all make every proper effort to catch Charles Payne and the few others who with him had followed the line of the hounds.

We should certainly tire and jolt our readers very grievously were we to presume to hustle them through the well-known and splendid run that ensued. Not only, however, do our limits forbid us to do so, but as we shall shortly have to quote hunting-anecdotes from a very superior pen, we willingly pull up to make, in cool blood instead of in hot, a very few remarks.

EFFECTS CAUSED BY THE SIGHT OF HOUNDS.

A description of a fox-hunt is not very agreeable either to read or to write,—firstly, because it records a series of events of no very great importance when they are over; and secondly, because the picture generally bears the appearance of exaggeration; the reason being, that it is composed of two parts, one of which it is almost impossible accurately to delineate. The danger or difficulty which a man and horse incur in taking any particular leap depends on the one hand upon the size of the fence, and on the other upon the combined amount of weight, strength, and activity which the horse can bring up to it. In trade, if a given weight, whether small or great, be put into one scale, it can be at once overbalanced by putting a still greater weight into the other scale. But while the dimensions of a fence can accurately be measured, it would be not only very difficult to determine the physical powers of a hunter, but, even if the statement could be made, ninety-nine people out of every hundred would most certainly disbelieve it; for, as the old proverb says, "seeing is believing;" so when a man has ridden a horse across his farm for many years, he is fully persuaded that,—to use another common expression,—"he knows what he is made of." But the truth is, he only knows what he has done, and what he can do under the maximum of excitement he hitherto has ever experienced; what he does *not* know, and indeed what without trial he can have no idea of, is the enormous amount of latent physical power in his horse which even the sight of hounds will develop.

For instance, in riding a hack along the road, the confidence or, as it may be termed, the courage of the rider depends not on himself, but on the strength and action of the animal he is bestriding. If the nag picks up his feet quickly, and pops them down firmly—if he goes stout in his canter and strong in his gallop, his owner rides *boldly*. If, however, the very same hero crosses a poor, weak, weedy animal, with strait action, tripping in all his paces, and with his toes sending almost every loose stone rolling on before him, he declares the instant he dismounts that he has been *frightened;* which difference, in truth, only means that, on trial, he has satisfactorily and unsatisfactorily ascertained the physical powers of the first horse to be amply sufficient, and those of the last totally insufficient, to perform the given amount of work he requires. Now it is really no exaggeration to say, that the excitement to a horse caused by the presence of hounds creates in his physical powers as wide a difference as exists between those of the two nags just described. The old, jaded, worn-out, "groggy" hunter, who came hobbling out of his stable, and who has been fumbling and blundering under his groom along the road, no sooner reaches the covert side than, like a lion "shaking the dew-drops from his shaggy mane," he in a moment casts away the ills which flesh is heir to—in short, his prostrated powers suddenly revive; and accordingly it is on record, that in one of the severest runs with staghounds ever known in Essex, the leading horse was aged, twenty-two. Again, on the road, when a horse has travelled thirty or forty miles, he usually becomes more or less tired; whereas, during the ten or twelve hours that a hunter is out of his stable, he will, with the utmost cheerfulness, besides trotting more than that distance on the road, follow the hounds for many hours across a heavy country and large fences; and as it is well known that, in harness, a horse is less fatigued by trotting before a carriage on a hard macadamized road for forty miles than in dragging it through an earth road for ten, it would appear almost fabulous to state how many miles on the road, or especially on dry turf, could be performed by the amount of excitement, activity, and strength expended by a hunter during a long and severe day's work.

For the foregoing reasons, if a man during summer rides his hunters, he will see a variety of fences which, as he quietly ruminates, he will pronounce to himself to be impracticable, simply because he can both see and feel that they are greater than the powers he is bestriding; and yet, when the trees are leafless and the hounds running, if he happens on the same horse to come to these very fences, he crosses them without the smallest thought or difficulty—not because *he* is excited (for the cooler he rides the better he will go), but because, while the height and breadth of each fence have not since he last saw them increased, the physical powers of his horse, developed by hunting, have been, to say the least, doubled. The scales which in summer had turned against him now preponderate in his favour; and accordingly Prudence, who but a few months before, with uplifted hand, had sternly warned him to "*beware!*" with smiling face and joyous aspect now beckons to him to "*Come on!*"

The feats which the mere skin and bones of a horse can perform during hunting are surprising. The comparatively small shin-bone of his hind legs will, without receiving the smallest blemish, smash any ordinary description of dry oak or elm-rail, and occasionally shiver the top of a five-barred gate, and yet, strange to say, though the frail bone so often fractures the timber, the timber is never able to fracture the frail bone, which, generally speaking, receives not the smallest injury from the conflict. Again, when even a singed horse at great speed has forced his way through a high, strong, spiteful-looking thorn-hedge, frightening almost into hysterics the poor little "bullfinch" that is sitting there, he almost invariably passes through the ordeal with his skin perfectly uncut, and often not even scratched !—nay, a horse going at great speed may be thrown head over heels by a wire fence without receiving from it the smallest blemish !

The trifling facts we have just stated will, we believe, not only explain the courage and physical powers of a hunter, but the difficulty of describing to non-hunting readers, without an appearance of exaggeration, the feats which, during a run, he can without danger or difficulty perform ; for, instead of boasting about a large fence, it is an indisputable fact that it is infinitely safer for the horse, and consequently for his rider, than a little one, at which almost all their worst accidents occur : indeed when a liberal landlord, for the benefit of his tenants, cuts through their fields a series of narrow deep drains, to be loosely filled up with earth, it is good-humouredly said by hunting men, that he is "*collar-boning*" them !

And now it is an extraordinary truth that the excitement which the horse feels in simply witnessing the chase of one set of animals after another, seems to pervade every living creature on the surface of the globe. In savage life, the whole object, occupation, and enjoyment of man, whenever he is not engaged in war, consists in catching and killing almost any of the creatures that inhabit the wilderness through which he roams. In a drop of putrid water a microscope informs us that animalcules of all shapes and sizes, with the same malice prepense, are hunting and slaying each other. The 600 boys at Eton, if collected together, would resolve readily among themselves to receive with decorum, and no doubt with youthful dignity, any great personages about to honour them with a visit; and yet, while the grand procession was approaching them, or even just after it had arrived, if a rat were to run about among them, all their good intentions in one moment would be destroyed.

During the grand reviews in France of the Allied armies under the command of Wellington, although the British troops had behaved steadily enough at Waterloo, it was found that the presence and authority of " the Iron Duke " were utterly unable to keep them immoveable as soon as the hares began to jump up among them. Nay, at Inkerman, while the battle was raging, several men of the Guards were observed by their officers suddenly to cease firing at the Russians, who were close to them, in order to "*prog*" with their bayonets a poor little scared hare that was running among their feet!

In like manner, although the Anglo-Saxon race are proverbially phlegmatic (a word described by Johnson to mean "dull; cold; frigid"), yet no sooner do they hear, in the language of Shakspeare,

"The musical confusion
Of hounds and echo in conjunction,"

than the windows of manufactories are crowded with pale eager faces, the lanes, paths, and fields become dotted with the feet and ankles of people of various classes and ages, whose eyes are all straining to get a glimpse of the run. If Dolly be among them, her cow, wherever she may be, is quite as curious as herself.

As the fox, who has distanced his pursuers, lightly canters along the hedge-side of a large grass field, the sheep instantly not only congregate to stare at him, but for a considerable time remain spell-bound, gazing in the direction of his course. Herds of bullocks with noses almost touching the ground, and with long straight tails slanting upwards, jump sometimes into the air, and sometimes sideways, with joy. As soon as the hounds appear, the timid sheep instantly follow them, and accordingly, almost before the leading rider can make for and get through perhaps the only gap in an impracticable fence, eighty or a hundred of these "muttons," with fat, throbbing, jolting sides, rush to and block up the little passage, in and around which they stand, forming a dense mass of panting wool, on which no blow from a hunting-whip or from a hedge-stake produces the slightest effect; and thus the whole field of gentlemen sportsmen, to their utter disgust, are completely stopped. "*I had no idea*," lisps a very young hard-riding dandy, in as feminine and drawling a voice as he can concoct, "*I really hadn't the* SLIGHTEST *idea, before, that sheep were súch —— fools!*" But their offspring are, in their generation, no wiser. A poor little lamb, almost just born, the instant it sees the hounds, will not only leave its mother to follow them, but under the legs of a crowd of horses—that if they can possibly avoid it will never tread upon it—canters along, until, its weak knees and lungs failing, it reels, and is left lying on its side, apparently dead.

CRUELTY OF HUNTING CONSIDERED.

Over the closed eyes, panting flank, and exhausted frame of this tiny, innocent, and yet seduced orphan, who had never known its father, and has just lost its mother, we will venture to offer to our readers a very few remarks on the strange dissolving view that has just vanished, or rather galloped, from their sight.

"It's just," said Andrew Fairservice to Frank Osbaldistone, "amaist as silly as our auld daft laird here and his gomerils o' sons, wi' his huntsmen and his hounds, and his hunting cattle and horns, riding haill days after a bit beast that winna weigh sax punds when they hae catched it."

To the foregoing observation it might also have been added, that in the extraordinary exertions we have described, the pleasures enjoyed by the "bit beast" in being hunted, when compared with those of the two or three hundred animals, human, equine, and canine, that are hunting him, are as disproportionate as is his weight when compared to the sum total of theirs.

"*No!*" said the haughty Countess of —— to an aged huntsman, who, cap in hand, had humbly invited her ladyship to do him the honour to come and see his hounds, "*No! I dislike everything belonging to hunting —it is so cruel.*"

"CRUEL!!" replied the old man, with apparent astonishment, "*why, my lady, it can't possibly be* CRUEL, *for,*" logically holding up three fingers in succession,

"*We all knows that the* GENTLEMEN *like it,*

"*And we all knows that the* HOSSES *like it,*

"*And we all knows that the* HOUNDS *like it,*

"*And,*" after a long pause, "*none on us, my lady, can know for certain, that the* FOXES *don't like it.*"

It may strongly be suspected, however, that they do not enjoy being hunted to death, and consequently that the operation, whenever and wherever it is performed, is, to a certain degree, an act of cruelty; which it is only hypocritical to vindicate by pretending to argue that Puggy has been sentenced to death to expiate his sins; for if, instead of robbing a hen roost, it had been his habit to come in all weathers secretly to sit on its nests to help and hatch the chickens, " *The Times* " news-paper would have advertised "hunting appointments." which would have been as numerously attended,—the hounds would have thrown off with the same punctuality, —and men and horses would have ridden just as eagerly and as gallantly to be in at the death of the saint as of a sinner, whose destruction all barn-door fowls, geese, tur-keys, pheasants, and rabbits in his neighbourhood would certainly not be disposed to regret.

As regards, however, the hunted animal, as well as the creatures that hunt him, we will observe that the sufferings of a fox that is eaten up by hounds are pro-bably not much greater and possibly a little less than those of the poor worm that on our hook catches the fish, —of the fish that catches the worm,—of the live eels that we skin,—or of the sheep and bullocks that are every day in thousands driven footsore to our slaughter-houses.

If our Arthingworth fox had taken in " *The Times*," the Waterloo covert, after all the preparations we have described, would most certainly have been drawn " blank."

L

But while undertakers in scarlet, in black, and in brown
coats, were expending many thousand pounds in preparations for his funeral, he, totally unconscious of them,
was creeping within it, in the rude health and perfect
happiness he had enjoyed in Leicestershire, his native
county.

All of a sudden he hears disagreeable sounds, and
encounters unpleasant smells, that sentence him without
delay "to return to the place from whence he came."
With elastic limbs, and a stout heart to propel them,
"away" he starts. Everything he does evinces extraordinary resolution, determination, and courage. While the
high-bred hounds that are following him over-top every
hedge, *he* dashes through their boughs, thorns, and briars,
as straight as an arrow from a bow. When, on reaching
the "earth" he has been making for, he finds that it is
stopped, instead of weakly dwelling there, "*away*" he
again starts for some other cunning hidingplace. As he
proceeds, his wind, but not his courage, fails him, until,
on the pack approaching him, though any one of them
would have yelped piteously had but one of his toes
been caught in a trap, yet, so soon as the leading hound
comes up, he pitches into him, and when the infuriated
pack rush in upon him, he invariably dies in the midst
of them, without the utterance of the smallest moan,
sigh, or sound. In fact, within the breasts of all who have

pursued him there does not exist a braver heart than that over which the huntsman, cracking his whip to keep the hounds at bay from it, is triumphantly crying "WHOO-OOP!" *

THE LAMB AND THE FOX.

But the plot of our drama thickens. For on the green carpet of our little theatre, on which so many actors have been performing, there now lie tragically before us, as it were side by side, the body of a swooned lamb, and the carcase of a dead fox. Let us therefore for a moment place each into one of the scales of Justice, to weigh the relative specific gravities of these two tiny emblems—

* Some seasons ago the master of the Pytchley determined "to give to the hounds" a fox that had run to ground in a narrow culvert communicating with the Reservoir at Maidwell.

To prevent the poor animal escaping from his doom, the hounds were made to surround the mouth of the drain before the order was given to "lift up the sluice."

On the words being uttered the eyes of all the riders who encircled the pack were, of course, concentrated on one point. A slight noise was heard, some dead sticks appeared, followed by a violent rush of water, in the midst of which, rolled up like an immense hedgehog, appeared the fox, who no sooner got into daylight, than, before a hound could snap hold of him, he jumped to the left, and, at almost the same instant, popping through the only little hole in the thick hedge that bounded the drain, burst away, distanced the pack of enemies, quadruped and biped, that followed him, and thus escaped a death from which nothing but his extraordinary quickness and determination could have saved him.

the one of innocence, the other of guilt—as regards their utility to man.

When a lamb has been nursed, reared, fattened, and killed, its quarters afford say four good dinners, or possibly one dish only at four great dinners, and as soon as, either above stairs or below, his bones have been cleanly picked, the history of his usefulness is at an end. But the benefits which a fox confers upon his country would, though stewed down for hours, require very many more dishes to contain them.

If an individual migrates in search of happiness, he not only may travel many a weary mile without attaining it, but sooner or later, foot-sore, leg-wearied, and dejected, he will be sure to discover that a very small proportion of the trouble, time, and money he has expended would have procured for him at home contentment or peace of mind, the greatest of all earthly blessings. For truly may it be said, that there exists nothing in a garden or in a field more easy to cultivate than domestic happiness, composed, as we all know, of innumerable small fibres, which, by the laws of Nature, taking root in every direction, attach a man, like Gulliver in the island of Lilliput, to the ground on which he has happened to take rest.

A cynic may sneer at the rich man who, with his own hands, and with bent back, sows flowers to deck his path, and who plants trees to grace shrubberies to harbour the birds that are to sing to him. He may despise him for delving and digging, for carpentering, lathe-turning, and for other labour which a paid workman could infinitely better perform. But if this labour sweetens the cup of human existence, by giving that health to the body, which invigorates the mind for its studies—in short, if this mixture of physical and mental exertion results in producing contentment, the labourer, however high his rank, without deigning to revile the philosopher, may justly return thanks to that Almighty Power which, by such simple means, has enabled him, by dulcifying his " domum," to produce for himself domestic happiness.

As, however, what is good for the parts must also be beneficial for the whole, it must be evident that, in spite of the sneers of the cynic, it is equally wise for a people to foster and encourage among themselves any description of healthy recreation or amusement that may have the effect of creating among the community not only a friendly acquaintance with each other, but an indissoluble attachment to " the land they live in." Indeed, if this salutary precaution were to be neglected, lamentable consequences must ensue; for, like two merchants dealing in the same article, so do Virtue and Vice strenuously compete against one another, by each, at the same moment, offering to mankind, pleasures for sale.

The great cities of the Continent, especially Paris, in

this respect possess powerful attractions, which, unless they were to be neutralized or rather counteracted by national attachments of still greater power, would inevitably drain from the United Kingdom, especially from the country, a large proportion of those wealthy classes whose presence, expenditure, and charity have proved so beneficial to their respective neighbourhoods. In like manner, as Nature abhors a vacuum, so, if the affluent among the middle and lower classes, with a little money and leisure on hand, were to find themselves without some wholesome recreation, it is proverbial that a certain sable personage, who delights in idleness, would very soon, in his own service and in his own peculiar way, "set them to work."

But however wise it may be for an individual within his own precincts to create recreation to suit his particular palate, it is not so very easy to concoct any amusement that shall be pleasing to the taste of many ranks of the community as well as be generally beneficial to the whole.

A public racket-court or fives-court can only contain a very small party.

The far-famed national game of cricket (the stock in trade of which consists of a ball, some bats, half-a-dozen stumps, and eleven players) is adapted only to that bright, joyous, sunshiny half of the year, which, with its flowers and fruits, hardly requires to be enlivened, leaving the

dreary months of winter totally unprovided with amusement.

What therefore, *pro bono publico*, we require is to
invent, if possible, some description of national recreation
which, in all weathers, shall concentrate in groups over
the whole superficies of the kingdom, people of all conditions, from the highest ranks down to the lowest, to
join together in a healthy, manly, harmless sport, requiring
coolness, good temper, science, and resolution: and lastly,
which shall manure, or top-dress, the entire surface of
the country by broad-casting over it, annually, a large
amount of gold, silver, and copper.

Now the invention of hunting produces all these beneficial results. At the appointed meet, classes in ordinary
life as distinctly separated from each other as the various
castes in India, first assemble together, and then, during a
good run, are jostled together in lumps, and by bumps,
which, by collision, produce many a spark of generous
feeling that, under ordinary circumstances, could not
possibly have been elicited. For instance, not very long
ago, during a run in Leicestershire, a well-dressed, good-
looking young stranger was seen to pull up, dismount,
and run to the assistance of an old man lying under a
horse that was struggling violently above him. In extri-
cating the prisoner the liberator was repeatedly kicked.
However, although his flesh and coat were cut, and a

silver flask flattened in his breast-pocket, he resolutely
effected his object and then cantered away. " *Who's
that?* " said a gentleman to a farmer who had gallantly
assisted in the extrication. " *I don't know his name,*"
was the reply, "*but, whoever he is, he stuck to him like
a* RIGHT GOOD 'UN ! " About a month afterwards it tran-
spired that the " right good 'un," who had risked his life
to help one he never before saw, and whom probably he
will never see again, was Lord C., now Marquis of H.,
and heir to the dukedom of D. In the hunting field,
unfettered by prescriptive rights or privileges, the head
and heart of man rise or sink to that level, whatever it
may be, that intrinsically is their due. In short, irre-
spective of parentage, education, or income, any rider may
assume whatever position he can take, and, so long as he
leads, no one can prevent his wearing the honours, whatever they may be, of the day.

Hunting is generally accused of being a very dangerous
amusement, and yet by medical returns it might easily
be demonstrated that it is not so injurious to a man's
health or so fatal to his life as going to a succession of
balls, or especially of good dinners; in fact, there can be
no doubt that a London season blanches, per cent. per
annum, more cheeks, and requires more physic and more
coffins, than a hunting season.

How little danger, instead of how much, belongs to

hunting, is daily proved by, comparatively speaking, the impunity with which inexperienced people join in the chase. If a crowd of 150 or 200 persons of all ages and shapes, none of whom had ever before been in a boat, were all of a sudden, say during Christmas holidays, to dress themselves like tars, and then compete with sailors in every sort of weather, the chances, or rather the certainty, would be, that, without any disparagement to the art of boating, at least half of them would be drowned from sheer ignorance and inexperience. Again, if an eccentric gentleman in London, making his coachman stand up behind his carriage, were to require his footman to drive it, the vehicle, before it could reach the Opera-house, would probably be either smashed or upset; and yet, its fate would not be admitted as proving that it is dangerous to drive. In fact, it is a common proverb, that, in order to be proficient in any trade, it is necessary to be first duly apprenticed to it. But in the hunting-field no education at all is deemed requisite. And, accordingly, so soon as a young man, " gentle or simple " (though oftener simple than gentle), can get hold of money, he buys a stud of horses and hacks, hires grooms, orders three or four scarlet coats with the appurtenances thereto, goes to Melton, makes his formal appearance at a crack meet, and his informal disappearance into the first brook, or on the other side of the first fence he comes

to, and yet, " *Oh!* PRAY *catch that horse if you please!* "
is usually the only result, repeated over and over again
without injury to anybody.   Now, if people who really
have never learned to ride, mounted on young horses
who have never learned to hunt, can thus attempt to
follow hounds without damaging much more than their
clothes, it *ought* to follow that an experienced rider on
a clever hunter has, at all events, not more danger to
apprehend than other people are liable to, who ride solely
on hard roads, on which a horse is very apt to travel
carelessly, and always falls heavily.   Will Williamson,
now upwards of eighty years of age, who has been huntsman to the Duke of Buccleugh for more than fifty years,
and whose worst accident was lately caused by being
overturned in a dog-cart, still follows his hounds; and,
in like manner, in every part of the kingdom are to be
found old men who, with very little to complain about,
have been hunting from their boyhood, and occasionally
from their childhood.

Charles Payne, the huntsman of the Pytchley, was
much damaged by being thrown out of a gig; while, a
short time ago, his head whip, who had fearlessly crossed
almost every fence in Northamptonshire, dislocated his
shoulder by slipping off a little deal table.   The gallant
master of the Tedworth hounds was severely injured in
his conservatory ; the huntsman of the Surrey fox-hounds

within his house by a fall. Lastly, it may truly be asserted, that, in hunting, more accidents occur from over caution in riders than from a combination of boldness and judgment; indeed, if hunters could but speak, they would often whisper to their riders, *" If you keep taking such affectionate care of* MY HEAD, *you'll throw me* DOWN."

The encouragement given to farmers to breed horses of the best description, the high prices paid to them for hay, oats, beans, and straw; the sums of money expended for the purchase or rent of hunting-boxes, lodgings, stables, carriage-houses, &c., added to a variety of other incidental expenses, large and small, amount to a grand total which it would be less easy to underrate than exaggerate.

But besides the sums which hunting-men, by maintaining from eight to fourteen hunters, with grooms and strappers in proportion, distribute in their various localities, in almost every county men of rank and fortune step forward to support, more or less at their own private cost, a huntsman, one or two whips, hounds, and a stable full of horses, for the recreation and amusement of the community.

With this generous object in view, the late Sir Richard Sutton, for many years, spent about 10,000*l.* a-year in maintaining two packs of hounds and a stud of about fifty horses, for which he readily paid enormous prices.

In any portion of the globe, except the United Kingdom, the price of dog-flesh in England would appear utterly incomprehensible. In 1812 Lord Middleton gave 1200 guineas for the pack he purchased. When Mr. Warde gave up the Craven country Mr. Horlock paid him 2000 guineas for his hounds; while Lord Suffield coolly handed over to Mr. Lambton 3000 guineas for his pack without seeing them. To Mr. Conyers the master of the Tedworth hounds offered for "Bashful" 100 guineas; and for another bitch, called "Careful," 400 guineas, or 10,080 francs; a sum which, in any village in France, would be considered for a peasant girl—though neither bashful nor careful—a splendid marriage portion.

Before Sir Richard's death, Lord Alford, Lord Hopetoun, Lord Southampton, and, since his decease, Lord Stamford, who keeps seventy horses, have come forward to bestow upon the hunting counties around them the same noble and munificent assistance which, on a smaller scale, is as liberally given in many other localities; and yet, without one minute item, the sum total of the enjoyment, the recreation, the health, the good fellowship, the hard riding, the enormous sums of money distributed over the United Kingdom to maintain that ancient, royal, loyal, noble, and national sport which seriatim we have endeavoured to describe would suddenly be annihilated, were we but to lose that tiny unclean beast, that dishonest little miscreant that everybody abuses—THE FOX.

Ille Jacet.

But the scene suddenly shifts,——a small cracked bell in a violent hurry rings,——the slight shuffling of a few running-away feet is heard,——the green curtain which scarcely half a minute ago had dropped slowly rises,—— and in the centre of the little stage there now appears, reposing by itself, a white wicker cradle containing a new-born baby, who will rapidly grow before our readers into a character intimately connected with the sayings and doings, the scenes and incidents we are endeavouring to describe.

THOMAS ASSHETON SMITH,

Born in Queen Anne Street, Cavendish Square, London, on the 2nd of August, 1776, was the grandson of Thomas Assheton, Esq., of Ashley Hall, near Bowden, in Cheshire, who assumed the name of Smith on the death of his uncle, Captain William Smith, son of the Right Honourable John Smith, Speaker of the House of Commons in the first two Parliaments of Queen Anne, and Chancellor of the Exchequer in the preceding reign.

As Shakspeare, in his immortal history of the Seven Ages of Man, briefly described the first as "the infant, mewling, &c., in its nurse's arms," so of the childhood of Tom Smith the only occurrence we are enabled to record is that his mother, one day, found him lying on his nurse's lap, gasping like a tench just landed from a pond.

"*What's the matter with the child?*" she eagerly inquired.

"*Nothin,*" replied the calm nurse; "*he's doing nicely.*"

As regarded the present tense, this answer was the truth, the whole truth, and nothing but the truth. Had, however, the question been "What *has been* the matter with him?" with the same grammatical accuracy the reply would have been, "If you please, Ma'am, he has just thrown up a large pin," which, unperceived, he had managed to swallow.

On his reaching the second age of man—that is to say, when he was but seven years old—he was sent "with his satchel and shining morning face" to Eton, where, on his arrival, he found himself the youngest boy in the school.

The busy hive of the United Kingdom, we all know, is divided into cells, in each of which, at this moment, a raw material is being converted by labour into some particular description of manufactured goods. In one cell, a Minister of State is concocting, from crude evidence, a speech, a budget, or a despatch. In another cell, a young woman, with a protuberant cushion on her lap, covered by an intricate pattern, marked by pins with heads of various colours, is as indefatigably labouring for the welfare of her country by twirling, twisting, and twiddling innumerable bobbins of fine thread into Honiton lace. In other cells, workpeople are converting broad-cloth into clothes, leather into shoes, horse-hair into wigs, medicine into pills, lead into bullets, brass and tin into cannon, iron into rifles, alkali and grease into soap. Within what is called a " scrap-mill," by the power of steam, controlled by a single man, broken bolts, bars, nuts, nails, screw-pins, &c., are made to revolve, until by rumbling, tumbling, rubbing, scrubbing, bruising, beating, hustling, and jostling each other, all are turned out clean and bright, fit to be welded together for any purpose that may be required.

At Eton, by a similar process, about 600 boys of all sizes and shapes—red-haired, white-haired, black-haired ; long-legged, short-legged, bandy-legged ; splay-footed, pigeon-toed ; proud, humble, noisy, silent, good-humoured, spiteful, brave, timid, pale-faced, sallow-faced, freckled and rosy-cheeked, weak and strong, clever and stupid, pliable and pigheaded—yet all controlled by that unwritten, immutable, imperishable code of *honour* which, like a halo, has always illuminated their play-ground and their school, are hustled together on water, in water, under water, and out of water, until, when the door of their scrap-mill is opened—although their minds and bodies are as dissimilar as ever—they all turn out polished *gentlemen*, prepared to encounter those hardships, dangers, vicissitudes, difficulties, and, above all, base temptations in life, which high-bred principles are so especially well adapted to resist.

For eleven years Tom Smith remained at this school, where he acquired a taste for classical literature, which characterised him through life. Pope, Shakspeare, and Horace, from which he used to quote long passages, were his favourite authors; he could also, without pressure, spout out the whole of the Epistle of Eloisa to Abelard. But what reigned at the back of his head and in the citadel of his heart was an ardent love for athletic exercises of any description, especially for cricket and boating. He was also, throughout his whole life, affectionately attached to fighting; and Etonians, old and young, to this day, record, as one of the severest contests in the history of youthful pugilism, the desperate battle he fought with Jack Musters, a kindred spirit, of whom it has been said that he could do seven things—namely, ride, fence, fight, swim, shoot, play at cricket and at tennis— as well as any man in Europe. His pugilistic propensity, which appeared so early, was conspicuous throughout his life. While hunting in Leicestershire he was prevailed upon to stand for the borough of Nottingham. On proceeding to the poll, he found not only the town placarded with "No foxhunting M.P.," but a guy in a red coat, tailed by a fox's brush, burning in effigy of him before the hustings. His appearance there elicited tremendous yells and hootings, which apparently no authority could subdue, until, with a stentorian voice, heard above the uproar, Tom Smith exclaimed, "Gentlemen! as you refuse to hear my political principles, be so kind as to listen to these few words: *I'll fight any man among ye, little or big*, and will have a round with him now for love!" In an instant, as if by magic, yells and groans were converted into rounds of cheers, demonstrating the strange stuff, be it good, bad, or indifferent, that Englishmen are made of.

On another occasion, while riding down the Gallowtree Gate, in Leicester, he struck the horse of a coal-heaver, who, in return, cut him sharply across the face. Smith jumped immediately from his horse, and the driver from his cart, the latter doffing his smock-frock, the former buttoning his coat and turning up his sleeves. The conflict was desperate; and from a fellow weighing fourteen stone, and standing six feet high, he was receiving severe punishment, when, by constables and a crowd of people, the combatants were separated. "You shall hear from me

M

again !" said Smith to his gallant smutty antagonist.
True to his word, the next morning the squire's groom
was seen inquiring where the coal-heaver lived.   On
finding the man, whose face, like his master's, had received
some heavy bruises, he said to him, "Mr. Smith has
sent me to give you this sovereign, and to tell you you're
the best man that ever stood before him."   "God bless
his honour !" replied the man, "and thank him a thousand
times."

When Tom Smith was at Eton, fighting had not cropped
to the surface of a schoolfellow and friend who in after
life, known by the name of WELLINGTON, greatly distinguished himself in this world by seeking and by
gaining pitched battles.   "I suppose, Smith," said the
old silver-haired Duke to him, one day, in London,
"you've done now with *fighting ?*"   "Oh, yes," replied
Smith, then in his sixtieth year, "I've quite given that
up ; but——" suddenly correcting himself, he added, "I'll
fight yet any man *of my age.*"

At Chapmansford, when upwards of seventy, a rough
country fellow, before a large field of sportsmen, threw a
stone at one of the hounds of the old squire, who instantly
struck him with his hunting whip.   "You daren't do that
if you were off your horse," said the man.   The words
were hardly out of the clodhopper's mouth when (in the
seventh age of man) Smith stood before him, with a pair

of fists clenched in his face, in so pugilistic an attitude that the fellow took to his heels, and, amidst the jeers of his comrades, ran away.

In 1794 Tom Smith quitted Eton to become a gentleman commoner at Christ Church, Oxford, where, with great diligence and assiduity, he hunted regularly in Oxfordshire and Northamptonshire,—became a fearless swimmer,—learnt to pull a sturdy oar on the Isis,—was a good shot and billiard-player,—and excelled as a batsman in the cricket-field on Cowley Marsh and Bullingdon. On leaving the University he became a member of the Marylebone Club and a regular attendant at Lord's during the summer; he was also a member of the Royal Yacht Club. Mr. Smith's love for science and shipbuilding induced him to build several sailing and steam yachts. He considered himself to be the practical originator of the wave line, and, by the advice of the Duke of Wellington, he submitted to the First Lord of the Admiralty some important hints for improving the construction of gunboats. In autumn, winter, and spring, he instinctively "went to the dogs," or, as in sporting phraseology it is termed, "took to hunting," so eagerly, that in 1800, when only twenty-four years old, he was signalized in song as a daring rider in that celebrated run from Billesden Coplow, in which but four gentlemen, with Jack Raven the Whip, were able to live with the hounds.

M 2

In 1806 he succeeded Lord Foley at Quorn, and for ten years hunted Leicestershire with first-rate hounds, for a portion of which he had paid to Mr. Musters 1000 guineas, until, in 1816, he took the place of Mr. Osbaldiston in Lincolnshire, where he hunted the Burton country for eight years. He then, ceasing for two years to be a master of hounds, hunted with the Duke of Rutland and in the neighbouring counties until 1826, when, taking up his residence at Penton Lodge, he created for himself a new country between Andover and Salisbury. In 1830 —two years after the death of his father, from whom he inherited a very large fortune—he removed to Tedworth, which he had lately rebuilt with magnificent kennels, and stables in which every hunter had a loose box. In these stables he had often as many as fifty horses, all in first-rate condition. For thirty-two years he hunted the Tedworth country without ever asking for subscriptions of any sort or kind. All he begged of the landowners and of those who hunted with him was to *preserve* foxes to enable him to kill them. At his meets his friend and guest the late Duke of Wellington often attended. In stature Mr. Smith was about 5 feet 10 inches high, athletic, well-proportioned, muscular, but slight. His weight was between eleven and twelve stone. With a highly-intelligent but resolute countenance, containing (as was observed of it) " a dash of the bulldog," he had plain features.

"*That fellow Jack Musters*," Tom Smith used to say, "*spoilt* MY *beauty*." For several years, though his name was seldom found in the debates, he represented in Parliament Carnarvonshire and Andover; and in 1832, in consequence of the riots which took place in that year, he raised, at his own expense, a corps of yeomanry cavalry, reviewed by the Duke of Wellington, the troopers of which were chiefly his own tenants or farmers of the neighbourhood. For upwards of fifty seasons he continued to be the master of hounds, until, after having been in his saddle for seventy years, the boy who in 1783 went to Eton when he was seven years old, died at Vaenol on the 9th of September, 1858, aged eighty-two.

At the earnest request of his widow, Sir John E. Eardley-Wilmot (assisted by extracts from the 'Field' newspaper), with considerable spirit and ability, has lately compiled a series of graphic incidents and sketches, forming altogether a memoir—or, as he terms them, 'Reminiscences'—of the life of one whom Napoleon I. addressed as "*le premier chasseur d'Angleterre*," and who was also called by the Parisians "*le grand chasseur* SMIT.*" From this volume we shall now submit to our readers a few extracts.

"Lord Foley," wrote 'Nimrod,' "was succeeded in the possession of the Quorn hounds by that most conspicuous sportsman of modern times, Thomas Assheton Smith. As combining the character of a skilful sportsman with that of a desperate horseman, perhaps his parallel is not to be found ; and his name will be handed down to posterity as a specimen of enthusiastic zeal in one individual pursuit, very rarely equalled. From the first day of the season to the last he was always the same man, the same desperate fellow over a country, and unquestionably possessing, *on every occasion and at every hour of the day*, the most bulldog nerve ever exhibited in the saddle. His motto was, ' I'll be with my hounds ; ' and all those who have seen him in the field must acknowledge he made no vain boast of his prowess. His falls were countless ; and no wonder, for he rode at places which *he knew* no horse could leap over ; but his object was to get, one way or the other, into the field with his hounds. As a horseman, however, he has ever been superexcellent. He sits in his saddle as if he were part of his horse, and his seat displays vast power over his frame. In addition to his power his hand is equal to Chifney's, and the advantage he experiences from it may be gleaned from the following expression. Being seen one day hunting his hounds on Radical, always a difficult, but at that time a more than commonly difficult, horse to ride, he was asked by a friend why he did not put a martingale on him, to give him more power over his mouth. ' Thank ye,' he replied, ' but my left hand shall be *my* martingale.' "

His fame and success in Lincolnshire were as great as at Quorn. The Melton men followed him, knowing they were sure of good sport wherever he went, although scarcely one of them was quite prepared for the formidable drains or dykes in the Burton Hunt. Shortly after their arrival there, they found a fox near the kennels that crossed a dyke called the Tilla. Tom Smith, the only one who rode at it, got in, but over, leaving behind him fourteen of the Meltonians floundering in the water at the same time, which so cooled their ardour that, excepting Sir H. Goodricke, gallant David Baird, and one or two others, they soon returned to Melton.

Mr. Delmé Ratcliffe, in his work on the 'Noble Science of Fox-hunting,' describes Tom Smith as follows :—

"I could nowhere find a more fitting model for the rising generation of sportsmen. . . . He was an instance of the very rare union of coolness and consummate skill as a huntsman, combined with the impetuosity of a most desperate rider; and not only was he the most determined of all riders, but equally remarkable as a horseman.

"Now I am not going to give merely my own opinion of Mr. Thomas Assheton Smith, as a horseman and rider to hounds, but shall lay before my readers that of all the sporting world, at least all who have seen him in the field; which is, that, taking him from the first day's hunting of the season to the last, place him on the best horse in his stable or on the worst, he is sure to be with his hounds, and *close to them too.* In fact, he has undoubtedly proved himself the best and hardest rider England ever saw, and it would be vain in any man to dispute his title to that character."

Again, says Mr. Apperley—

"Let us look at him in his saddle. Does he not look like a workman? Observe how lightly he sits! No one could suppose him to be a twelve-stone man. And what a firm hand he has on his horses! How well he puts them at their fences, and what chances he gives them to extricate themselves from any scrape they may have gotten into! He never hurries them then; no man ever saw Tom Smith ride fast at his fences, at least at large ones (brooks excepted), let the pace be what it may; and what a treat it is to see him jump water! His falls, to be sure, have been innumerable; but what very hard-riding man does not get falls? Hundreds of Mr. Smith's falls may be accounted for :

he has measured his horses' pluck by his own, and ridden at hundreds of non-feasible places, with the chance of getting over them somehow."

Again : "No man," says Dick Christian, "that ever came into Leicestershire could beat Mr. Smith—I do not care what any of them say ;" while "The Druid," in ' Silk and Scarlet,' after giving some very interesting anecdotes of Tom Smith, says of him, "However hasty in temper and action he might be in the field or on the flags, he was the mightiest hunter that ever ' rode across Belvoir's sweet vale ' or wore a horn at his saddle-bow."

"His wonderful influence," he adds, "over his hunters was strongly exemplified at another time, but in rather a different manner. He had mounted a friend, who complained of having nothing to ride, on his celebrated horse Cicero. The hounds were running breast-high across the big pasture lands of Leicestershire, and Cicero was carrying his rider like a bird, when a strong flight of rails had almost too ugly an aspect of height, strength, and newness for the liking of our friend on his 'mount.' The keen eye of Assheton Smith, as he rode beside him, at once discerned that he had no relish for the timber, and seeing that he was likely to make the horse refuse, he cried out, ' Come up, Cicero ! ' His well-known voice had at once the desired effect; but Cicero's rider, by whom the performance was not intended, left his ' seat ' vacant, fortunately without any other result than a roll upon the grass."

"I have said," remarks Nimrod, "that Mr. Smith's make and shape, together with a fine bridle-hand, have assisted him in rising to perfection as a horseman."

" I once saw," relates a friend, " a fine specimen of Mr. Smith's hand and nerve in the going off of a frost, when the *bone* was not quite out of the ground. We were running a fox hard over Salisbury Plain, when all at once his horse came on a treacherous flat, greasy at top, as sportsmen say, but hard and slippery underneath. The horse he rode was a hard puller, and very violent, named Piccadilly; and the least check from the bridle, when the animal began to blunder, would have to a certainty made him slip up. Here the fine riding of the squire shone conspicuously. He left his horse entirely alone, as if he were swimming; and after floundering about and swerving for at least a hundred yards, Piccadilly recovered himself, and went on as if nothing had happened."

"At the end of a desperate run, he once charged the river Welland, which divides the counties of Leicester, Northampton, and Rutland, and is said to be altogether impracticable. The knack he had of getting across water is to be attributed to his resolute way of riding to hounds, by which his horses knew that it was in vain to refuse whatever he might put them at."

One day when Smith was drawing for a fox on his famous horse Fire-King, he came to a precipitous bank at the end of a meadow, with a formidable drop into a hard road. "*You can't get out there, Sir,*" said a civil farmer. "*I should like very much to see the place where* WE" (patting Fire-King) "*cannot go,*" was the reply, as down he rode, to the astonishment of the field.

"In falling," says Sir J. Eardley Wilmot, "he always contrived to fall clear of his horse. The bridle-rein, which fell as lightly as breeze of zephyr on his horse's neck, was then held as in a vice. In some instances, with horses whom he knew well, he would ride for a fall, where he knew it was not possible for him to clear a fence. With Jack-o'-Lantern he was often known to venture on this experiment, and he frequently said there was not a field in Leicestershire in which he had not had a fall. 'I never see you in the Harborough country,' he observed to a gentleman who occasionally hunted with the Quorn. 'I don't much like your Harborough country,' replied the other, 'the fences are so large.' 'Oh! ' observed Mr. Smith, 'there is no place you cannot get over with a fall.' To a young supporter of his pack, who was constantly falling and *hurting* himself, he said, 'All who profess to ride should know *how to fall.*' "

The author of ' Silk and Scarlet ' says :—

"It was a great speech of Mr. Smith's, if ever he saw a horse refuse with his Whips, ' *Throw your* HEART *over, and your horse will follow.*' He never rode fast at his fences. I have heard him say scores of times, 'When a man rides at fences a hundred miles an hour, *depend upon it he funks.*' "

Sir William Miles confirms this statement :—

"Mr. Smith," he remarks, "always said, ' *Go slow at all fences, except water.* It makes a horse know the use of his legs, and by so riding he can put down a leg wherever it is wanted.' "

Long Wellesley had a horse which he declared no man could see a run on. " He only requires *a rider*," said the squire. " Will *you* ride him, then, at Glen Gorse ? " " Willingly !" replied Smith, who, after several falls, killing his fox, was presented with the animal, which he accordingly named " Gift."

The history of the education of Smith's favourite horse, Jack-o'-Lantern, is described as follows :—

"We were riding," said Tom Edge, "to covert through a line of bridle-gates, when we came to a new double oaken post and rail fence. 'This is just the place to make my colt a good timber jumper,' said the squire ; 'so you shut the gate, and ride away fast.' This was no sooner done than the squire rode at the rails, which Jack taking with his breast, gave both himself and his rider such a fall, that their respective heads were looking towards the fence they had ridden at. Up rose both at the same time, as if nothing very particular had happened. 'Now,' said Tom Smith, 'this will be the *making* of the horse; just do as you did before, and ride away.' Edge did so, and Jack flew the rails without touching, and from that day was a first-rate timber fencer."

Only on two occasions, while hunting, did Tom Smith succeed in breaking a bone: once at Melton, when he consoled himself by learning arithmetic from the pretty damsel at the post-office; and afterwards, when one of his ribs was fractured, owing, as he said, to his having a knife in his breast-pocket:—

"And yet," says Sir J. Eardley Wilmot, "notwithstanding the gallant manner in which he always rode, never turning from any fence that intervened between him and his hounds, he never had a horse drop dead under him, or die from the effects of a severe day's riding. It is also a fact well recorded that he was never known to strike a horse unfairly. 'How is it,' asked a friend, 'that horses and hounds seem never to provoke you?' '*They* are brutes, and know no better, but *men* do,' was the reply."

The most extraordinary hunter in his stable, "Ayston," was pigeon-toed, and so bad a hack, that he had to be led to covert; and yet at no time would his master have taken a thousand guineas for him.

After the famous Billesden Coplow run, in which Tom Smith maintained so prominent a place, he sold the horse he that day rode, called Furze-cutter, for which he had given 26*l.*, to Lord Clonbrock for 400*l.*

The Rev. Francis Dyson, now rector of Creeklande, on

being ordained, was appointed to assist his father, the clergyman at Tedworth :—

"Mr. Smith," says Sir J. Eardley Wilmot, "was so pleased with his first sermon, that, on coming out of church, he slapped the young curate on the back, and said, 'Well done, Frank! you shall have a mount on Rory O'More next Thursday.' Young Dyson had many a run afterwards out of the squire's stables, for his performances in the field pleased as much as those in the pulpit.

"Once, when the hounds were running short with a sinking fox, a person clad in a long black coat, and evidently thinking scorn of the fun, inquired of the Whip what the *dogs were then doing*. 'Why, Sir,' said Dick Burton, throwing a keen glance down the inquirer's person, 'they are preaching his funeral sermon.' "

In 1840 Tom Smith proposed to pay a visit to his old friend Sir Richard Sutton, whose hunting had been stopped by a severe accident. On hearing of this movement, Mr. Greene of Rolleston, who had been one of his best pupils in his Leicestershire days, requested him, in his way to Lincolnshire, to bring his hounds once more into his old country, Mr. Hodgson, who then hunted Leicestershire, having handsomely placed the best meet at his disposal. The veteran, for he was then sixty-four, accepted the challenge, bringing with him eighteen couples of his finest hounds, of great substance, open-chested, and in splendid condition.

"It would be vain," writes Sir J. Eardley Wilmot, "to endeavour to commemorate the scene which took place when Tom Smith, surrounded by his hounds, met the field at Shankton Holt on Friday, the 20th of March. More than two thousand horsemen, one-third of whom appeared in pink, were assembled. Men of the highest birth and station, men who had served their country with deeds of most daring gallantry by sea and land, men who in political or social life were the most brilliant in repute, thronged to do honour to the first fox-hunter of the day. They had come from remote counties, and more were pouring in along the grassy slopes and vales, or skirting the well-known gorse covers. As Dick Christian remarked, 'the first lot were at Shankton Holt when the tail end weru't out of Rolleston gates.' Cold must have been the heart of him who could behold without joyous emotion the crowds of grey-headed horsemen hurrying forward to shake hands with their old friend and fellow-sportsman, each calling vividly to memory some scene where he had acted the most conspicuous part. More than twenty years had rolled away since he had resigned the lead in that magnificent country. There had been splendid riders since his day ; and while time had thinned the ranks of the veterans, younger men had either achieved or were achieving fame—Frank Holyoake, now Sir Francis Goodricke, well known for his splendid feats on Brilliant; Colonel Lowther, Lord Wilton, Lord Archibald Seymour, George Payne, Little * Gilmour, Lord Gardner, George Anson, and a host of sportsmen, well deserving the reputation they had won, yet all strangers to the doings of this hero of the Quorn, except through anecdotes familiar to them as 'household words.' In addition to these were a very goodly display of carriages-and-four filled with ladies, and pedestrians without number. The hounds with Dick Burton were drawn up on the lawn, while the vast group of horsemen formed a circle, with the carriages and assembled crowd outside. After the friendly salutations were over, and their enthusiastic character astonished no one but the Illustrious Stranger†present, Mr. Smith took his hounds to Shankton Holt, where he drew only the bottom of the covert; thence to Norton Gorse, Stanton Wood, Glooston Wood, and Fallow Close, all blank. It

---

* Like William of Deloraine, "*good at need.*"
† Prince Ernest, brother to Prince Albert.

was an unfavourable day for scent,—a bright sun with north-
easterly wind, not a cloud to be seen, and the cold intense. A fox
having been found by Mr. Hodgson, in Vowes Covert, as already
stated, away went the hounds towards Horringhold, leaving Blaston
to the right. Here Mr. Smith took a strong flight of rails into a
road, quite like a ' young 'un.' The fox soon afterwards crossed the
Welland, and went away for Rockingham Park, where, it being late,
they whipped off."

From 1830 to 1856—that is to say, until Tom Smith
had reached the age of eighty—with his indomitable
energy and undaunted courage he continued to hunt his
hounds at Tedworth, spending his summers at Vaenol
on board his yacht. His head was as clear and his hand
as firm as they had been twenty years ago. If he felt not
quite well in a morning, plunging his head into cold
water, he used to hold it there as long as he could, which
he said always put him to rights. It is true he had
curtailed his meets to four only a week, but on these
days the farmers were delighted to see " the old Squire "
vault on horseback, as usual, blow his horn while his
horse was carrying him over a five-barred gate, and, with
a loose rein, gallop down the sheep-fed hill-sides with all
the alacrity of a boy. But although the hourglass of his
existence appeared to be still as bright and clear as
ever, the sand within the upper portion of the crystal
was now running to its end. In September, 1856, while
at his summer residence in North Wales, he was suddenly
seized with an alarming attack of asthma, which, by the

use of stimulants and by the assiduous attention of Mrs. Smith,—at this period herself in a very weak state of health,—was so far subdued that on one of his horses saddled appearing at the door—although five minutes before he had been gasping for breath on the sofa—he mounted the animal, and broke away, as if instinctively, to seek for himself a stronger stimulant than his physician could prescribe—*the sight once again of his hounds.*

" Although," writes Sir J. Eardley Wilmot, very feelingly, " he rallied from this attack in an astonishing manner, he was no longer the same man. The erect gait was bent, and the eagle eye had lost its lustre."

The able writer of ' Silk and Scarlet' gives the following graphic and affecting description of Tom Smith the last time he appeared at the meet with his hounds :—

" The covert side knew him no more after the October of 1857, when he just cantered up to Willbury on his chestnut hack Blemish, to see his hounds draw. Carter got his orders to bring the choicest of the 1858 entry, and he and Will Bryce arrived at the usual rendezvous with five couple of bitches by the Fitzwilliam Hardwicke and Hermit. He looked at them a short time, and exclaimed, ' WELL, THEY 'RE AS BEAUTIFUL AS THEY CAN BE,' bade both his men good-bye, and they saw him no more."

He returned to Tedworth as usual—

" But," writes Sir J. Eardley Wilmot, " at the annual meet on the 1st of November, 1857, the hounds met without the accustomed centre figure of their master, who slowly rode up to them without his scarlet. He remarked, quite seriously, that if he had worn his hunting gear, and his pack should observe that he could not follow them, they would show their sorrow by refusing to hunt the fox. A universal gloom pervaded the field; he looked wistfully and lovingly at his old favourites, the heroes of many a well-fought field; and as he quickly went back into the hall, shrinking almost from the outer air, while the horsemen and pack turned away slowly towards the shrubberies, every one felt with a heavy heart that the glory of the old foxhunter had at length departed."

The state of Mrs. Smith's health having for many years caused her husband great anxiety, in 1845, in order, as he said, " to bring Madeira to England," he constructed for her at Tedworth a magnificent conservatory or crystal palace, 315 feet in length and 40 in width, in which, enjoying the temperature of a warm climate, she might take walking exercise during the winter months. A Wiltshire farmer, on first seeing this building, observed, he supposed it was for the 'Squire to hunt there whenever a frost stopped him in the field.

"It was a melancholy spectacle," writes Sir J. Eardley Wilmot, "to see Tom Smith the winter before his death, when he could no longer join his hounds, mount one of his favourite hunters—Euxine, Paul Potter, or Blemish—with the assistance of a chair, and take his exercise for an hour at a foot's pace up and down this conservatory, often with some friend at his side to cheer him up and while away the time until he re-entered the house, for he was not allowed at that period to go out of doors. Even in this feeble condition, 'quantùm mutatus ab illo Hectore,' once on horseback, he appeared to revive; and the dexterity and ease with which he managed, like a plaything, the spirited animal under him, which had scarcely left its stable for months, was most surprising."

During the last days of his existence he rested rather than took exercise on that noble animal the horse, which for seventy years he had so resolutely and yet so considerately governed. His mind, in its declining hours, had also its support. Throughout his life, without ostentation and often in secret, he had been charitable to people of various conditions. Of the two thousand workmen in his quarries, scarcely one of them had ever been taken before a magistrate for dishonesty. Never was he known, if properly requested, to refuse to give a site for a church or even for a Dissenting chapel. Both he and Mrs. Smith invariably went to church on foot, it being a rule with them never, except in case of illness, to have either carriage or horse out on Sundays.

A few weeks after he had completed his eighty-second year he had a sudden attack of the same symptoms which had shaken him so severely in 1856. In a moment of consciousness, evidently aware of his approaching end, pointing to his faithful valet, he said to his devoted wife, " *Take care of that man !* " and when Mrs. Smith left the room, he said to her maid, " *Watch over your mistress ; take care of* HER." A few hours afterwards—

" Last scene of all,
That ends this strange eventful history "—

on the 9th of September, 1858, while Mrs. Smith's sister was watching by his bedside, a slight change came over

N

his countenance, but before the doctors or even his valet could be summoned,—with a gentle sigh expired Thomas Assheton Smith, bequeathing, on half a sheet of writing-paper, the whole of his vast possessions, producing from 50,000*l.* to 55,000*l.* a year, to his widow (who survived him only a few months); and moreover leaving behind him a name that will long be remembered not only by the farmers and riding men of the counties he hunted, but by all who are disposed fairly and justly to appreciate the lights and shadows which constitute the character of " The English Country Gentleman," one only of whose recreations we have endeavoured to delineate to our readers in the foregoing slight sketches of those three gallant animals—the HORSE, the FOX, and last, though not least, the FOXHUNTER.

THE ROYAL ENGINEER TRAIN PRACTISING LASSO DRAUGHT.

To face page 165.

ON MILITARY HORSE-POWER.

As the momentum or force of a shot is said to be its weight multiplied by its velocity, so the strength of an army may not unjustly be estimated by multiplying its physical powers by the rate at which (if necessary) it can be made to travel: in short, activity is to an army what velocity is to a shot, or what the rigging of a vessel is to its hull. But, although we refuse to increase the weight of a shot unless we can proportionately preserve our power to propel it, yet, in European warfare, this principle, as regards the " matériel " of an army, has not always been kept in mind. Inventions have very easily been admitted, which afterwards have not been so easy to carry. It is true, they have added to the powers of the army, but they have so diminished its speed, that, encumbered by its implements and accoutrements, a European, like an East Indian army, has often felt that it requires less science to fight than to march; and thus, when Bonaparte, in his retreat from Moscow, was surrounded by Cossacks, which his troops were unable to crush only because they could not get at them, his well-known confession proves that when the field is vast, and its resources feeble, the distance between regular and irregular warfare " is but a step,"—the reason being,

N 2

that the superior strength of the former is worn out by the superior activity of the latter, or, as Marshal Saxe expressed it, "its arms are of less value than its legs."

Now, it is undeniable that this want of activity proceeds partly from the weight of the "matériel," but principally from the following very remarkable imperfection in the military equipment of Europe.

It is well known that not only every soldier, but every human being following an army, is subject to military discipline, and that his labour may, at any time, and for any purpose, be required of him; but, although the rational being is thus called upon to work with cheerful obedience for the grand objects of the army, the physical powers of the brute beast have never yet been developed; and accordingly for the various, sudden, and momentary emergencies for which horse-power has often and urgently in vain been required, horse-power (the cavalry) to an enormous extent has existed upon the spot, a military element which it has hitherto been considered so impracticable to control, that the guns, ammunition, treasure, &c., which European cavalry have oftentimes bravely won, their horses have been supposed totally incapable to carry away; and the laurel which was positively in their hands they have thus been obliged to abandon. Again, for sieges in countries which have been drained by the artillery and cavalry, not only of horses, but of sustenance to maintain them, it has often been absolutely necessary to bring forward, by bullocks and other inefficient means, the battering train, ammunition, entrenching tools, materials, &c., amounting in weight, even for the attack of a second-rate fortress, to several thousand tons. In moments of such distress the infantry working in the trenches have often severely suffered from the delay occasioned by the want of horse-power, while their comrades, the cavalry, have been deemed incapable of sharing the honour and fatigue of the day, from the anomalous conclusion that, although it is easy to extract from men manual labour, it is impossible to extract from horses horse-power; and yet there exists no reason why, in moments of emergency, cavalry horses should not be required to work (most particularly at drag-ropes) as well as infantry soldiers; for although the patient endurance of hardships and privations is one of the noblest features in military life, yet absolutely to suffer from the want of what one positively possesses is, even in common life, a discreditable misfortune, indicating not bodily weakness, but mental imbecility.

Even in that noble department, the Horse Artillery itself, there existed throughout the Peninsular War a striking example of latent power which had never been exerted. To each gun there were attached twelve horses trained to draught. Of these, only eight possessed the means of drawing: the gun might therefore, in mechanical calculation, be said to be propelled by an engine of eight horse-power; and if a morass, or any other obstacle, over-balanced this power, the gun was either deserted, or (as was customary) the infantry were harnessed to it, by drag-ropes, in the immediate presence of four draught-horses, whose powers (besides officers' horses) it was conceived that we were unable to command.*

Now, to awaken, *at no expense,* the important, natural, yet dormant powers, not only of cavalry but of all other horses, and, consequently, to afford the means of accelerating (when required) the movements, grand or small, of an army, would surely be more beneficial than even to suggest an improvement in its arms; for it may justly be said that our present weapons are destructive enough —that even if we could succeed in making them more so, still our enemies would retort them upon us—that the advantage, or rather the disadvantage, would then be mutual—and that, eventually, war would only be made still more destructive; but by giving activity and mobility to European armies, the science of war is promoted; and even if the benefit to the civilized nations

---

* To the 12-pounder Armstrong gun (which sighted to 8° gives a range of 3000 yards) are now attached eight horses in harness, and eight more on which the non-commissioned officers and men, including horse holders, are mounted. Of these, four are supplied with web breast harness and traces: to a proportion of the remainder lassos are supplied.

of Europe should be equal (but this, from the superior size and strength of English horses, would evidently be in our favour), yet it would at least shield the profession from the disgrace of being again persecuted, in any country, by an uncivilized army; and if the navy of England, laden with its immense weight of metal, is endeavouring, by science and reflection, to accelerate its rate of sailing, so that it can not only stand against the largest fleet, but can chase and run down the smallest pirate, surely the British army, already distinguished by its heart and its arm, should never rest satisfied until it can sufficiently develop its locomotive powers to be able to overtake and punish the insults of irregular troops.

Having now endeavoured to prove, 1st, That in European warfare there positively does exist a serious imperfection; and 2ndly, That it is for the interest, and due to the character, of the profession, that this imperfection should be corrected, we will proceed to explain the reasons which have lately induced the Duke of Cambridge by the following order to direct the attention of the British cavalry to the practice of lasso draught, (which for more than two years, by order of the Inspector-General of Fortifications, General Sir John Burgoyne, has been most successfully and scientifically adopted, by Captain Siborne, R.E., commanding the Royal Engineer Train, under the intelligent superintendence of Colonel Henry Sandham, Director of the Royal Engineers' Establishment at Chatham.)

Extract from the Queen's Regulations, page 126.

" In order that the cavalry may, upon emergencies, be available for the purposes of draught, such as assisting artillery, &c., through deep roads, and in surmounting other impediments and obstacles which the carriages of the army have frequently to encounter in the course of active service, ten men per troop are to be equipped with the tackle of the lasso."

In Europe, Asia, Africa, North America, and a considerable portion of South America, for every purpose of drawing, a horse is confined between two traces; and accordingly, whenever for the first time in his life he is placed in this predicament, so soon as one of them touches or tickles him on one side, he flies from it to the other trace, which suddenly arrests him, and, usually blindfolded by blinkers, being ignorant of, as well as alarmed at, the unknown objects that are restraining him, he occasionally endeavours to disperse them by kicking; and even if he submits, it requires some little experience to tranquillize his fears. For these reasons, throughout the regions enumerated, a horse that has never been in harness, however valuable he may be, is *totally* useless in a moment of emergency for the purposes of draught.

Now throughout that region of South America which extends in 35° south latitude from Buenos Ayres on the Atlantic, to Santiago and to Valparaiso on the Pacific Ocean, harness is composed of nothing but a surcingle and a single trace, by which the horse draws as a man would drag a garden-roller, by one hand instead of by two.

By this simple mode all the merchandise, and all the travellers that have ever traversed on wheels those immense plains that separate the two great oceans of the world, have been transported.

For military purposes its efficiency has been thus substantiated by General Miller in his history of 'The War for Independence :'—

"Our corps consisted of ten six-pounders and one howitzer. Each gun was drawn by four horses, and each horse ridden by a gunner, there being no corps of drivers in the service. A non-commissioned officer and seven drivers were, besides the four already mentioned, attached to each piece of artillery. Buckles, collars, cruppers, and breast-plates were not in use; the horses simply drew from the saddle, and with this equipment our guns have travelled nearly 100 miles in a day."

But besides its efficiency for all the requirements of either peace or war, the singular advantage of this simple harness is that any description of horse, tame or wild, uses it without noticing it; for if the single trace which passes immediately beneath his hip bone happens (which it ought not) to press against his side, by shrinking from it only an inch it instantly ceases to touch him; and as there then remains nothing to confine, tickle, or alarm him, he refrains from kicking, simply because there is nothing to kick at, and from quarrelling because he can see nothing in the world to quarrel with.

With this equipment, if a party of native riders, hunting ostriches in South America, are requested to help the horses of a carriage across a river, and up a steep bank, similar, for instance, to that of the Alma, in a moment they affix their lassos, conquer the difficulty, attain the summit, and then, with tobacco smoke steaming from their mouths, gallop away to follow their sport.

The Royal Engineer Train have demonstrated by public experiments in this country, that with this simple equipment, which would injure neither the efficiency nor the appearance of the cavalry, any number of horses, whether accustomed to draught or not, are capable of being at once harnessed to any description of carriage, not only (*see sketch*) in front to draw it forward, but in rear to hold it back, or even sideways to prevent its oversetting—in short, that it is a power which can be made to radiate in any direction; and as its character stands upon a much firmer foundation—as it is *bonâ fide* the common mode of draught in South America—

in constant use for all military and civil purposes—a practical invention which, under all circumstances, has been always found to answer, it is evident to demonstration,—1st. That if it can transport artillery, &c., across the lofty, vast, and rugged features of uncultivated America, it would surely be serviceable on the roads and bridges of civilized countries. 2ndly, That if it can be adapted to unbroken horses, it cannot be inapplicable to the trained horses of our cavalry. And, 3rdly, That as both the surcingle and trace are made, in America, of nothing but the skins of bullocks, we should, on active service, be able in all countries at least to obtain this material, and generally many others.

It must, moreover, be observed, that as a mounted horse (*i. e.* a horse and man) are heavier than an unmounted horse, the former with a lasso can drag a heavier weight than the latter with a collar and traces.*

Now, supposing for a moment that not only our cavalry were to be furnished with, but that every saddle-horse receiving rations in a European army was to be ordered to wear the South American surcingle (*which costs less than English girths and surcingle,* and which experience has proved to be, merely as a girth, superior to a common

---

* On active service, when a gun sticks in very heavy ground, it has been usual to place a gunner upon every unmounted horse, and, if necessary, behind every driver on the mounted ones. By this additional weight or power a gun has repeatedly been extricated and brought into action.

one), and to carry a halter of the usual regulation length, but long enough for a single trace, without detailing the various important as well as trifling services which might be performed, is it not evident that the general activity of the army would most materially be increased? that, in fact, this equipment would form an era in military warfare? that it would be an enormous, and, in Europe, an unheard-of engine of say twenty or thirty thousand horses' power, which, at a moment's warning, could either be called forward or dismissed, and, after all, maintained at no expense whatever? for it must ever be kept in mind, THAT WE POSSESS, AND ALWAYS HAVE POSSESSED, THE POWER; all that, for five and thirty years, we have until lately in vain proposed, is—to rouse it into action.

If the propriety and future utility of this project should be admitted, there is one most important observation to be made. The characteristic feature of this simple harness is, that having been invented for unbroken horses, it possesses the singular military advantage of being at once applicable to any sort or description of horse. But it is well known to every reflecting mind, that there is no useful art which does not, somewhere or other, require attention; and to this general rule the American harness is certainly no exception; for though any horse will draw in it, yet it does require, on the part of *the rider*, considerable experience and attention. The single trace must be managed in a particular manner, or, in turning, it gets under the horse's tail: unless it is properly held in the hand at starting, the horse may break it by the jerk. There are several other little precautions necessary, most particularly in the mode of adjusting the surcingle, which requires considerable practice and attention.

The many curious and indeed scientific applications and combinations of power of which this simple harness is capable, form a beautiful example of what even uncivilised man can contrive when his attention has been long and steadily directed to a solitary object. And surely the ingenuity and practical experience of one nation are worthy the patient attention of another. But the apparent simplicity of many a useful invention has often been its ruin; and this observation is most particularly applicable to lasso harness, which is, in appearance, so very simple, that it seems to require only to be seen to be perfectly understood: yet, efficient as it is in America, and efficient as it will be to any nation in Europe that will give to its merits sufficient time and a fair trial,— yet, on some little experience and reflection, it is most confidently stated that, as a theory, it certainly is *of no use at all;* and the truth of this observation will at once be proved by the complete failure and confusion which will inevitably take place if our cavalry try the harness without first not only patiently but cordially and zealously learning how to use it. Yet this ought not, in common justice, to condemn the principle; for, could cavalry, without some little instruction, succeed in driving even with our own harness?—Could French coachmen, without practice, drive our mails?—Could our English postilions drive the five horses of a French diligence? And if driving is thus a science of many departments, it would not be reasonable to expect that our cavalry should be able to *drive*, merely because they have learnt to *ride*.

How to Hobble and Anchor Horses.

"*Hard pummelling*," said the Duke of Wellington to the Guards at Waterloo, "*Hard pummelling, Gentlemen! Well, we must just see who'll pummel the* HARDEST."

During the reign of Brown Bess the great battles of Europe were decided very much in the manner above described.

Two armies met on a battle-field, or two fleets on "the wide, rude sea," as in England two prize-fighters have entered a small space encircled by ropes, to "see who'll pummel the hardest." In all three cases, endur-

ance, indomitable courage, and physical strength sooner
or later conquered.

As, however, in mechanics, a timid, puny boy, with
the assistance of a pulley, could drag towards him Mars
or Hercules, so must the new arms of precision lately
invented, give victory, not to the bravest or the strongest,
but to whichever of two combatant armies shall exercise
their deadly weapons with the greatest amount of science.

And, as fortification has justly been defined "the art
of enabling a small body of men to resist for a considerable
time the attack of a greater number," so will, in future,
the science of war consist in the art of concealing by every
possible artifice the general commanding, his staff, his
artillery, cavalry, and infantry, from the fire of rifled
cannon and Minié muskets, of which, when properly
directed, it may be said that almost "every bullet will
have its billet."

On this principle, if England were to be invaded, it
would be the endeavour and the duty of the general
on whose intellectual powers the destiny of the empire
would hang, to direct his army to take against their
enemy (after, in spite of his utmost efforts, they had effected
a landing), not, as in by-gone days, "*the field*," but rather
possession of the banks, hedges, and ditches thereof; to
make every great mansion, building, or village, by loop-
holing their walls, a Hougoumont; every railway embank-

ment a covert-way and parapet; every hollow road a pro-
tector or ambuscade for cavalry or infantry; the scarped
summit of every hill a battery; in short, by avoiding
exposure, and by every means that ingenuity can devise,
to make the invaders, during every step of their advance,
smart under a lash, and fall from blows, administered
by a nimble, intellectual army which they feel, which
they are literally dying to see, but which is skilfully
continuing, out of their reach, to decimate their ranks,
in order that when the great battle is given, the invading army—though infinitely superior when it disem-
barked—shall be reduced to a force inferior in number to
that of the stern, steady, stalwart defenders of their native
soil.

It is evident, however, that to carry on war on the
above principle, it will be necessary that cavalry, in their
equipment as well as drill, should undergo a complete
revolution, with a view to enable them in future, in addition to the use of their sabres, to help artillery with their
lassos,—act as *mounted infantry*,—in short, make themselves generally useful; for, at present, they form on a
field of battle so large a target, that under existing circumstances they would have, either out of harm's way to
sit on their horses all day long waiting for an opportunity
not likely to occur, or be destroyed by rifled guns and
muskets before their services could be required: in fact,

as it would be impossible for them to charge men in squares, or even in position armed with muskets of unerring aim, they could be of little use until after the battle was *won*, by following up the enemy in their retreat.

Now, instead of being the dearest and the most useless, they would become the cheapest and most efficient branch of the army, if, besides occasionally using their lassos to help our Armstrong guns, &c., they had power to skim along hollow roads, &c., to the vicinity of the summit of a hill or any other position, from which, half or wholly hidden, they could, with short Minié rifles, direct a deadly fire upon an overwhelming amount of advancing troops, from whom they could gallop away—only to re-attack them—the instant it became prudent to do so.

But to enable cavalry or volunteer mounted yeomanry to act in this manner, how, it will be asked, could they manage to leave their horses?

To this important question we will reply, not by any theoretical project, but by a statement of facts, which, though generally unknown in England, have for many generations been in constant practice in other parts of the world.

1. Throughout Russia, the Cossacks,—whenever for any reason, small or large, they have wished to leave one horse, or a regiment of horses, to stand alone, to ruminate

o

either in the snow or on a verdant plain—have, for ages, been in the habit of, as it were, riveting them to the ground, by tying together their two fore fetlocks by a pair of hobbles, to the centre of which is affixed a narrow strap that buckles over the hock of one hind leg. By this triangular apparatus (weighing less than one pound), which out of four legs leaves only one at liberty, the animal physically and morally is completely paralysed; indeed he is not only unable to move away, but after his first fall is afraid again to try to do so.

2. In South Africa, farmers and sportsmen of all descriptions have long been in the habit of what they term "anchoring" their horses by a lump of lead, from three to five pounds in weight, carried in a small pocket buckled to the outside of their near or left holster.

To this "anchor" is attached a piece of cord about ten feet long, which, passing and running freely through both rings of the curb bit, and hanging from them like a loose rein, is fastened to a **D** or ring on the off-side of the saddle.

No time need be lost in displacing the lead from its pocket when necessary, as it can be jerked out on the ground in the act of dismounting.

When a horse has been thus anchored, if he attempts to move on, his nose is brought down to his breast by the cord, which, tightening equally on both sides, acts exactly like a bridle in the hand of a rider; and as the pressure of the curb-chain ceases so soon as he stops, he soon finds out that the best thing he can do is to stand still and graze.

As the cord is not *fastened* to either ring of the bit, but merely runs through both, the pressure it exerts when the horse tries to move is equal on both sides; and therefore, on the pulley principle, a lead of four pounds weight makes it necessary for the horse to overcome with his mouth a steady and continuous pressure of eight pounds on the extremity of the bit lever before he can move forward. On mounting hurriedly the cord is grasped with the reins, the anchor is raised, and while galloping away is adjusted in its pocket.

Although this invention has proved to be admirably adapted for farmers, for hunting and shooting, or for staff or engineer officers while reconnoitring or surveying (for which purpose General Sir John Michel, now commanding a brigade in China, has used it with great success), it could not safely be applied to cavalry; for as the horse has power, if he chooses to endure the pain inflicted by his bit, to "pull" or drag the anchor, were he to run away with it, its oscillations would be very dangerous in a camp.

To carry the additional weight of the anchor would also be considered as an objection; but this could be entirely

· got rid of by any intelligent staff officer affixing to a rope,
—whenever he wished for reconnoitring to tether his
horse,—a stone, a piece of wood, or any other heavy substance, which he would unlash and leave behind him so
soon as his object on foot had been accomplished.

3. In Mendoza, San Luis, Santiago, Buenos Ayres, and
all other cities in the provinces of Rio de la Plata, in
Chili, and in Peru, whenever a young dandy, calling
upon his innamorata, is informed that she is "en casa,"
that is at home, he dismounts, extracts from his waistcoat
pocket a beautiful pair of slight hobbles (weighing only
two ounces), which by two silver buttons he affixes to the
fetlocks of his high-bred horse, who, swishing with his
long tail the innumerable flies that assail him, and looking
at every animal that canters by him, stands stock still,
until within the house all the compliments of the season
have been paid, and all the songs to the guitar exhausted.

In those countries every cavalry soldier carries a pair
of such hobbles for his horse, not in his pocket, but as an
ornament dangling from the throat-lash of the bridle.

By this invention a horse is not so thoroughly secured
as by that used by the Cossacks; and accordingly, if he be
overfed, very fresh, and greatly alarmed, he has power in
a very awkward gait to move away.

On active service, however, where horses have more

work than food, it would prove efficient for a single horse, and would completely arrest a troop when connected together by their collar chains, by which arrangement a movement, however slight, by any one horse would be restrained by the vis inertiæ of all the rest.

On the above suggestion being submitted by us about six months ago to General Sir John Burgoyne, with the vivacity and energy that distinguish him, he instantly directed it to be properly tested by the mounted troop of the Royal Engineer Train, who, as regards both bridles and saddles, are equipped as cavalry.

The result of the experiments, under the superintendence of Colonel Henry Sandham, and the able assistance of Captain Duff, R.E., has proved so eminently successful, that any one visiting Aldershott is now enabled to see six or eight horses hobbled at intervals of about thirty feet asunder, standing motionless, while the riders of the rest of the troop to which they belong, with drawn sabres flashing in the sun, are galloping through them backwards and forwards; and as of course cavalry horses could be made to do the same, it has been substantiated that that noble branch of our army, as also our volunteer yeomanry, by merely carrying hobbles, which only weigh two ounces per pair, would at once be enabled, in addition to other services, to act, whenever requisite, as *mounted infantry*.

To an officer of the staff or engineers, sent to deliver

an order to, or to reconnoitre a locality which on horseback it would be certain death to him to attempt to approach, a pair of hobbles would enable him, or, in case of
invasion, any possessor of a horse and a Minié rifle, to
ride as far as with safety he could advance, and then by
dismounting and securing his animal to creep, or if necessary, crawl onwards along the bottom of a ditch, or behind
any bank or hedge, sufficient to conceal him from the fire
of an army of unerring marksmen to whom, after making
all necessary observations, he could invisibly administer
deadly blows.

As, however, in future warfare it will of course constantly occur, that appropriate cover in appropriate situ-
ations and directions will not be available, our army, however perfect it may be made in the light infantry rifle
movements above described, should be discouraged from
relying on them, lest such an idea should lead, not only
to a timid course of procedure on the part of the General
commanding, but to a conception in the minds of British
soldiers, whose favourite weapon has hitherto been their
bayonets, that the odds will be much against them unless
they be hidden from the fire of their enemy.

On Chloroforming Horses.

In the first book of Genesis, although on the bursting out of light; on the gathering together of the waters to let the dry land appear; on the creation of the grass, the herb, and the fruit-tree; of the sun, moon, and stars; of the fishes of the sea; of the fowls of the air; of the beast of the earth, of the cattle, of every living creature, and everything that creepeth upon the earth, we are informed by Moses that on each of these successive formations "God saw that it was good;" yet, the same six important words of approval were not (as in all the previous instances they had been) especially uttered on the creation of man, the reason possibly being that of the works of creation every thing was fixed, and "of its kind" immutably "good," save human reason, which, for the weal or woe of the favoured race on whom alone it was bestowed, was gifted with an elasticity by which its character, capable of being elevated or depressed to almost immeasurable distances above or below the level of its original creation, might become either "good" or evil.

And accordingly, while the heat of the sun, the light of the moon, the brightness of the stars, the force of the hurricane, the velocity of light, the movements of the heavenly bodies, the return of the seasons, have neither increased nor diminished in the smallest degree; yet human reason, since the moment of its creation, has never continued within the same limits, simply because its cumulative powers have enabled it to inherit, increase, and transmit knowledge which, by the triumph of reason over immutable instinct, has, in accordance with the Almighty decree, given to man dominion over the fish of the sea, and over the fowl of the air, and over the cattle, and over all the earth, and over every creeping thing that creepeth on the earth.

As property, however, in animals as well as in acres, " has its duties as well as its rights," it might have been expected (at least by *them*) that when the Lord of the creation thus obtained possession of the superior physical strength of brute beasts, he would deem it just to impart to them in return a small tithe or share of any discovery by human reason that could alleviate the work which, in subjection to its power, they were required to perform ; and as in mercantile firms it is usual for the partners to expend for their mutual benefit the amount of the capital they respectively contribute, it might have been expected that in the alliance which has taken place between men and horses, a similar division of profits would have been adopted. But like " Irish reciprocity," the advantages are all on one side ; or in plainer terms, Reason screws all it can out of Instinct, giving to the poor brute, its owner, nothing in return.

For instance, when man found that his unshod horse could only carry him per day a small number of miles, he invented for and presented him with iron shoes, in return for which he required the wearer thereof to carry him more than double that distance.

To the old fashioned lever, attached to the extremity of which a horse revolving a mill could only draw up per day a small quantity of water, or knead a small quantity of clay, man as he improved in mechanical knowledge added a wheel, in return for which he required the quadruped worker thereof to lift treble the amount of water, or to knead treble the amount of clay.

Along the rough muddy roads that existed throughout Europe half a century ago, a horse could with difficulty draw a single man seated in his gig or "buggy." As soon, however, as by human science roads were macadamised, *i.e.*, levelled and improved, there arose as it were out of them (like mushrooms in a meadow) innumerable descriptions of four-wheeled carriages, in which the horse, simply because he was enabled, was required to draw, in addition to his master, his wife and three or four of their children.

When by the invention of railways the locomotive engine suddenly superseded animal power, the horses, instead of sharing in a discovery by human reason which seemed to promise to them emancipation from

slavery, found that by it they were merely to be transferred from good highways to bad bye-ways.

If thousands of omnibuses, cabs, and canal-boats, which
have been plying seven days in the week, are suddenly
restrained by human laws from running on the Sabbath,
the proprietors instantly diminish the number of their
horses, expressly for the purpose of continuing to give to
each the same amount of work and of rest, the latter, like
" the best of oats, beans, and chopped hay," being bestowed
upon him solely to enable him to perform the maximum
amount of work.

In short, by the common rule of three, as well as by
the common rule of life, quaintly exemplified by the following extract, human reason calculates that if 7000 horses
are necessary to work for seven days per week, only 6000
will be wanted to work for six days.

"SUNDAY AND WEEKDAY RELIGIONS.—The tides come twice a-
day in New York Harbour, but they only come once in seven days
in God's harbour of the sanctuary. They rise on Sunday, but ebb
on Monday, and are down and out all the rest of the week. Men
write over their store door, 'Business is business,' and over the
church door, 'Religion is religion ;' and they say to Religion, 'Never
come in here,' and to Business, 'Never go in there.' 'Let us have
no secular things in the pulpit,' they say ; 'we get enough of them
through the week in New York. There all is stringent and biting
selfishness, and knives, and probes, and lancets, and hurry, and
work, and worry. Here we want repose, and sedatives, and healing
balm. All is prose over there; here let us have poetry. We want

to sing hymns, and to hear about heaven and Calvary; in short, we want the pure Gospel without any worldly intermixture.' And so they desire to spend a pious, quiet Sabbath, full of pleasant imaginings and peaceful recollections; but when the day is gone, all is laid aside. They will take by the throat the first debtor whom they meet, and exclaim, 'Pay me what thou owest. It is *Monday*.' And when the minister ventures to hint to them something about their duty to their fellow-men, they say, 'Oh, you stick to your preaching. You do not know how to collect your own debts, and cannot tell what a man may have to do in his intercourse with the world.' God's law is not allowed to go into the week. If the merchant spies it in his store, he throws it over the counter. If the clerk sees it in the bank, he kicks it out at the door. If it is found in the street, the multitude pursue it, pelting it with stones, as if it were a wolf escaped from a menagerie, and shouting, 'Back with you ! You have got out of *Sunday*.' There is no religion in all this. It is mere sentimentalism. Religion belongs to every day—to the place of business as much as to the church. High in an ancient belfry there is a clock, and once a week the old sexton winds it up; but it has neither dial plate nor hands. The pendulum swings, and there it goes, ticking, ticking, day in and day out, unnoticed and useless. What the old clock is in its dark chamber, keeping time to itself, but never showing it, that is the mere sentimentality of religion, high above life, in the region of airy thought; perched up in the top of Sunday, but without dial or pointer to let the week know what o'clock it is, of time or of eternity."—*American Paper*.

It may be impracticable to prevent man from taking to himself the *whole* benefit of every ingenious invention by which the physical power of the horse can be increased, yet surely, either by legislation or by the power of public opinion, he should be required to grant or rather transmit to the poor animal, as a gift from Heaven, the benefit of any scientific discovery that may save him from unnecessary and indescribable agony under operations almost all of which are prescribed either for the self interest, pride, or fashions of his master.

But although the avowed object of the criminal laws of England is to prevent crime by the infliction of a scale of punishments which, fearful enough to deter the guiltiest, are all divested, so far as science can devise, of bodily pain; although we deprecate any suffering on the tread-mill beyond that of ordinary hard labour; and although even for the murderer we have invented a machinery of rope, planks, and bolts to produce a sudden and almost painless death, yet, until lately, people of both sexes, of all ages, and of every sort and condition, have under the surgeon's knife been subjected to tortures which it would have been beyond the ingenuity of the most merciless tyrant that ever existed to have invented.

The screams, however, which have resounded throughout the civilized world—in private houses, in palaces, in cottages, on the field of battle, between the decks of men-of-war, and through the doors and windows of all public hospitals,—have lately, by the command and blessing of Almighty God, been suddenly stopped by the administration of chloroform, which now, diluted in the proportion of three parts of vapour to ninety-seven parts of atmospheric air, causes a patient, at no risk whatever of his life, and at a cost amounting to less than two-pence, to be bereft, not necessarily of his senses, but merely of sensation, while the knife, without the infliction of the slightest pain, is performing on his living body the most appalling operations.

" And the Lord God caused a deep sleep to fall upon Adam, and he slept : and he took one of his ribs, and closed up the flesh instead thereof."

Now, if in return for this extraordinary alleviation, or rather annihilation of all sufferings under surgical treatment, man should deem it his duty to render public thanks to that Omnipotent. Power from which it has proceeded, is it possible for him practically to perform any more acceptable act of acknowledgment than to allow the dumb creatures in his service to participate in a blessing which, by Divine authority, has been imparted to the possessors, not exclusively of human reason, but without favour or exception, of animal life ?

As regards his horses, the performance of this duty is especially incumbent : for not only, like all other animals, are they liable to the accidents and ills that flesh is heir to, but some of the cruelest operations to which they are subjected—such, for instance, as cutting off and cauterising their tails, burning their sinews with red hot irons, dividing and cutting out a portion of a nerve, with other excruciating operations on young horses, under which they are often heard to squeal from pain—are inflicted on them, to comply with either a useless as well as a barbarous fashion ;—or to enable them " to go for another season's hunting ; "—or to make them " sound enough to sell ; " or for the attainment of conveniences of which the horse derives not the smallest share: and as the high-bred, broken-down hunter has no voice to ask for mercy,—as he cannot boast of possessing reason,—as he has inherited no knowledge,—as he has no power to bequeath any,—as his whole energies have been devoted to the service and enjoyments of man, by whose mechanical contrivances he is now " cast " with his four feet shackled together, lying prostrate on a heap of straw ;—just before the red-hot iron sears his over-strained sinews, or the sharp knife is inserted into his living flesh—surely, in a civilized country like England, some high power should be authorized to exclaim, not " Woodman, spare that tree ! " but " *Sportsman*, SAVE *that horse !* " by chloroform, from the agonising torture to which you have sentenced him !

You are a man of *pleasure* :—save him from unnecessary *pain*. You are a man of business :—inscribe in that ledger in which every one of the acts of your life is recorded, on one side how much *he* will gain, and on the other, per contrà, how very little *you* will lose, by the evaporation of a fluid that will not cost you the price of the shoes of the poor animal whose marketable value you have determined, by excruciating agony *to him*, to increase.

As he lies prostrate, all that is necessary to save him from suffering the smallest amount of pain is, to desire the operator with his left hand to close the animal's upper nostril, while beneath the lower one he places a quarter of a pint tin pot, containing a sponge, on which is gradually. dropped, from a little vial, chloroform sufficient to deprive him of sensation, which can readily be tested by the occasional slight prick of a pin; and although, when thus lulled into an unconscious state, the noble animal may, during a dreadful operation, possibly dream that

> " He sees war's lightning flashing,
> Sees the claymore and bayonet clashing,
> Sees through the blood the warhorse dashing "—

yet, on the restoration of sensation, which usually occurs some minutes after the operation is over, he calmly awakens, raises his head, and looks around, perfectly unconscious of all that has occurred to him !

In every point of view in which it can be considered,

this boon, granted by Heaven to the brute beast, should not be withheld from him by man.

On Mr. Henry Thompson, the celebrated practising surgeon at University College Hospital, and also at Marylebone Dispensary, being lately asked " What are the occasions on which you are in the habit of administering chloroform ? " he energetically replied, " *For everything that gives* PAIN."

If, therefore, man to this enormous extent is benefited by chloroform, what right has he to withhold it from his own animals, to whom, not only in equity, but by the laws of God, it belongs as much as it belongs to him ?

Their claims are so affecting, and so obvious, the remedy that would save them from all pain is so cheap and simple, that it is, we feel, only necessary to appeal to the public to obtain by acclamation a verdict in their favour.

Professor Spooner, in an address delivered by him to the students of the Veterinary College in October last, stated that in the two chief Veterinary Colleges in France— at Alfort and at Lyons—pupils, twice a week for seven hours a day, are instructed in surgery by the *"vivisection"* or cutting up of living horses, who, until they actually expire, are subjected to a series of cruelties which, although Mr. Spooner professionally described and deprecated, we dare not repeat.

What a disgrace it is to France, and especially to her brave army, that while every cavalry soldier who distinguishes himself in action, covered with medals and "glory," may proudly end his days in the Hôtel des Invalides,—the horse that carried him in all his brilliant charges, &c., when *he* is worn out and unfit for service, is liable to be led into an arena in the heart of "The Empire," to be, before the public, not honoured nor rewarded, but, inch by inch, and bit by bit, to be dissected alive, until by the last sigh from his lungs, and by the last pulsation from his heart, he ends his account with his inconsiderate, ungenerous, and ungrateful country !

The *English* veterinary surgeons of the present day are so far superior to those of the last generation—they are so willing and so proud to follow in their important vocation whatever new discoveries may be humanely and successfully practised in our public hospitals, that if our Sovereign, the Commander-in-Chief of our army, our noblemen, sportsmen, and men of education, character, and wealth, would but combine together in determining to *require* that chloroform shall invariably be administered to their creatures " for everything that gives pain," the "fashion" would quickly be followed, even by the most unreflecting portion of our community ; and England, "great, glorious, and free," would then stand distinguished in the world, not only for the strength,

P

stoutness, endurance, weight, and swiftness of her animals, but by her *merciful* protection of them under surgical operations.

"𝔄 righteous man regardeth his beast: but the tender mercies of the wicked are cruel."

IN GRATITUDE TO

THE HORSE,

THE FOREGOING IMPERFECT OBSERVATIONS,

APPLICABLE TO ALL LIVING CREATURES,

ARE RESPECTFULLY SUBMITTED

TO THE CONSIDERATION OF THE PUBLIC,

BY

HIS RIDER.

LONDON: PRINTED BY WILLIAM CLOWES AND SONS, STAMFORD STREET,
AND CHARING CROSS.

ALBEMARLE STREET, LONDON,
September, 1868.

MR. MURRAY'S

GENERAL LIST OF WORKS.

ALBERT'S (PRINCE) SPEECHES AND ADDRESSES ON PUBLIC OCCASIONS; with an Introduction giving some Outlines of his Character. Portrait. 8vo. 10s. 6d.; or *Popular Edition*. Portrait. Fcap. 8vo. 1s.

ABBOTT'S (REV. J.) Philip Musgrave; or, Memoirs of a Church of England Missionary in the North American Colonies. Post 8vo. 2s.

ABERCROMBIE'S (JOHN) Enquiries concerning the Intellectual Powers and the Investigation of Truth. Fcap. 8vo. 6s. 6d.

———————————— Philosophy of the Moral Feelings. Fcap. 8vo. 4s.

ACLAND'S (REV. CHARLES) Popular Account of the Manners and Customs of India. Post 8vo. 2s.

ÆSOP'S FABLES. A New Translation. With Historical Preface. By Rev. THOMAS JAMES. With 100 Woodcuts, by TENNIEL and WOLF. 50th Thousand. Post 8vo. 2s. 6d.

AGRICULTURAL (THE ROYAL) SOCIETY'S JOURNAL. 8vo. Published half-yearly.

AIDS TO FAITH: a Series of Theological Essays. By various Writers. Edited by WILLIAM THOMSON, D.D., Archbishop of York. 8vo. 9s.

AMBER-WITCH (THE). A most interesting Trial for Witchcraft. Translated from the German by LADY DUFF GORDON. Post 8vo. 2s.

ARMY LIST (THE). *Published Monthly by Authority*. 18mo. 1s. 6d.

ARTHUR'S (LITTLE) History of England. By LADY CALLCOTT. New Edition, continued to 1862. Woodcuts. Fcap. 8vo. 2s. 6d.

ATKINSON'S (MRS.) Recollections of Tartar Steppes and their Inhabitants. Illustrations. Post 8vo. 12s.

AUNT IDA'S Walks and Talks; a Story Book for Children. By a LADY. Woodcuts. 16mo. 5s.

AUSTIN'S (JOHN) LECTURES ON JURISPRUDENCE; or, the Philosophy of Positive Law. New and Cheaper Edition. 2 Vols. 8vo.

———————— (SARAH) Fragments from German Prose Writers. With Biographical Notes. Post 8vo. 10s.

B

ADMIRALTY PUBLICATIONS; Issued by direction of the Lords
Commissioners of the Admiralty:—

A MANUAL OF SCIENTIFIC ENQUIRY, for the Use of Travellers.
Edited by Sir JOHN F. HERSCHEL, and Rev. ROBERT MAIN, M.A.
Third Edition. Woodcuts. Post 8vo. 9s.

AIRY'S ASTRONOMICAL OBSERVATIONS MADE AT GREENWICH.
1836 to 1847. Royal 4to. 50s. each.

———— ASTRONOMICAL RESULTS. 1848 to 1858. 4to. 8s. each.

———— APPENDICES TO THE ASTRONOMICAL OBSERVA-
TIONS.

1836.—I. Bessel's Refraction Tables.
 II. Tables for converting Errors of R.A. and N.P.D. } 6s.
  into Errors of Longitude and Ecliptic P.D. }
1837.—I. Logarithms of Sines and Cosines to every Ten } 8s.
  Seconds of Time. }
 II. Table for converting Sidereal into Mean Solar Time. }
1842.—Catalogue of 1439 Stars. 8s.
1845.—Longitude of Valentia. 8s.
1847.—Twelve Years' Catalogue of Stars. 14s.
1851.—Maskelyne's Ledger of Stars. 6s.
1852.—I. Description of the Transit Circle. 5s.
 II. Regulations of the Royal Observatory. 2s.
1853.—Bessel's Refraction Tables. 8s.
1854.—I. Description of the Zenith Tube. 3s.
 II. Six Years' Catalogue of Stars. 10s.
1856.—Description of the Galvanic Apparatus at Greenwich Observatory. 8s.
1862.—I. Seven Years' Catalogue of Stars. 10s.
 II. Plan of the Building and Ground of the Royal Ob- }
  servatory, Greenwich. } 3s.
 III. Longitude of Valentia. }

———— MAGNETICAL AND METEOROLOGICAL OBSERVA-
TIONS. 1840 to 1847. Royal 4to. 50s. each.

———— ASTRONOMICAL, MAGNETICAL, AND METEOROLO-
GICAL OBSERVATIONS, 1848 to 1864. Royal 4to. 50s. each.

———— ASTRONOMICAL RESULTS. 1848 to 1864. 4to.

———— MAGNETICAL AND METEOROLOGICAL RESULTS.
1848 to 1864. 4to. 8s. each.

———— REDUCTION OF THE OBSERVATIONS OF PLANETS.
1750 to 1830. Royal 4to. 50s.

——————————————————— LUNAR OBSERVATIONS. 1750
to 1830. 2 Vols. Royal 4to. 50s. each.

——————————————— 1831 to 1851. 4to. 20s.

BERNOULLI'S SEXCENTENARY TABLE. *London*, 1779. 4to.

BESSEL'S AUXILIARY TABLES FOR HIS METHOD OF CLEAR-
ING LUNAR DISTANCES. 8vo.

———— FUNDAMENTA ASTRONOMIÆ: *Regiomontii*, 1818. Folio. 60s.

BIRD'S METHOD OF CONSTRUCTING MURAL QUADRANTS.
London, 1768. 4to. 2s. 6d.

———— METHOD OF DIVIDING ASTRONOMICAL INSTRU-
MENTS. *London*, 1767. 4to. 2s. 6d.

COOK, KING, AND BAYLY'S ASTRONOMICAL OBSERVATIONS.
London, 1782. 4to. 21s.

ENCKE'S BERLINER JAHRBUCH, for 1830. *Berlin*, 1828. 8vo. 9s.

GROOMBRIDGE'S CATALOGUE OF CIRCUMPOLAR STARS.
4to. 10s.

HANSEN'S TABLES DE LA LUNE. 4to. 20s.

ADMIRALTY PUBLICATIONS—*continued.*

HARRISON'S PRINCIPLES OF HIS TIME-KEEPER. PLATES. 1797. 4to. 5s.

HUTTON'S TABLES OF THE PRODUCTS AND POWERS OF NUMBERS. 1781. Folio. 7s. 6d.

LAX'S TABLES FOR FINDING THE LATITUDE AND LONGITUDE. 1821. 8vo. 10s.

LUNAR OBSERVATIONS at GREENWICH. 1783 to 1819. Compared with the Tables, 1821. 4to. 7s. 6d.

MASKELYNE'S ACCOUNT OF THE GOING OF HARRISON'S WATCH. 1767. 4to. 2s. 6d.

MAYER'S DISTANCES of the MOON'S CENTRE from the PLANETS. 1822, 3s.; 1823, 4s. 6d. 1824 to 1835, 8vo. 4s. each.

———— THEORIA LUNÆ JUXTA SYSTEMA NEWTONIANUM. 4to. 2s. 6d.

—— TABULÆ MOTUUM SOLIS ET LUNÆ. 1770. 4to. 5s.

—— ASTRONOMICAL OBSERVATIONS MADE AT GOTTINGEN, from 1756 to 1761. 1826. Folio. 7s. 6d.

NAUTICAL ALMANACS, from 1767 to 1871. 8vo. 2s. 6d. each.

———————— SELECTIONS FROM THE ADDITIONS up to 1812. 8vo. 5s. 1834-54. 8vo. 5s.

———————— SUPPLEMENTS, 1828 to 1833, 1837 and 1838 8vo. 2s. each.

———————— TABLE requisite to be used with the N.A. 1781. 8vo. 5s.

POND'S ASTRONOMICAL OBSERVATIONS. 1811 to 1835. 4to. 21s. each.

RAMSDEN'S ENGINE for DIVIDING MATHEMATICAL INSTRUMENTS. 4to. 5s.

———————— ENGINE for DIVIDING STRAIGHT LINES. 4to. 5s.

SABINE'S PENDULUM EXPERIMENTS to DETERMINE THE FIGURE OF THE EARTH. 1825. 4to. 40s.

SHEPHERD'S TABLES for CORRECTING LUNAR DISTANCES. 1772. Royal 4to. 21s.

———————— TABLES, GENERAL, of the MOON'S DISTANCE from the SUN, and 10 STARS. 1787. Folio. 5s. 6d.

TAYLOR'S SEXAGESIMAL TABLE. 1780. 4to. 15s.

———————— TABLES OF LOGARITHMS. 4to. 3l.

TIARK'S ASTRONOMICAL OBSERVATIONS for the LONGITUDE of MADEIRA. 1822. 4to. 5s.

———————— CHRONOMETRICAL OBSERVATIONS for DIFFERENCES of LONGITUDE between DOVER, PORTSMOUTH, and FALMOUTH. 1823. 4to. 5s.

VENUS and JUPITER: OBSERVATIONS of, compared with the TABLES. *London*, 1822. 4to. 2s.

WALES' AND BAYLY'S ASTRONOMICAL OBSERVATIONS. 1777. 4to. 21s.

WALES' REDUCTION OF ASTRONOMICAL OBSERVATIONS MADE IN THE SOUTHERN HEMISPHERE. 1764—1771. 1788. 4to. 10s. 6d.

B 2

BARBAULD'S (Mrs.) Hymns in Prose for Children. With 112
Original Designs. Small 4to. 5s.; or *Fine Paper*, 7s. 6d.

BARROW'S (Sir John) Autobiographical Memoir. From Early
Life to Advanced Age. Portrait. 8vo. 16s.

———— (John) Life, Exploits, and Voyages of Sir Francis
Drake. With numerous Original Letters. Post 8vo. 2s.

BARRY'S (Sir Charles) Life. By Alfred Barry, D.D. With
Portrait, and Illustrations. Medium 8vo. 24s.

BATES' (H. W.) Records of a Naturalist on the River Amazons
during eleven years of Adventure and Travel. *Second Edition*. Illustrations. Post 8vo. 12s.

BEAUCLERK'S (Lady Di) Summer and Winter in Norway.
Second Edition. With Illustrations. Small 8vo. 6s.

BEES AND FLOWERS. Two Essays. By Rev. Thomas James.
Reprinted from the "Quarterly Review." Fcap. 8vo. 1s. each.

BERTHA'S Journal during a Visit to her Uncle in England.
Containing a Variety of Interesting and Instructive Information. *Seventh
Edition*. Woodcuts. 12mo. 7s. 6d.

BERTRAM'S (Jas. G.) Harvest of the Sea: a Contribution to the
Natural and Economic History of British Food Fishes. *Second and
Cheaper Edition*. With 50 Illustrations. 8vo.

BICKMORE'S (Albert S., M.A.) Travels in the East Indian Archi-
pelago. With Maps and Illustrations. 8vo. (*In preparation*.)

BIRCH'S (Samuel) History of Ancient Pottery and Porcelain:
Egyptian, Assyrian, Greek, Roman, and Etruscan. With 200 Illustrations. 2 Vols. Medium 8vo. 42s.

BISSET'S (Andrew) History of the Commonwealth of England,
from the Death of Charles I. to the Expulsion of the Long Parliament
by Cromwell. Chiefly from the MSS. in the State Paper Office. 2 vols.
8vo. 30s.

BLAKISTON'S (Capt.) Narrative of the Expedition sent to ex-
plore the Upper Waters of the Yang-Tsze. Illustrations. 8vo. 18s.

BLOMFIELD'S (Bishop) Memoir, with Selections from his Correspondence. By his Son. *Second Edition*. Portrait, post 8vo. 12s.

BLUNT'S (Rev. J. J.) Undesigned Coincidences in the Writings of
the Old and New Testament, an Argument of their Veracity: containing
the Books of Moses, Historical and Prophetical Scriptures, and the
Gospels and Acts. *Ninth Edition*. Post 8vo. 6s.

———— History of the Church in the First Three Centuries.
Third Edition. Post 8vo. 7s. 6d.

———— Parish Priest; His Duties, Acquirements and Obliga-
tions. *Fourth Edition*. Post 8vo. 7s. 6d.

———— Lectures on the Right Use of the Early Fathers.
Second Edition. 8vo. 15s.

———— Plain Sermons Preached to a Country Congregation.
Fifth and Cheaper Edition. 2 Vols. Post 8vo.

———— Essays on various subjects. 8vo. 12s.

BOOK OF COMMON PRAYER. Illustrated with Coloured Borders, Initial Letters, and Woodcuts. A new edition. 8vo. 18s. cloth ; 31s. 6d. calf; 36s. morocco.

BORROW'S (GEORGE) Bible in Spain; or the Journeys, Adventures, and Imprisonments of an Englishman in an Attempt to circulate the Scriptures in the Peninsula. 3 Vols. Post 8vo. 27s.; or *Popular Edition*, 16mo, 3s. 6d.

——————— Zincali, or the Gipsies of Spain; their Manners, Customs, Religion, and Language. 2 Vols. Post 8vo. 18s.; or *Popular Edition*, 16mo, 3s. 6d.

——————— WILD WALES : its People, Language, and Scenery. *Third Edition*. With Introductory Remarks. Post 8vo. 6s.

——————— Lavengro ; The Scholar—The Gipsy—and the Priest. Portrait. 3 Vols. Post 8vo. 30s.

——————— Romany Rye ; a Sequel to Lavengro. *Second Edition*. 2 Vols. Post 8vo. 21s.

BOSWELL'S (JAMES) Life of Samuel Johnson, LL.D. Including the Tour to the Hebrides. Edited by Mr. CROKER. Portraits. Royal 8vo. 10s.

BRACE'S (C. L.) History of the Races of the Old World. Post 8vo. 9s.

BRAY'S (MRS.) Life of Thomas Stothard, R.A. With Personal Reminiscences. Illustrated with Portrait and 60 Woodcuts of his chief works. 4to. 21s.

BREWSTER'S (SIR DAVID) Martyrs of Science; or, Lives of Galileo, Tycho Brahe, and Kepler. *Fourth Edition*. Fcap. 8vo. 4s. 6d.

——————— More Worlds than One. The Creed of the Philosopher and the Hope of the Christian. *Eighth Edition*. Post 8vo. 6s.

——————— Stereoscope : its History, Theory, Construction, and Application to the Arts and to Education. Woodcuts. 12mo. 5s. 6d.

——————— Kaleidoscope: its History, Theory, and Construction, with its application to the Fine and Useful Arts. *Second Edition*. Woodcuts. Post 8vo. 5s. 6d.

BRITISH ASSOCIATION REPORTS. 8vo.

York and Oxford, 1831-32, 13s. 6d.
Cambridge, 1833, 12s.
Edinburgh, 1834, 15s.
Dublin, 1835, 13s. 6d.
Bristol, 1836, 12s.
Liverpool, 1837, 16s. 6d.
Newcastle, 1838, 15s.
Birmingham, 1839, 13s. 6d
Glasgow, 1840, 15s.
Plymouth, 1841, 13s. 6d.
Manchester, 1842, 10s. 6d.
Cork, 1843, 12s.
York, 1844, 20s.
Cambridge, 1845, 12s.
Southampton, 1846, 15s.
Oxford, 1847, 18s.
Swansea, 1848, 9s.
Birmingham, 1849, 10s.

Edinburgh, 1850, 15s.
Ipswich, 1851, 16s. 6d.
Belfast, 1852, 15s.
Hull, 1853, 10s. 6d.
Liverpool, 1854, 18s.
Glasgow, 1855. 15s.
Cheltenham, 1856, 18s.
Dublin, 1857. 15s.
Leeds. 1858. 20s.
Aberdeen, 1859, 15s.
Oxford, 1860, 25s.
Manchester, 1861, 15s.
Cambridge, 1862, 20s.
Newcastle, 1863, 25s.
Bath, 1864, 18s.
Birmingham, 1865. 25s
Nottingham 1866, 24s.
Dundee, 1867, 26s.

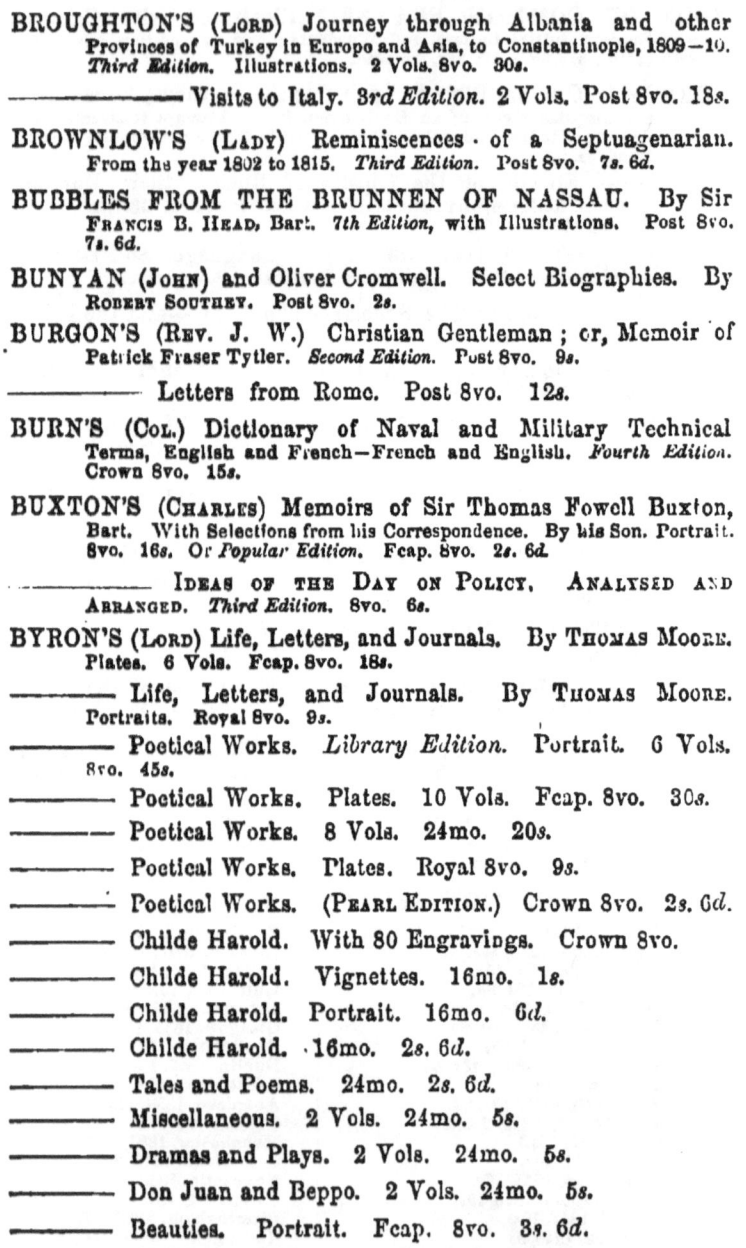

BROUGHTON'S (LORD) Journey through Albania and other
Provinces of Turkey in Europe and Asia, to Constantinople, 1809—10.
Third Edition. Illustrations. 2 Vols. 8vo. 30*s.*

———— Visits to Italy. 3rd *Edition.* 2 Vols. Post 8vo. 18*s.*

BROWNLOW'S (LADY) Reminiscences · of a Septuagenarian.
From the year 1802 to 1815. *Third Edition.* Post 8vo. 7*s.* 6*d.*

BUBBLES FROM THE BRUNNEN OF NASSAU. By Sir
FRANCIS B. HEAD, Bart. 7*th Edition,* with Illustrations. Post 8vo.
7*s.* 6*d.*

BUNYAN (JOHN) and Oliver Cromwell. Select Biographies. By
ROBERT SOUTHEY. Post 8vo. 2*s.*

BURGON'S (REV. J. W.) Christian Gentleman ; or, Memoir of
Patrick Fraser Tytler. *Second Edition.* Post 8vo. 9*s.*

———— Letters from Rome. Post 8vo. 12*s.*

BURN'S (COL.) Dictionary of Naval and Military Technical
Terms, English and French—French and English. *Fourth Edition.*
Crown 8vo. 15*s.*

BUXTON'S (CHARLES) Memoirs of Sir Thomas Fowell Buxton,
Bart. With Selections from his Correspondence. By his Son. Portrait.
8vo. 16*s.* Or *Popular Edition.* Fcap. 8vo. 2*s.* 6*d.*

———— IDEAS OF THE DAY ON POLICY, ANALYSED AND
ARRANGED. *Third Edition.* 8vo. 6*s.*

BYRON'S (LORD) Life, Letters, and Journals. By THOMAS MOORE.
Plates. 6 Vols. Fcap. 8vo. 18*s.*

———— Life, Letters, and Journals. By THOMAS MOORE.
Portraits. Royal 8vo. 9*s.*

———— Poetical Works. *Library Edition.* Portrait. 6 Vols.
8vo. 45*s.*

———— Poetical Works. Plates. 10 Vols. Fcap. 8vo. 30*s.*

———— Poetical Works. 8 Vols. 24mo. 20*s.*

———— Poetical Works. Plates. Royal 8vo. 9*s.*

———— Poetical Works. (PEARL EDITION.) Crown 8vo. 2*s.* 6*d.*

———— Childe Harold. With 80 Engravings. Crown 8vo.

———— Childe Harold. Vignettes. 16mo. 1*s.*

———— Childe Harold. Portrait. 16mo. 6*d.*

———— Childe Harold. 16mo. 2*s.* 6*d.*

———— Tales and Poems. 24mo. 2*s.* 6*d.*

———— Miscellaneous. 2 Vols. 24mo. 5*s.*

———— Dramas and Plays. 2 Vols. 24mo. 5*s.*

———— Don Juan and Beppo. 2 Vols. 24mo. 5*s.*

———— Beauties. Portrait. Fcap. 8vo. 3*s.* 6*d.*

BURR'S (G. D.) Instructions in Practical Surveying, Topographical Plan Drawing, and on sketching ground without Instruments. *Fourth Edition.* Woodcuts. Post 8vo. 6s.

BUTTMAN'S LEXILOGUS; a Critical Examination of the Meaning of numerous Greek Words, chiefly in Homer and Hesiod. Translated by Rev. J. R. FISULAKE. *Fifth Edition.* 8vo. 12s.

—— CATALOGUE OF IRREGULAR GREEK VERBS. With all the Tenses extant—their Formation, Meaning, and Usage, accompanied by an Index. Translated, with Notes, by Rev. J. R. FISHLAKE. *Fifth Edition.* Revised by Rev. E. VENABLES. Post 8vo. 6s.

CALLCOTT'S (LADY) Little Arthur's History of England. *New Edition, brought down to 1832.* With Woodcuts. Fcap. 8vo. 2s. 6d.

CAMPBELL'S (LORD) Lives of the Lord Chancellors and Keepers of the Great Seal of England. From the Earliest Times to the Death of Lord Eldon in 1838. *Fourth Edition.* 10 Vols. Crown 8vo. 6s. each.

—— Lives of the Chief Justices of England. From the Norman Conquest to the Death of Lord Tenterden. *Second Edition.* 3 Vols. 8vo. 42s.

—— Shakspeare's Legal Acquirements Considered. 8vo. 5s. 6d.

—— Life of Lord Chancellor Bacon. Fcap. 8vo. 2s. 6d.

—— (GEORGE) Modern India. A Sketch of the System of Civil Government. With some Account of the Natives and Native Institutions. *Second Edition.* 8vo. 16s.

—— India as it may be. An Outline of a proposed Government and Policy. 8vo. 12s.

—— (THOS.) Short Lives of the British Poets. With an Essay on English Poetry. Post 8vo. 3s. 6d.

CARNARVON'S (LORD) Portugal, Gallicia, and the Basque Provinces. From Notes made during a Journey to those Countries. *Third Edition.* Post 8vo. 3s. 6d.

—— Recollections of the Druses of Lebanon. With Notes on their Religion. *Third Edition.* Post 8vo. 5s. 6d.

CASTLEREAGH (THE) DESPATCHES, from the commencement of the official career of the late Viscount Castlereagh to the close of his life. Edited by the MARQUIS OF LONDONDERRY. 12 Vols. 8vo. 14s. each.

CATHCART'S (SIR GEORGE) Commentaries on the War in Russia and Germany, 1812-13. Plans. 8vo. 14s.

CAVALCASELLE AND CROWE'S History of Painting in Italy, from the Second to the Sixteenth Century, from recent researches, as well as from personal inspection of the Works of Art in that Country. With 100 Illustrations. 3 Vols. 8vo. 63s.

—— History of Painting in North Italy, including Venice, Lombardy, Padua, Vicenza, Verona, Parma, Friuli, Ferrara, and Bologna. With Illustrations. 2 Vols. 8vo. (*In preparation.*)

—— Notices of the Lives and Works of the Early Flemish Painters. Woodcuts. Post 8vo. 12s.

CHILD (G. CHAPLIN, M.D.) Benedicite; or, Song of the Three Children; being Illustrations of the Power, Wisdom, and Goodness of the Creator. *New and Cheaper Edition.* Post 8vo.

CHURTON'S (ARCHDEACON) Gongora. An Historical Essay on the Age of Philip III. and IV. of Spain. With Translations. Portrait. 2 Vols. Small 8vo. 15s.

CICERO'S LIFE AND TIMES. With his Character viewed as a Statesman, Orator, and Friend, and a Selection from his Correspondence and Orations. By WILLIAM FORSYTH, Q.C. *New Edition.* With Illustrations. 8vo. 16s.

CLIVE'S (LORD) Life. By REV. G. R. GLEIG, M.A. Post 8vo. 3s. 6d.

COLCHESTER (THE) PAPERS. The Diary and Correspondence of Charles Abbott, Lord Colchester, Speaker of the House of Commons, 1802–1817. Portrait. 3 Vols. 8vo. 42s.

COLERIDGE'S (SAMUEL TAYLOR) Table-Talk. *New Edition.* Portrait. Fcap. 8vo. 6s.

COLLINGWOOD'S (CUTHBERT) Rambles of a Naturalist on the Shores and Waters of the China Sea. Being Observations in Natural History during a Voyage to China, Formosa, Borneo, Singapore, &c., during 1866—67. With Illustrations. 8vo. 16s.

COLONIAL LIBRARY. [See Home and Colonial Library.]

COOK'S (Canon) Sermons Preached at Lincoln's Inn Chapel, and on Special Occasions. 8vo. 9s.

COOKERY (MODERN DOMESTIC). Founded on Principles of Economy and Practical Knowledge, and adapted for Private Families. By a Lady. *New Edition.* Woodcuts. Fcap. 8vo. 5s.

CORNWALLIS (THE) Papers and Correspondence during the American War,—Administrations in India,—Union with Ireland, and Peace of Amiens. *Second Edition.* 3 Vols. 8vo. 63s.

COWPER'S (MARY, COUNTESS) Diary while Lady of the Bedchamber to Caroline Princess of Wales, 1714–20. Edited by Hon. SPENCER COWPER. *Second Edition.* Portrait. 8vo. 10s. 6d.

CRABBE'S (REV. GEORGE) Life and Poetical Works. Plates. 8 vols. Fcap. 8vo. 24s.; or Complete in 1 Vol. Plates. Royal 8vo. 7s.

CREE'S (E. D.) Portrait of the Primitive Church. Fcap. 8vo. 1s.

CROKER'S (J. W.) Progressive Geography for Children. *Fifth Edition.* 18mo. 1s. 6d.

———— Stories for Children, Selected from the History of England. *Fifteenth Edition.* Woodcuts. 16mo. 2s. 6d.

———— Boswell's Life of Johnson. Including the Tour to the Hebrides. Portraits. Royal 8vo. 10s.

———— Essays on the Early Period of the French Revolution. 8vo. 15s.

———— Historical Essay on the Guillotine. Fcap. 8vo. 1s.

CROMWELL (OLIVER) and John Bunyan. By ROBERT SOUTHEY. Post 8vo. 2s.

CROWE'S AND CAVALCASELLE'S Notices of the Early Flemish Painters. Woodcuts. Post 8vo. 12s.

———— History of Painting in Italy, from 2nd to 16th Century. Derived from Historical Researches as well as Inspection of the Works of Art in that Country. With 100 Illustrations. 3 Vols. 8vo. 21s. each.

———————— North Italy, including Venice, Lombardy, Padua, Vicenza, Verona, Parma. Friuli, Ferrara, and Bologna. With Illustrations. 2 Vols. 8vo. (In preparation.)

CUMMING'S (R. GORDON) Five Years of a Hunter's Life in the Far Interior of South Africa; with Anecdotes of the Chace, and Notices of the Native Tribes. New Edition. Woodcuts. Post 8vo. 5s.

CUNNINGHAM'S (ALLAN) Poems and Songs. Now first collected and arranged, with Biographical Notice. 24mo. 2s. 6d.

CURTIUS' (PROFESSOR) Student's Greek Grammar, for Colleges and the Upper Forms. Edited by DR. WM. SMITH. Third Edition. Post 8vo. 6s.

——— Smaller Greek Grammar for the Middle and Lower Forms. 12mo. 3s 6d.

CURZON'S (HON. ROBERT) ARMENIA AND ERZEROUM. A Year on the Frontiers of Russia, Turkey, and Persia. Third Edition. Woodcuts. Post 8vo. 7s. 6d.

———— Visits to the Monasteries of the Levant. Fifth Edition. Illustrations. Post 8vo. 7s. 6d.

CUST'S (GENERAL) Warriors of the 17th Century—The Thirty Years' War—and the Civil Wars of France and England. 4 Vols. Post 8vo. 8s. each.

——— Annals of the Wars—18th & 19th Century, 1700—1815. Compiled from the most Authentic Sources. With Maps. 9 Vols. Post 8vo. 5s. each.

DARWIN'S (CHARLES) Journal of Researches into the Natural History of the Countries visited during a Voyage round the World. Post 8vo. 9s.

——— Origin of Species by Means of Natural Selection; or, the Preservation of Favoured Races in the Struggle for Life. Fourth Edition, revised. Post 8vo. 15s.

——— Fertilization of Orchids through Insect Agency, and as to the good of Intercrossing. Woodcuts. Post 8vo. 9s.

——— Variation of Animals and Plants under Domestication. With Illustrations. 2 Vols. 8vo. 28s.

——————— Fact and Argument for. By FRITZ MULLER. With numerous Illustrations and Additions by the Author. Translated from the German by W. S. DALLAS. 8vo. (Nearly ready.)

DAVIS'S (NATHAN) Visit to the Ruined Cities of Numidia and Carthaginia. Illustrations. 8vo. 16s.

——— (SIR J. F.) Chinese Miscellanies: a Collection of Essays and Notes. Post 8vo. 6s.

DAVY'S (SIR HUMPHRY) Consolations in Travel; or, Last Days of a Philosopher. Fifth Edition. Woodcuts. Fcap. 8vo. 6s.

——— Salmonia; or, Days of Fly Fishing. Fourth Edition. Woodcuts. Fcap. 8vo. 6s.

DELEPIERRE'S (OCTAVE) History of Flemish Literature. From the Twelfth Century. 8vo. 9s.

—— Historical Difficulties and Contested Events. Being Notes on some Doubtful Points of History. Post 8vo. 6s.

DENISON'S (E. B.) Life of Bishop Lonsdale, D.D. With Selections from his Writings. With Portrait. Crown 8vo. 10s. 6d.

DERBY'S (EARL OF) Translation of the Iliad of Homer into English Blank Verse. *Fifth Library Edition*, 2 vols. 8vo. 24s.; or *Seventh Edition*, with Translations from the Poets, Ancient and Modern. 2 Vols. Post 8vo. 10s.

  ₊ Translations from the Poets, may be had separately. 8vo. 3s. 6d.

DE ROS'S (LORD) Memorials of the Tower of London. *Second Edition.* With Illustrations. Crown 8vo. 12s.

—— Young Officer's Companion; or, Essays on Military Duties and Qualities: with Examples and Illustrations from History. *New Edition.* Post 8vo.

DIXON'S (W. HEPWORTH) Story of the Life of Lord Bacon. *Second Edition.* Portrait. Fcap. 8vo. 7s. 6d.

DOG-BREAKING; the Most Expeditious, Certain, and Easy Method, whether great excellence or only mediocrity be required. With a Few Hints for those who Love the Dog and the Gun. By LIEUT.-GEN. HUTCHINSON. *Fourth Edition.* With 40 Woodcuts. Crown 8vo. 15s.

DOMESTIC MODERN COOKERY. Founded on Principles of Economy and Practical Knowledge, and adapted for Private Families. *New Edition.* Woodcuts. Fcap. 8vo. 5s.

DOUGLAS'S (SIR HOWARD) Life and Adventures. By S. W. FULLOM. Portrait. 8vo. 15s.

—— Theory and Practice of Gunnery. *Fifth Edition.* Plates. 8vo. 21s.

—— Military Bridges. *Third Edition.* Plates. 8vo. 21s.

—— Naval Warfare with Steam. 8vo. 8s. 6d.

—— Modern Systems of Fortification. Plans. 8vo. 12s.

DRAKE'S (SIR FRANCIS) Life, Voyages, and Exploits, by Sea and Land. By JOHN BARROW. *Third Edition.* Post 8vo. 2s.

DRINKWATER'S (JOHN) History of the Siege of Gibraltar, 1779-1783. With a Description and Account of that Garrison from the Earliest Periods. Post 8vo. 2s.

DU CHAILLU'S (PAUL B.) EQUATORIAL AFRICA, with Accounts of the Gorilla, the Nest-building Ape, Chimpanzee, Crocodile, &c. Illustrations. 8vo. 21s.

—— Journey to Ashango Land; and Further Penetration into Equatorial Africa. Illustrations. 8vo. 21s.

DUFFERIN'S (LORD) Letters from High Latitudes; an Account of a Yacht Voyage to Iceland, Jan Mayen, and Spitzbergen. *Fifth Edition.* Woodcuts. Post 8vo. 7s. 6d.

DYER'S (THOS. H.) History of Modern Europe, from the taking of Constantinople by the Turks to the close of the War in the Crimea. 4 Vols. 8vo.

EASTLAKE'S (SIR CHARLES) Italian Schools of Painting. From the German of KUGLER. Edited, with Notes. *Third Edition.* Illustrated from the Old Masters. 2 Vols. Post 8vo. 30s.

EDWARDS' (W. H.) Voyage up the River Amazon, including a Visit to Para. Post 8vo. 2s.

ELDON'S (Lord) Public and Private Life, with Selections from his Correspondence and Diaries. By Horace Twiss. *Third Edition*. Portrait. 2 Vols. Post 8vo. 21s.

ELLESMERE'S (Lord) Two Sieges of Vienna by the Turks. Translated from the German. Post 8vo. 2s.

ELLIS'S (W.) Visits to Madagascar, including a Journey to the Capital, with notices of Natural History, and Present Civilisation of the People. *Fifth Thousand*. Map and Woodcuts. 8vo. 16s.

Madagascar Revisited. Setting forth the Persecutions and Heroic Sufferings of the Native Christians. Illustrations. 8vo. 16s.

- (Mrs.) Education of Character, with Hints on Moral Training. Post 8vo. 7s. 6d.

ELPHINSTONE'S (Hon. Mountstuart) History of India—the Hindoo and Mahomedan Periods. *Fifth Edition*. Map. 8vo. 18s.

ENGEL'S (Carl) Music of the Most Ancient Nations; particularly of the Assyrians, Egyptians, and Hebrews; with Special Reference to the Discoveries in Western Asia and in Egypt. With 100 Illustrations. 8vo. 16s.

ENGLAND (History of) from the Peace of Utrecht to the Peace of Versailles, 1713–83. By Lord Mahon (now Earl Stanhope). *Library Edition*, 7 Vols. 8vo. 93s.; or *Popular Edition*, 7 Vols. Post 8vo. 35s.

—— —— From the First Invasion by the Romans. By Mrs. Markham. *New and Cheaper Edition, continued to 1863*. Woodcuts. 12mo. 4s.

—— From the Invasion of Julius Cæsar to the Revolution of 1688. By David Hume. Corrected and continued to 1858. Edited by Wm. Smith, LL.D. Woodcuts. Post 8vo. 7s. 6d.

—— — (Smaller History of). By Wm. Smith, LL.D. *New Edition, continued to 1865*. Woodcuts. 18mo. 3s. 6d.

—— —— Little Arthur's. By Lady Callcott. *New Edition, continued to 1862*. Woodcuts. 18mo. 2s. 6d.

ENGLISHWOMAN IN AMERICA. Post 8vo. 10s. 6d.

ESKIMAUX and English Vocabulary, for Travellers in the Arctic Regions. 16mo. 3s. 6d.

ESSAYS FROM "THE TIMES." Being a Selection from the Literary Papers which have appeared in that Journal. 2 vols. Fcap. 8vo. 8s.

ETHNOLOGICAL SOCIETY'S TRANSACTIONS. New Series. Vols. I. to VI. 8vo. 10s. 6d. each.

EXETER'S (Bishop of) Letters to Charles Butler, on his Book of the Roman Catholic Church. *New Edition*. Post 8vo. 6s.

FAMILY RECEIPT-BOOK. A Collection of a Thousand Valuable and Useful Receipts. Fcap. 8vo. 5s. 6d.

FARRAR'S (A. S.) Critical History of Free Thought in reference to the Christian Religion. Being the Bampton Lectures, 1862. 8vo. 16s.

—— —— (F. W.) Origin of Language, based on Modern Researches. Fcap. 8vo. 5s.

FERGUSSON'S (JAMES) Palaces of Nineveh and Persepolis Restored. Woodcuts. 8vo. 16s.

—— —— History of Architecture in all Countries: from the Earliest Times to the Present Day. With 1200 Illustrations and au Index. Vols. I. and II. 8vo. 42s. each.

—— —— History of Architecture. Vol. III.—The Modern Styles. With 312 Illustrations, and an Index. 8vo. 31s. 6d.

—— —— Holy Sepulchre and the Temple at Jerusalem; being the Substance of Two Lectures delivered at the Royal Institution, 1862 and '65. Woodcuts. 8vo. 7s. 6d.

FISHER'S (REV. GEORGE) Elements of Geometry, for the Use of Schools. *Fifth Edition.* 18mo. 1s. 6d.

—— —— First Principles of Algebra, for the Use of Schools. *Fifth Edition.* 18mo. 1s. 6d.

FLEMING (WM.) Student's Manual of Moral Philosophy. Post 8vo. 7s. 6d.

FLOWER GARDEN (THE). By REV. THOS. JAMES. Fcap. 8vo. 1s.

FONNEREAU'S (T. G.) Diary of a Dutiful Son. Fcap. 8vo. 4s. 6d.

FORBES' (C. S.) Iceland; its Volcanoes, Geysers, and Glaciers. Illustrations. Post 8vo. 14s.

FORSTER'S (JOHN) Arrest of the Five Members by Charles the First. A Chapter of English History re-written. Post 8vo.

—— —— Grand Remonstrance, 1641. With an Essay on English freedom under the Plantagenet and Tudor Sovereigns. *Second Edition.* Post 8vo. 12s.

—— —— Sir John Eliot: a Biography, 1590—1632. With Portraits. 2 Vols. Crown 8vo. 30s.

—— —— Biographies of Oliver Cromwell, Daniel De Foe, Sir Richard Steele, Charles Churchill, Samuel Foote. *Third Edition.* Post 8vo. 12s.

FORD'S (RICHARD) Gatherings from Spain. Post 8vo. 3s. 6d.

FORSYTH'S (WILLIAM) Life and Times of Cicero. With Selections from his Correspondence and Orations. *New Edition.* Illustrations. 8vo. 16s.

FORTUNE'S (ROBERT) Narrative of Two Visits to the Tea Countries of China, 1843-52. *Third Edition.* Woodcuts. 2 Vols. Post 8vo. 18s.

—— —— Third Visit to China. 1853-6. Woodcuts. 8vo. 16s.

—— —— Yedo and Peking. With Notices of the Agriculture and Trade of China, during a Fourth Visit to that Country. Illustrations. 8vo. 16s.

FOSS' (Edward) Judges of England. With Sketches of their Lives, and Notices of the Courts at Westminster, from the Conquest to the Present Time. 9 Vols. 8vo. 126s.

———— Tabulæ Curiales ; or, Tables of the Superior Courts of Westminster Hall. Showing the Judges who sat in them from 1066 to 1864 ; with the Attorney and Solicitor Generals of each reign. To which is prefixed an Alphabetical List of all the Judges during the same period. 8vo. 10s. 6d.

FRANCE (HISTORY OF). From the Conquest by the Gauls. By Mrs. MARKHAM. New and Cheaper Edition, continued to 1856. Woodcuts. 12mo. 4s.

———— From the Earliest Times to the Establishment of the Second Empire, 1852. By W. H. PEARSON. Edited by WM. SMITH, LL.D. Woodcuts. Post 8vo. 7s. 6d.

FRENCH (THE) in Algiers ; The Soldier of the Foreign Legion— and the Prisoners of Abd-el-Kadir. Translated by Lady DUFF GORDON. Post 8vo. 2s.

FRERE'S (M.) Old Deccan Days ; or, Hindoo Fairy Legends Current in Southern India. Collected from Oral Tradition. Illustrated by C. F. FRERE. With an Introduction and Notes, by SIR BARTLE FRERE. Crown 8vo. 12s.

GALTON'S (FRANCIS) Art of Travel ; or, Hints on the Shifts and Contrivances available in Wild Countries. Fourth Edition. Woodcuts. Post 8vo. 7s. 6d.

GEOGRAPHY (ANCIENT). By Rev. W. L. BEVAN. Woodcuts. Post 8vo. 7s. 6d.

———— (MODERN). By Rev. W. L. BEVAN. Woodcuts. Post 8vo. In the Press.

———— Journal of the Royal Geographical Society of London. 8vo.

GERMANY (HISTORY OF). From the Invasion by Marius, to Recent times. By Mrs. MARKHAM. New and Cheaper Edition. Woodcuts. 12mo. 4s.

GIBBON'S (EDWARD) History of the Decline and Fall of the Roman Empire. A New Edition. Preceded by his Autobiography. And Edited, with Notes, by Dr. WM. SMITH. Maps. 8 Vols. 8vo. 60s.

———— (The Student's Gibbon) ; Being an Epitome of the above work, incorporating the Researches of Recent Commentators. By Dr. WM. SMITH. Woodcuts. Post 8vo. 7s. 6d.

GIFFARD'S (EDWARD) Deeds of Naval Daring ; or, Anecdotes of the British Navy. Fcap. 8vo. 3s. 6d.

GLADSTONE'S (W. E.) Financial Statements of 1853, 60, 63, and 64 ; with Speeches on Tax-Bills and Charities. Second Edition. 8vo. 12s.

———— Speeches on Parliamentary Reform. Third Edition. Post 8vo. 5s.

GLEIG'S (G. R.) Campaigns of the British Army at Washington and New Orleans. Post 8vo. 2s.

———— Story of the Battle of Waterloo. Post 8vo. 3s. 6d.

———— Narrative of Sale's Brigade in Affghanistan. Post 8vo. 2s.

———— Life of Robert Lord Clive. Post 8vo. 3s. 6d.

———— Sir Thomas Munro. Post 8vo. 3s. 6d.

GOLDSMITH'S (OLIVER) Works. A New Edition. Edited with
Notes by PETER CUNNINGHAM. Vignettes. 4 Vols. 8vo. 30s.

GONGORA; An Historical Essay on the Times of Philip III. and
IV. of Spain. With Illustrations. By ARCHDEACON CHURTON. Portrait. 2 vols. Post 8vo. 15s.

GORDON'S (SIR ALEX. DUFF) Sketches of German Life, and Scenes
from the War of Liberation. From the German. Post 8vo. 3s. 6d.

————— (LADY DUFF) Amber-Witch: A Trial for Witchcraft. From the German. Post 8vo. 2s.

— ————— French in Algiers. 1. The Soldier of the Foreign
Legion. 2. The Prisoners of Abd-el-Kadir. From the French.
Post 8vo. 2s.

GOUGER'S (HENRY) Personal Narrative of Two Years' Imprison-
ment in Burmah. Second Edition. Woodcuts. Post 8vo. 12s.

GRAMMARS (LATIN and GREEK). See CURTIUS; SMITH; KING
EDWARD VITH., &c. &c.

GREECE (HISTORY OF). From the Earliest Times to the Roman
Conquest. By WM. SMITH, LL.D. Woodcuts. Post 8vo. 7s. 6d.

— (SMALLER HISTORY OF). By WM. SMITH, LL.D. Woodcuts. 16mo. 3s. 6d.

GRENVILLE (THE) PAPERS. Being the Public and Private
Correspondence of George Grenville, including his PRIVATE DIARY.
Edited by W. J. SMITH. 4 Vols. 8vo. 16s. each.

GREY'S (EARL) Correspondence with King William IVth. and
Sir Herbert Taylor, from November, 1830, to the Passing of the Reform
Act in 1832. 2 Vols. 8vo. 30s.

————— ————— Parliamentary Government and Reform; with
Suggestions for the Improvement of our Representative System.
Second Edition. 8vo. 9s.

—·——— (SIR GEORGE) Polynesian Mythology, and Ancient
Traditional History of the New Zealand Race. Woodcuts. Post
8vo. 10s. 6d.

GRUNER'S (LEWIS) Terra-Cotta Architecture of North Italy,
From careful Drawings and Restorations. With Illustrations, engraved
and printed in Colours. Small folio. 5l. 5s.

GROTE'S (GEORGE) History of Greece. From the Earliest Times
to the close of the generation contemporary with the death of Alexander
the Great. Fourth Edition. Maps. 8 Vols. 8vo. 112s.

— — ——— PLATO, and the other Companions of Socrates.
Second Edition. 3 Vols. 8vo. 45s.

——— (MRS.) Memoir of Ary Scheffer. Post 8vo. 8s. 6d.

GUIZOT'S (M.) Meditations on Christianity, and on the Religious
Questions of the Day. Part I. The Essence. Part II. The Present
State. 2 Vols. Post 8vo. 20s.

————— Meditations on Christianity. Part III. Its Relation
to the State of Society and Progress of the Human Mind. Post 8vo.
(Nearly Ready.)

HALLAM'S (HENRY) Constitutional History of England, from the Accession of Henry the Seventh to the Death of George the Second. *Seventh Edition.* 3 Vols. 8vo. 30s.

———— History of Europe during the Middle Ages. *Tenth Edition.* 3 Vols. 8vo. 30s.

———— The Student's Hallam. An Epitome of the History of Europe during the Middle Ages. With Additional Notes and Illustrations. By WM. SMITH, LL.D. Post 8vo. Uniform with the "Student's Hume." (*In Preparation.*)

———— Literary History of Europe, during the 15th, 16th and 17th Centuries. *Fourth Edition.* 3 Vols. 8vo. 36s.

———— Historical Works. Containing History of England, —Middle Ages of Europe,—Literary History of Europe. 10 Vols. Post 8vo. 6s. each.

———— (ARTHUR) Remains; in Verse and Prose. With Preface, Memoir, and Portrait. Fcap. 8vo. 7s. 6d.

HAMILTON'S (JAMES) Wanderings in North Africa. With Illustrations. Post 8vo. 12s.

HANNAH'S (REV. DR.) Bampton Lectures for 1863; the Divine and Human Elements in Holy Scripture. 8vo. 10s. 6d.

HART'S ARMY LIST. (*Quarterly and Annually.*) 8vo.

HAY'S (J. H. DRUMMOND) Western Barbary, its Wild Tribes and Savage Animals. Post 8vo. 2s.

HEAD'S (SIR FRANCIS) Horse and his Rider. Woodcuts. Post 8vo. 5s.

———— Rapid Journeys across the Pampas. Post 8vo. 2s.

———— Bubbles from the Brunnen of Nassau. Illustrations. Post 8vo. 7s. 6d.

———— Emigrant. Fcap. 8vo. 2s. 6d.

———— Stokers and Pokers ; or, the London and North Western Railway. Post 8vo. 2s.

———— (SIR EDMUND) Shall and Will; or, Future Auxiliary Verbs. Fcap. 8vo. 4s.

HEBER'S (BISHOP) Journey through the Upper Provinces of India, from Calcutta to Bombay, with an Account of a Journey to Madras and the Southern Provinces. *Twelfth Edition.* 2 Vols. Post 8vo. 7s.

———— Poetical Works, including Palestine, Europe, The Red Sea, Hymns, &c. *Sixth Edition.* Portrait. Fcap. 8vo. 6s.

———— Hymns adapted to the Weekly Church Service of the Year. 16mo. 1s. 6d.

HERODOTUS. A New English Version. Edited, with Notes and Essays, historical, ethnographical, and geographical, by Rev. G. RAWLINSON, assisted by SIR HENRY RAWLINSON and SIR J. G. WILKINSON. *Second Edition.* Maps and Woodcuts. 4 Vols. 8vo. 48s.

FOREIGN HANDBOOKS.

HAND-BOOK—TRAVEL-TALK. English, French, German, and Italian. 18mo. 3s. 6d.

——————— NORTH GERMANY,—HOLLAND, BELGIUM, PRUSSIA, and the Rhine from Holland to Switzerland. Map. Post 8vo. 10s.

——————— SOUTH GERMANY, Bavaria, Austria, Styria, Salzberg, the Austrian and Bavarian Alps, the Tyrol, Hungary, and the Danube, from Ulm to the Black Sea. Map. Post 8vo. 10s.

——————— KNAPSACK GUIDE TO THE TYROL. Post 8vo. 6s.

——————— PAINTING. German, Flemish, and Dutch Schools. Woodcuts. 2 Vols. Post 8vo. 24s.

——————— LIVES OF THE EARLY FLEMISH PAINTERS. By CROWE and CAVALCASELLE. Illustrations. Post 8vo. 12s.

——————— SWITZERLAND, Alps of Savoy, and Piedmont. Maps. Post 8vo. 10s.

——————— KNAPSACK GUIDE TO SWITZERLAND. Post 8vo. 5s.

——————— FRANCE, Normandy, Brittany, the French Alps, the Rivers Loire, Seine, Rhone, and Garonne, Dauphiné, Provence, and the Pyrenees. Maps. Post 8vo. 12s.

——————— CORSICA and SARDINIA. Maps. Post 8vo. 4s.

——————— PARIS, and its Environs. Map and Plans. Post 8vo. 3s. 6d.

** MURRAY'S PLAN OF PARIS, mounted on canvas. 3s 6d.

——————— SPAIN, Andalusia, Ronda, Granada, Valencia, Catalonia, Gallicia, Arragon, and Navarre. Maps. Post 8vo. (In the Press.)

——————— PORTUGAL, LISBON, &c. Map. Post 8vo. 9s.

——————— NORTH ITALY, Piedmont, Liguria, Venetia, Lombardy, Parma, Modena, and Romagna. Map. Post 8vo. 12s.

——————— CENTRAL ITALY, Lucca, Tuscany, Florence, The Marches, Umbria, and the Patrimony of St. Peter's. Map. Post 8vo. 10s.

——————— ROME AND ITS ENVIRONS. Map. Post 8vo. 9s.

——————— SOUTH ITALY, Two Sicilies, Naples, Pompeii, Herculaneum, and Vesuvius. Map. Post 8vo. 10s.

——————— KNAPSACK GUIDE TO ITALY. Post 8vo. 6s.

——————— SICILY, Palermo, Messina, Catania, Syracuse, Etna, and the Ruins of the Greek Temples. Map. Post 8vo. 12s.

——————— PAINTING. The Italian Schools. Edited by Sir CHARLES EASTLAKE, R.A. Woodcuts. 2 Vols. Post 8vo. 30s.

——————— LIVES OF ITALIAN PAINTERS, FROM CIMABUE to BASSANO. By Mrs. JAMESON. Portraits. Post 8vo. 10s. 6d.

——————— DENMARK, SWEDEN, and NORWAY. New Edition. Maps. Post 8vo. (In Preparation.)

HOME AND COLONIAL LIBRARY. A Series of Works adapted for all circles and classes of Readers, having been selected for their acknowledged interest and ability of the Authors. Post 8vo Published at 2s. and 3s. 6d. each, and arranged under two distinctive heads as follows :—

CLASS A.
HISTORY, BIOGRAPHY, AND HISTORIC TALES.

1. SIEGE OF GIBRALTAR. By JOHN DRINKWATER. 2s.

2. THE AMBER-WITCH. By LADY DUFF GORDON. 2s.

3. CROMWELL AND BUNYAN. By ROBERT SOUTHEY. 2s.

4. LIFE OF SIR FRANCIS DRAKE. By JOHN BARROW. 2s.

5. CAMPAIGNS AT WASHING-TON. By REV. G. R. GLEIG. 2s.

6. THE FRENCH IN ALGIERS. By LADY DUFF GORDON. 2s.

7. THE FALL OF THE JESUITS. 2s.

8. LIVONIAN TALES. 2s.

9. LIFE OF CONDE. By LORD MA-HON. 3s. 6d.

10. SALE'S BRIGADE. By REV. G. R. GLEIG. 2s.

11. THE SIEGES OF VIENNA. By LORD ELLESMERE. 2s.

12. THE WAYSIDE CROSS. By CAPT. MILMAN. 2s.

13. SKETCHES OF GERMAN LIFE. By SIR A. GORDON. 3s. 6d.

14. THE BATTLE OF WATERLOO. By REV. G. R. GLEIG. 3s. 6d.

15. AUTOBIOGRAPHY OF STEF-FENS. 2s.

16. THE BRITISH POETS. By THOMAS CAMPBELL. 3s. 6d.

17. HISTORICAL ESSAYS. By LORD MAHON. 3s. 6d.

18. LIFE OF LORD CLIVE. By REV. G. R. GLEIG. 3s. 6d.

19. NORTH - WESTERN RAIL-WAY. By SIR F. B. HEAD. 2s.

20. LIFE OF MUNRO. By REV. G. R. GLEIG. 3s. 6d.

CLASS B.
VOYAGES, TRAVELS, AND ADVENTURES.

1. BIBLE IN SPAIN. By GEORGE BORROW. 3s. 6d.

2. GIPSIES OF SPAIN. By GEORGE BORROW. 3s. 6d.

3 & 4. JOURNALS IN INDIA. By BISHOP HEBER. 2 Vols. 7s.

5. TRAVELS IN THE HOLY LAND. By IRBY and MANGLES. 2s.

6. MOROCCO AND THE MOORS. By J. DRUMMOND HAY. 2s.

7. LETTERS FROM THE BALTIC. By a LADY. 2s.

8. NEW SOUTH WALES. By MRS. MEREDITH. 2s.

9. THE WEST INDIES. By M. G. LEWIS. 2s.

10. SKETCHES OF PERSIA. By SIR JOHN MALCOLM. 3s. 6d.

11. MEMOIRS OF FATHER RIPA. 2s.

12. 13. TYPEE AND OMOO. By HERMANN MELVILLE. 2 Vols. 7s.

14. MISSIONARY LIFE IN CAN-ADA. By REV. J. ABBOTT. 2s.

15. LETTERS FROM MADRAS. By a LADY. 2s.

16. HIGHLAND SPORTS. By CHARLES ST. JOHN. 3s. 6d.

17. PAMPAS JOURNEYS. By SIR F. B. HEAD. 2s.

18 GATHERINGS FROM SPAIN. By RICHARD FORD. 3s. 6d.

19. THE RIVER AMAZON. By W. H. EDWARDS. 2s.

20. MANNERS & CUSTOMS OF INDIA. By REV. C. ACLAND. 2s.

21. ADVENTURES IN MEXICO. By G. F. RUXTON. 3s. 6d.

22. PORTUGAL AND GALLICIA. By LORD CARNARVON. 3s. 6d.

23. BUSH LIFE IN AUSTRALIA. By REV. H. W. HAYGARTH. 2s.

24. THE LIBYAN DESERT. By BAYLE ST. JOHN. 2s.

25. SIERRA LEONE. By a LADY. 3s. 6d.

₄ Each work may be had separately.

HORACE (WORKS OF.) Edited by DEAN MILMAN. With 100
Woodcuts. Crown 8vo. 7s. 6d.
——————— (Life of). By DEAN MILMAN. Woodcuts, and coloured
Borders. 8vo. 9s.
HOUGHTON'S (LORD) Poetical Works. Fcap. 8vo. 6s.
HUME (THE STUDENT'S) A History of England, from the Invasion
of Julius Cæsar to the Revolution of 1688. Corrected and continued
to 1858. Edited by DR. WM. SMITH. Woodcuts. Post 8vo. 7s. 6d.
HUTCHINSON (GEN.) on the most expeditious, certain, and
easy Method of Dog-Breaking. *Fourth Edition.* Enlarged and
revised, with 40 Illustrations. Crown 8vo. 15s.
HUTTON'S (H. E.) Principia Græca; an Introduction to the Study
of Greek. Comprehending Grammar, Delectus, and Exercise-book,
with Vocabularies. *Sixth Edition.* 12mo. 3s. 6d.
IRBY AND MANGLES' Travels in Egypt, Nubia, Syria, and
the Holy Land. Post 8vo. 2s.
JAMES' (REV. THOMAS) Fables of Æsop. A New Translation, with
Historical Preface. With 100 Woodcuts by TENNIEL and WOLF.
Fiftieth Thousand. Post 8vo. 2s. 6d.
JAMESON'S (MRS.) Lives of the Early Italian Painters—
and the Progress of Painting in Italy—Cimabue to Bassano. *New
Edition.* With 50 Portraits. Post 8vo. 10s. 6d.
JENNINGS' (L. J.) Eighty Years of Republican Government in
the United States. Post 8vo. 10s. 6d.
JESSE'S (EDWARD) Gleanings in Natural History. *Eighth Edition.*
Fcp. 8vo. 6s.
JOHNS' (REV. B. G.) Blind People; their Works and Ways. With
Sketches of the Lives of some famous Blind Men. With Illustrations.
Post 8vo. 7s. 6d.
JOHNSON'S (DR. SAMUEL) Life. By James Boswell. Including
the Tour to the Hebrides. Edited by MR. CROKER. Portraits.
Royal 8vo. 10s.
——————— Lives of the English Poets. Edited by PETER
CUNNINGHAM. 3 vols. 8vo. 22s. 6d.
KEN'S (BISHOP) Life. By a LAYMAN. Portrait. 2 Vols. 8vo. 18s.
——————— Exposition of the Apostles' Creed. Fcap. 1s. 6d.
——————— Approach to the Holy Altar. Fcap. 8vo. 1s. 6d.
KENNEDY'S (GENERAL) Notes on the Battle of Waterloo. With
a Memoir of his Life and Services, and a Plan for the Defence of Canada.
With Map and Plans. 8vo. 7s. 6d.
KERR'S (ROBERT) GENTLEMAN'S HOUSE; OR, HOW TO PLAN
ENGLISH RESIDENCES, FROM THE PARSONAGE TO THE PALACE. With
Tables and Cost. Views and Plans. *Second Edition.* 8vo. 24s.
——————— Ancient Lights; a Book for Architects, Surveyors,
Lawyers, and Landlords. 8vo. 5s. 6d.
——————— (R. MALCOLM) Student's Blackstone. A Systematic
Abridgment of the entire Commentaries, adapted to the present state
of the law. Post 8vo. 7s. 6d.
KING'S (REV. C. W.) Antique Gems; their Origin, Use, and
Value, as Interpreters of Ancient History, and as illustrative of Ancient
Art. *Second Edition.* Illustrations. 8vo. 24s.
KING EDWARD VIth's Latin Grammar; or, an Introduction
to the Latin Tongue. *Seventeenth Edition.* 12mo. 3s. 6d.
——————— First Latin Book; or, the Accidence,
Syntax, and Prosody, with an English Translation. *Fifth Edition.* 12mo.
2s. 6d.

KING GEORGE THE THIRD'S CORRESPONDENCE WITH LORD NORTH, 1769-82. Edited, with Notes and Introduction, by W. BODHAM DONNE. 2 vols. 8vo. 32s.

KIRK'S (J. FOSTER) History of Charles the Bold, Duke of Burgundy. Portrait. 3 Vols. 8vo. 45s.

KUGLER'S Italian Schools of Painting. Edited, with Notes, by SIR CHARLES EASTLAKE. *Third Edition.* Woodcuts. 2 Vols. Post 8vo. 30s.

———— German, Dutch, and Flemish Schools of Painting. Edited, with Notes, by DR. WAAGEN. *Second Edition.* Woodcuts. 2 Vols. Post 8vo. 24s.

LAYARD'S (A. H.) Nineveh and its Remains. Being a Narrative of Researches and Discoveries amidst the Ruins of Assyria. With an Account of the Chaldean Christians of Kurdistan; the Yezedis, or Devil-worshippers; and an Enquiry into the Manners and Arts of the Ancient Assyrians. *Sixth Edition.* Plates and Woodcuts. 2 Vols. 8vo. 36s.
   ⁎ A POPULAR EDITION. With Illustrations. Post 8vo. 7s. 6d.

———— Nineveh and Babylon; being the Narrative of a Second Expedition to Assyria. Plates. 8vo. 21s.
   ⁎ A POPULAR EDITION. With Illustrations. Post 8vo. 7s. 6d.

LEATHES' (STANLEY) Short Practical Hebrew Grammar. With an Appendix, containing the Hebrew Text of Genesis i.—vi., and Psalms i.—vi. Grammatical Analysis and Vocabulary. Post 8vo. 7s. 6d.

LENNEP'S (REV. H. J. VAN) Missionary Travels in Asia Minor. With Illustrations. 2 Vols. Post 8vo. (*In preparation.*)

LESLIE'S (C. R.) Handbook for Young Painters. With Illustrations. Post 8vo. 10s. 6d.

———— Autobiographical Recollections, with Selections from his Correspondence. Edited by TOM TAYLOR. Portrait. 2 Vols. Post 8vo. 18s.

———— Life and Works of Sir Joshua Reynolds. Portraits and Illustrations. 2 Vols. 8vo. 42s.

LETTERS FROM THE BALTIC. By a LADY. Post 8vo. 2s.

———— MADRAS. By a LADY. Post 8vo. 2s.

———— SIERRA LEONE. By a LADY. Post 8vo. 3s. 6d.

LEVI'S (LEONE) Wages and Earnings of the Working Classes. With some Facts Illustrative of their Economic Condition. 8vo. 6s.

LEWIS (SIR G. C.) On the Government of Dependencies. 8vo. 12s.

———— Glossary of Provincial Words used in Herefordshire, &c. 12mo. 4s. 6d.

———— (M. G.) Journal of a Residence among the Negroes in the West Indies. Post 8vo. 2s.

LIDDELL'S (DEAN) History of Rome. From the Earliest Times to the Establishment of the Empire. With the History of Literature and Art. 2 Vols. 8vo. 28s.

———— Student's History of Rome, abridged from the above Work. With Woodcuts. Post 8vo. 7s. 6d.

LINDSAY'S (LORD) Lives of the Lindsays; or, a Memoir of the Houses of Crawfurd and Balcarres. With Extracts from Official Papers and Personal Narratives. *Second Edition.* 3 Vols. 8vo. 24s.

LISPINGS from LOW LATITUDES; or, the Journal of the Hon. Impulsia Gushington. Edited by LORD DUFFERIN. With 24 Plates. 4to. 21s.

LITTLE ARTHUR'S HISTORY OF ENGLAND. By LADY
CALLCOTT. *New Edition, continued to* 1862. With 20 Woodcuts.
Fcap. 8vo. 2s. 6d.

LIVINGSTONE'S (DR.) Popular Account of his Missionary
Travels in South Africa. Illustrations. Post 8vo. 6s.

———————— Narrative of an Expedition to the Zambezi and
its Tributaries; and of the Discovery of Lakes Shirwa and Nyassa.
1858-64. Map and Illustrations. 8vo. 21s.

LIVONIAN TALES. By the Author of " Letters from the
Baltic." Post 8vo. 2s.

LOCKHART'S (J. G.) Ancient Spanish Ballads. Historical and
Romantic. Translated, with Notes. *New Edition.* Post 8vo. 2s. 6d.

———————— Life of Theodore Hook. Fcap. 8vo. 1s.

LONDON (OLD). A series of Essays on its Archæology and
Antiquities, by DEAN STANLEY; A. J. BERESFORD HOPE, M.P.; G. G.
SCOTT, R.A.; R. WESTMACOTT. R.A.; E. FOSS, F.S.A.; G. T. CLARK;
JOSEPH BURTT; REV. J. R GREEN; and G. SCHARF, F.S.A. 8vo. 12s.

LONDON'S (BISHOP OF) Dangers and Safeguards of Modern
Theology. Containing Suggestions to the Theological Student under
present difficulties. *Second Edition.* 8vo. 9s.

LONSDALE'S (BISHOP) Life. With Selections from his Writings.
By E. B. DENISON, Q.C. With Portrait. Crown 8vo. 10s. 6d.

LOUDON'S (MRS.) Instructions in Gardening. With Directions
and Calendar of Operations for Every Month. *Eighth Edition.* Woodcuts. Fcap. 8vo. 5s.

LUCAS' (SAMUEL) Secularia; or, Surveys on the Main Stream of
History. 8vo. 12s.

LUCKNOW: a Lady's Diary of the Siege. Fcap. 8vo. 4s. 6d.

LYELL'S (SIR CHARLES) Elements of Geology; or, the Ancient
Changes of the Earth and its Inhabitants as illustrated by Geological
Monuments. *Sixth Edition.* Woodcuts. 8vo. 18s.

———————— Principles of Geology; or, the Modern Changes
of the Earth and its Inhabitants considered as illustrative of Geology.
Tenth Edition. With Illustrations. 2 Vols. 8vo. 32s.

———————— Geological Evidences of the Antiquity of Man.
Third Edition. Illustrations. 8vo. 14s.

LYTTELTON'S (LORD) Ephemera. Post 8vo. 10s. 6d.

LYTTON'S (LORD) Poems. *New Edition.* Post 8vo. 10s. 6d.

———————— Lost Tales of Miletus. *Second Edition.* Post 8vo. 7s. 6d.

MACPHERSON'S (MAJOR S. C.) Memorials of Service in India,
while Political Agent at Gwalior during the Mutiny. With Portrait
and Illustrations. 8vo. 12s.

MAHON'S (LORD) Works. See STANHOPE (Earl of).

McCLINTOCK'S (SIR L.) Narrative of the Discovery of the
Fate of Sir John Franklin and his Companions in the Arctic Seas.
Twelfth Thousand. Illustrations. 8vo. 16s.

M'CULLOCH'S (J. R.) Collected Edition of RICARDO's Political
Works. With Notes and Memoir. 8vo. 16s.

MacDOUGALL'S (COL.) Modern Warfare as Influenced by Modern
Artillery. With Plans. Post 8vo. 12s.

MAINE (H. SUMNER) On Ancient Law: its Connection with the
Early History of Society, and its Relation to Modern Ideas. 8vo. 12s.

MALCOLM'S (Sir John) Sketches of Persia. Post 8vo. 3s. 6d.

MANSEL (Canon) Limits of Religious Thought Examined. Being the Bampton Lectures for 1858. Post 8vo. 8s. 6d.

MANSFIELD (Sir William) On a Gold Currency for India. 8vo. 3s. 6d.

MANTELL'S (Gideon A.) Thoughts on Animalcules; or, the Invisible World, as revealed by the Microscope. Plates. 16mo. 6s.

MANUAL OF SCIENTIFIC ENQUIRY. For the Use of Travellers. Edited by Sir J. F. Herschel and Rev. R. Main. Maps. Post 8vo. 9s. (Published by order of the Lords of the Admiralty.)

MARKHAM'S (Mrs.) History of England. From the First Invasion by the Romans, down to Recent Times. New Edition, continued to 1863. Woodcuts. 12mo. 4s.

———————— History of France. From the Conquest by the Gauls, to Recent Times. New Edition, continued to 1856. Woodcuts. 12mo. 4s.

———————— History of Germany. From the Invasion by Marius, to Recent Times. New Edition. Woodcuts. 12mo. 4s.

———————— (Clements R.) Travels in Peru and India. Maps and Illustrations. 8vo. 16s.

MARRYAT'S (Joseph) History of Modern and Mediæval Pottery and Porcelain. With a Description of the Manufacture. Third and revised and enlarged Edition. Plates and Woodcuts. 8vo. (Nearly Ready.)

———————— (Horace) Jutland, the Danish Isles, and Copenhagen. Illustrations. 2 Vols. Post 8vo. 24s.

———————— Sweden and Isle of Gothland. Illustrations. 2 Vols. Post 8vo. 28s.

MARSH'S (G. P.) Student's Manual of the English Language. Post 8vo. 7s. 6d.

MAUREL'S (Jules) Essay on the Character, Actions, and Writings of the Duke of Wellington. Second Edition. Fcap. 8vo. 1s. 6d.

MAYNE'S (Capt.) Four Years in British Columbia and Vancouver Island. Its Forests, Rivers, Coasts, and Gold Fields, and Resources for Colonisation. Illustrations. 8vo. 16s.

MELVILLE'S (Hermann) Typee and Omoo; or, Adventures amongst the Marquesas and South Sea Islands. 2 Vols. Post 8vo. 7s.

MILLS' (Rev. John) Three Months' Residence at Nablus, with an Account of the Modern Samaritans. Illustrations. Post 8vo. 10s. 6d.

MILMAN'S (Dean) Historical Works. Containing: 1. History of the Jews, 3 Vols. 2. History of Early Christianity, 3 Vols. 3. History of Latin Christianity, 9 Vols. Post 8vo. 6s. each.

———— Annals of St. Paul's Cathedral. Portrait and Illustrations. 8vo. (In preparation.)

———————— Character and Conduct of the Apostles considered as an Evidence of Christianity. 8vo. 10s. 6d.

———— Translations from the Agamemnon of Æschylus and Bacchanals of Euripides. With Illustrations. Crown 8vo. 12s.

———————— Works of Horace. With 100 woodcuts. Small 8vo. 7s. 6d.

———————— Life of Horace. Woodcuts. 8vo. 9s.

———————— Poetical Works. Plates. 3 Vols. Fcap. 8vo. 18s.

———————— Fall of Jerusalem. Fcap. 8vo. 1s.

———————— (Capt. E. A.) Wayside Cross. A Tale of the Carlist War. Post 8vo. 2s.

MEREDITH'S (MRS. CHARLES) Notes and Sketches of New South
Wales. Post 8vo. 2s.

MESSIAH (THE): A Narrative of the Life, Travels, Death,
Resurrection, and Ascension of our Blessed Lord. By the Author of
"Life of Bishop Ken." Map. 8vo. 18s.

MICHIE'S (ALEXANDER) Siberian Overland Route from Peking
to Petersburg, through the Deserts and Steppes of Mongolia, Tartary,
&c. Maps and Illustrations. 8vo. 16s.

MODERN DOMESTIC COOKERY. Founded on Principles of
Economy and Practical Knowledge and adapted for Private Families.
New Edition. Woodcuts. Fcap. 8vo. 5s.

MOORE'S (THOMAS) Life and Letters of Lord Byron. Plates.
6 Vols. Fcap. 8vo. 18s.; or 1 Vol. Portraits. Royal 8vo. 9s.

MOTLEY'S (J. L.) History of the United Netherlands : from the
Death of William the Silent to the Twelve Years' Truce, 1609. Embrac-
ing the English-Dutch struggle against Spain; and a detailed Account
of the Spanish Armada. Portraits. 4 Vols. 8vo. 60s. Or Popular
Edition. 4 Vols. Post 8vo. 6s. each.

MOUHOT'S (HENRI) Siam, Cambojia, and Lao ; a Narrative of
Travels and Discoveries. Illustrations. 2 vols. 8vo. 32s.

MOZLEY'S (REV. J. B.) Treatise on Predestination. 8vo. 14s.

———— Primitive Doctrine of Baptismal Regeneration. 8vo. 7s.6d.

MUNDY'S (GENERAL) Pen and Pencil Sketches in India.
Third Edition. Plates. Post 8vo. 7s. 6d.

MUNRO'S (GENERAL SIR THOMAS) Life and Letters. By the REV.
G. R. GLEIG. Post 8vo. 3s. 6d.

MURCHISON'S (SIR RODERICK) Russia in Europe and the Ural
Mountains. With Coloured Maps, Plates, Sections, &c. 2 Vols.
Royal 4to. 5l. 5s.

———————— Siluria ; or, a History of the Oldest Rocks containing Organic Remains. Fourth Edition. Map and Plates. 8vo. 30s.

MURRAY'S RAILWAY READING. Containing :—

WELLINGTON. By LORD ELLESMERE, 6d.	HALLAM's LITERARY ESSAYS. 2s.
NIMROD ON THE CHASE, 1s.	MAHON's JOAN OF ARC. 1s.
ESSAYS FROM "THE TIMES." 2 Vols. 8s.	HEAD's EMIGRANT. 2s. 6d.
MUSIC AND DRESS. 1s.	NIMROD ON THE ROAD. 1s.
LAYARD's ACCOUNT OF NINEVEH. 5s.	CROKER ON THE GUILLOTINE. 1s.
MILMAN's FALL OF JERUSALEM. 1s.	HOLLWAY's NORWAY. 2s.
MAHON's "FORTY-FIVE." 3s.	MAUREL's WELLINGTON. 1s. 6d.
LIFE OF THEODORE HOOK. 1s.	CAMPBELL's LIFE OF BACON. 2s. 6d.
DEEDS OF NAVAL DARING. 3s. 6d.	THE FLOWER GARDEN. 1s.
THE HONEY BEE. 1s.	LOCKHART's SPANISH BALLADS. 2s. 6d.
JAMES' ÆSOP's FABLES. 2s. 6d.	TAYLOR's NOTES FROM LIFE. 2s.
NIMROD ON THE TURF. 1s. 6d.	REJECTED ADDRESSES. 1s.
ART OF DINING. 1s. 6d.	PENN's HINTS ON ANGLING. 1s.

MUSIC AND DRESS. By a LADY. Reprinted from the " Quarterly
Review." Fcap. 8vo. 1s.

NAPIER'S (SIR CHAS.) Life; chiefly derived from his Journals
and Letters. By SIR W. NAPIER. Second Edition. Portraits. 4 Vols.
Post 8vo. 48s.

———— (SIR WM.) Life and Letters. Edited by H. A. BRUCE,
M.P. Portraits. 2 Vols. Crown 8vo. 28s.

———————— English Battles and Sieges of the Peninsular
War. Fourth Edition. Portrait. Post 8vo. 9s.

NAUTICAL (THE) ALMANACK. Royal 8vo. 2s. 6d. (By Authority.)

NAVY LIST (THE). (Published Quarterly, by Authority.) 16mo. 2s. 6d.

NEW TESTAMENT (ILLUSTRATED). With Explanatory Commentary. Edited by ARCHDEACON CHURTON, M.A., and BASIL JONES, M.A. With 110 authentic Views of Places, from Sketches and Photographs taken on the spot. 2 Vols. Crown 8vo. 30s. cloth; 52s. 6d. calf; 63s. morocco.

NICHOLLS' (SIR GEORGE) History of the English, Irish and Scotch Poor Laws. 4 Vols. 8vo.

———— (Rev. H. G.) Historical Account of the Forest of Dean. Woodcuts, &c. Post 8vo. 10s. 6d.

NICOLAS' (SIR HARRIS) Historic Peerage of England. Exhibiting the Origin, Descent, and Present State of every Title of Peerage which has existed in this Country since the Conquest. By WILLIAM COURTHOPE. 8vo. 30s.

NIMROD On the Chace—The Turf—and The Road. Woodcuts. Fcap. 8vo. 3s. 6d.

OLD LONDON; Papers read at the London Congress of the Archæological Institute, July, 1866. By A. J. B. BERESFORD HOPE, M.P.; DEAN STANLEY, D.D.; G. T. CLARK, Esq.; G. GILBERT SCOTT, R.A.; PROFESSOR WESTMACOTT, R.A.; EDWARD FOSS, F.S.A.; JOSEPH BURTT, Esq.; REV. J. R. GREEN; GEORGE SCHARF, F.S.A. With Illustrations. 8vo. 12s.

OXENHAM'S (REV. W.) English Notes for Latin Elegiacs; designed for early Proficients in the Art of Latin Versification, with Prefatory Rules of Composition in Elegiac Metre. Fourth Edition. 12mo. 3s. 6d.

OXFORD'S (BISHOP OF) Popular Life of William Wilberforce. Portrait. Post 8vo. 10s. 6d.

PARIS' (Dr.) Philosophy in Sport made Science in Earnest; or, the First Principles of Natural Philosophy inculcated by aid of the Toys and Sports of Youth. Ninth Edition. Woodcuts. Post 8vo. 7s. 6d.

PARKYNS' (MANSFIELD) Life in Abyssinia: During a Three Years' Residence and Travels in that Country. New Edition, with Map and 30 Illustrations. Post 8vo. 7s. 6d.

PEEL'S (SIR ROBERT) Memoirs. Edited by EARL STANHOPE and Mr. CARDWELL. 2 Vols. Post 8vo. 7s. 6d. each.

PENN'S (RICHARD) Maxims and Hints for an Angler and Chessplayer. New Edition. Woodcuts. Fcap. 8vo. 1s.

PENROSE'S (F. C.) Principles of Athenian Architecture, and the Optical Refinements exhibited in the Construction of the Ancient Buildings at Athens, from a Survey. With 40 Plates. Folio. 5l. 5s.

PERCY'S (JOHN, M.D.) Metallurgy of Fuel, Coal, Fire-Clays, Copper, Zinc, Brass, &c. Illustrations. 8vo. 21s.

———— Metallurgy of Iron and Steel. Illustrations. 8vo. 42s.

———— Metallurgy of Lead, Silver, Gold, Platinum, Nickel, Cobalt, Antimony, Bismuth, Arsenic, &c. Illustrations. 8vo. (In the Press.)

PHILLIPP (C. S. M.) On Jurisprudence. 8vo. 12s.

PHILLIPS' (JOHN) Memoirs of William Smith, (the Father of Geology). Portrait. 8vo. 7s. 6d.

———— Geology of Yorkshire, The Coast, and Limestone District. Plates. 4to. Part I., 20s.—Part II., 30s.

———— Rivers, Mountains, and Sea Coast of Yorkshire. With Essays on the Climate, Scenery, and Ancient Inhabitants. Second Edition, Plates. 8vo. 15s.

PHILPOTTS' (Bishop) Letters to the late Charles Butler, on his
" Book of the Roman Catholic Church." *New Edition.* Post 8vo. 6s.

POPE'S (Alexander) Life and Works. *A New Edition.* Containing nearly 500 unpublished Letters. Edited, with a New Life,
Introductions and Notes, by Rev. Whitwell Elwin. Portraits
8vo. (*In the Press.*)

PORTER'S (Rev. J. L.) Five Years in Damascus. With Travels to
Palmyra, Lebanon and other Scripture Sites. Map and Woodcuts.
2 Vols. Post 8vo. 21s.

————— Handbook for Syria and Palestine: including an Account
of the Geography, History, Antiquities, and Inhabitants of these Countries,
the Peninsula of Sinai, Edom, and the Syrian Desert. Maps. 2 Vols.
Post 8vo. 24s.

PRAYER-BOOK (Illustrated), with Borders, Initials, Vignettes, &c. Edited, with Notes, by Rev. Thos. James. Medium
8vo. 18s. cloth; 31s. 6d. calf; 36s. morocco.

PUSS IN BOOTS. With 12 Illustrations. By Otto Speckter.
16mo. 1s. 6d. or Coloured, 2s. 6d.

QUARTERLY REVIEW (The). 8vo. 6s.

RAMBLES among the Turkomans and Bedaweens of the Syrian
Deserts. Post 8vo. 10s. 6d.

RANKE'S (Leopold) History of the Popes of Rome during the
16th and 17th Centuries. Translated from the German by Sarah
Austin. 3 Vols. 8vo. 30s.

RAWLINSON'S (Rev. George) Herodotus. A New English
Version. Edited with Notes and Essays. Assisted by Sir Henry
Rawlinson and Sir J. G. Wilkinson. *Second Edition.* Maps and
Woodcut. 4 Vols. 8vo. 48s.

————————— Five Great Monarchies of the Ancient World,
Chaldæa, Assyria, Media, Babylonia, and Persia. With Maps and 650
Illustrations. 4 Vols. 8vo. 16s. each.

————————— Historical Evidences of the truth of the Scripture
Records stated anew. *Second Edition.* 8vo. 14s.

REED'S (E. J.) Practical Treatise on Shipbuilding in Iron and
Steel. With 250 Illustrations. 8vo. (*In the Press*)

REJECTED ADDRESSES (The). By James and Horace Smith.
Fcap. 8vo. 1s.

RENNIE'S (D. F.) British Arms in Peking, 1860; Kagosima,
1862. Post 8vo. 12s.

————————— Peking and the Pekingese: Being a Narrative of
the First Year of the British Embassy in China. Illustrations. 2 Vols.
Post 8vo. 24s.

————————— Story of Bhotan and the Dooar War; including Sketches of a Residence in the Himalayas and Visit to Bhotan in
1865. Map and Woodcut. Post 8vo. 12s.

REYNOLDS' (Sir Joshua) Life and Times. Commenced by
C. R. Leslie, R.A., continued and concluded by Tom Taylor. Portraits
and Illustrations. 2 Vols. 8vo. 42s.

————— Descriptive Catalogue of his Works. With Notices
of their present owners and localities. By Tom Taylor and Charles
W. Franks. With Illustrations. Fcap. 4to. (*In the Press.*)

RICARDO'S (David) Political Works. With a Notice of his
Life and Writings. By J. R. M'Culloch. *New Edition.* 8vo. 16s.

RIPA'S (Father) Memoirs during Thirteen Years' Residence at the
Court of Peking. From the Italian. Post 8vo. 2s.

ROBERTSON'S (Canon) History of the Christian Church, from the Apostolic Age to the Death of Boniface VIII., A.D. 1122—1304. 3 Vols. 8vo.

ROBINSON'S (Rev. Dr.) Biblical Researches in Palestine and the Adjacent Regions; a Journal of Travels in 1838 and 1852. *Third Edition.* Maps. 3 Vols. 8vo. 42s.

———————— Physical Geography of the Holy Land. Post 8vo. 10s. 6d.

ROME (Student's History of). From the Earliest Times to the Establishment of the Empire. By Dean Liddell. Woodcuts. Post 8vo. 7s. 6d.

——— (Smaller History of). By Wm. Smith, LL.D. Woodcuts. 16mo. 3s. 6d.

ROWLAND'S (David) Manual of the English Constitution; Its Rise, Growth, and Present State. Post 8vo. 10s. 6d.

———————— Laws of Nature the Foundation of Morals. Post 8vo. 6s.

RUNDELL'S (Mrs.) Domestic Cookery, adapted for Private Families. *New Edition.* Woodcuts. Fcap. 8vo. 5s.

RUSSELL'S (Rutherfurd) History of the Heroes of Medicine. Portraits. 8vo. 14s.

RUXTON'S (George F.) Travels in Mexico; with Adventures among the Wild Tribes and Animals of the Prairies and Rocky Mountains. Post 8vo. 3s. 6d.

SALE'S (Sir Robert) Brigade in Affghanistan. With an Account of the Defence of Jellalabad. By Rev. G. R. Gleig. Post 8vo. 2s.

SALLESBURY'S (Edward) "Children of the Lake." A Poem. Fcap. 8vo. 4s. 6d.

SANDWITH'S (Humphry) Siege of Kars. Post 8vo. 3s. 6d.

SCOTT'S (G. Gilbert) Secular and Domestic Architecture, Present and Future. 8vo. 9s.

– – ——— (Master of Baliol) University Sermons. Post 8vo. 8s. 6d.

SCROPE'S (G. P.) Geology and Extinct Volcanoes of Central France. Illustrations. Medium 8vo. 30s.

SHAW'S (T. B.) Manual of English Literature. Edited, with Notes and Illustrations, by Dr. Wm. Smith. Post 8vo. 7s. 6d.

———————— Specimens of English Literature. Selected from the Chief Writers. Edited by Wm. Smith, LL.D. Post 8vo. 7s. 6d.

SHIRLEY (Evelyn P.) on Deer and Deer Parks, or some Account of English Parks, with Notes on the Management of Deer. Illustrations. 4to. 21s.

SIERRA LEONE; Described in Letters to Friends at Home. By A Lady. Post 8vo. 3s. 6d.

SIMMONS (Capt. T. F.) on the Constitution and Practice of Courts-Martial; with a Summary of the Law of Evidence. *Sixth and Revised Edition.* 8vo. (*In the Press.*)

SMITH'S (Rev. A. C.) Attractions of the Nile and its Banks. A Journal of Travels in Egypt and Nubia. Woodcuts. 2 Vols. Post 8vo.

SOUTH'S (John F.) Household Surgery; or, Hints on Emergencies. *Seventeenth Thousand.* Woodcuts. Fcp. 8vo. 4s. 6d.

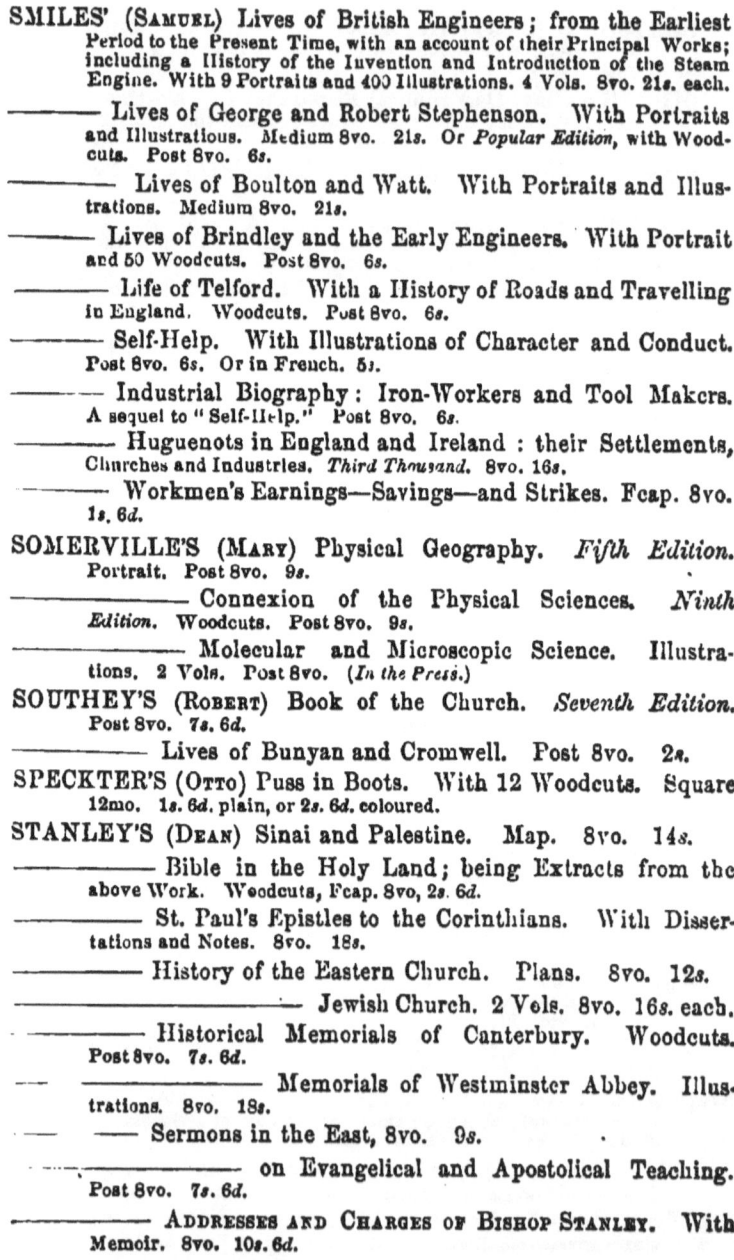

SMILES' (SAMUEL) Lives of British Engineers; from the Earliest Period to the Present Time, with an account of their Principal Works; including a History of the Invention and Introduction of the Steam Engine. With 9 Portraits and 400 Illustrations. 4 Vols. 8vo. 21s. each.

————— Lives of George and Robert Stephenson. With Portraits and Illustrations. Medium 8vo. 21s. Or *Popular Edition*, with Woodcuts. Post 8vo. 6s.

————— Lives of Boulton and Watt. With Portraits and Illustrations. Medium 8vo. 21s.

————— Lives of Brindley and the Early Engineers. With Portrait and 50 Woodcuts. Post 8vo. 6s.

————— Life of Telford. With a History of Roads and Travelling in England. Woodcuts. Post 8vo. 6s.

————— Self-Help. With Illustrations of Character and Conduct. Post 8vo. 6s. Or in French. 5s.

————— Industrial Biography: Iron-Workers and Tool Makers. A sequel to "Self-Help." Post 8vo. 6s.

————— Huguenots in England and Ireland : their Settlements, Churches and Industries. *Third Thousand.* 8vo. 16s.

————— Workmen's Earnings—Savings—and Strikes. Fcap. 8vo. 1s. 6d.

SOMERVILLE'S (MARY) Physical Geography. *Fifth Edition.* Portrait. Post 8vo. 9s.

————— Connexion of the Physical Sciences. *Ninth Edition.* Woodcuts. Post 8vo. 9s.

————— Molecular and Microscopic Science. Illustrations. 2 Vols. Post 8vo. (*In the Press.*)

SOUTHEY'S (ROBERT) Book of the Church. *Seventh Edition.* Post 8vo. 7s. 6d.

————— Lives of Bunyan and Cromwell. Post 8vo. 2s.

SPECKTER'S (OTTO) Puss in Boots. With 12 Woodcuts. Square 12mo. 1s. 6d. plain, or 2s. 6d. coloured.

STANLEY'S (DEAN) Sinai and Palestine. Map. 8vo. 14s.

————— Bible in the Holy Land; being Extracts from the above Work. Woodcuts. Fcap. 8vo, 2s. 6d.

————— St. Paul's Epistles to the Corinthians. With Dissertations and Notes. 8vo. 18s.

————— History of the Eastern Church. Plans. 8vo. 12s.

————— Jewish Church. 2 Vols. 8vo. 16s. each.

————— Historical Memorials of Canterbury. Woodcuts. Post 8vo. 7s. 6d.

————— Memorials of Westminster Abbey. Illustrations. 8vo. 18s.

————— Sermons in the East, 8vo. 9s.

————— on Evangelical and Apostolical Teaching. Post 8vo. 7s. 6d.

————— ADDRESSES AND CHARGES OF BISHOP STANLEY. With Memoir. 8vo. 10s. 6d.

SMITH'S (Dr. Wm.) Dictionary of the Bible; its Antiquities, Biography, Geography, and Natural History. Illustrations. 3 Vols. 8vo. 105s.

———— Concise Bible Dictionary, for Families and Students. Illustrations. Medium 8vo. 21s.

———— Smaller Bible Dictionary, for Schools and Young Persons. Illustrations. Post 8vo. 7s. 6d.

———— Dictionary of Christian Antiquities: from the Times of the Apostles to the Age of Charlemagne. Illustrations. Medium. 8vo. (In preparation.)

———— Biblical Atlas. Folio. (In preparation.)

———— Greek and Roman Antiquities. Woodcuts. 8vo. 42s.

———— Greek and Roman Biography and Mythology. Woodcuts. 3 Vols. 8vo. 5l. 15s. 6d.

———— Greek and Roman Geography. Woodcuts. 2 Vols. 8vo. 80s.

———— Classical Atlas. Folio. (In preparation.)

———— Classical Dictionary, for the Higher Forms. With 750 Woodcuts. 8vo. 18s.

———— Smaller Classical Dictionary. With 200 Woodcuts. Crown 8vo. 7s. 6d.

———— Smaller Dictionary of Greek and Roman Antiquities. With 200 Woodcuts. Crown 8vo. 7s. 6d.

———— Copious and Critical English-Latin Dictionary. 8vo and 12mo. (Nearly Ready.)

———— Complete Latin English Dictionary. With Tables of the Roman Calendar, Measures, Weights, and Money. 8vo. 21s.

———— Smaller Latin-English Dictionary. 12mo. 7s. 6d.

———— Latin-English Vocabulary; for Phædrus, Cornelius Nepos, and Cæsar. 12mo. 3s. 6d.

———— Principia Latina—Part I. A Grammar, Delectus, and Exercise Book, with Vocabularies. Sixth Edition. 12mo. 3s. 6d.

———————————— Part II. A Reading-book of Mythology, Geography, Roman Antiquities, and History. With Notes and Dictionary. Third Edition. 12mo. 3s. 6d.

———————————— Part III. A Latin Poetry Book. Hexameters and Pentameters; Eclog. Ovidianæ; Latin Prosody, &c. Second Edition. 12mo. 3s. 6d.

———————————— Part IV. Latin Prose Composition. Rules of Syntax, with Examples, Explanations of Synonyms, and Exercises on the Syntax. Second Edition. 12mo. 3s. 6d.

———————————— Part V. Short Tales and Anecdotes for Translation into Latin. 12mo. 3s.

———— Student's Latin Grammar for the Higher Forms. Post 8vo. 6s.

———— Smaller Latin Grammar, for the Middle and Lower Forms. 12mo. 3s. 6d.

———— Initia Græca, Part I. An Introduction to Greek; comprehending Grammar, Delectus, and Exercise-book. With Vocabularies. 12mo. 3s. 6d.

———— Initia Græca, Part II. A Reading Book. Containing Short Tales, Anecdotes, Fables, Mythology, and Grecian History. Arranged in a systematic Progression, with a Lexicon. 12mo. 3s. 6d.

———— Initia Græca, Part III. Greek Prose Composition. Containing the Rules of Syntax, with copious Examples and Exercises. 12mo. (In preparation.)

SMITH'S (Dr. Wm.) Student's Greek Grammar for the Higher Forms. By Professor Curtius. Post 8vo. 6s.
———— Smaller Greek Grammar for the Middle and Lower Forms. 12mo. 3s. 6d.
———— Smaller History of England. With Illustrations. 16mo. 3s. 6d.
———— History of Greece. With Illustrations. 16mo. 3s. 6d.
———— History of Rome. With Illustrations. 16mo. 3s. 6d.
———— Classical Mythology. With Translations from the Ancient Poets. Illustrations. 12mo. 3s. 6d.
———— Scripture History. With Woodcuts. 16mo. (In preparation.)

STUDENT'S HUME. A History of England from the Invasion of Julius Cæsar to the Revolution of 1688. By David Hume. Corrected and continued to 1858. Woodcuts. Post 8vo. 7s. 6d.
  *** Questions on the above Work, 12mo. 2s.
———— HISTORY OF FRANCE; from the Earliest Times to the Establishment of the Second Empire, 1852. By W. H. Pearson, M.A. Woodcuts. Post 8vo. 7s. 6d.
———— HISTORY OF GREECE; from the Earliest Times to the Roman Conquest. With the History of Literature and Art. By Wm. Smith, LL.D. Woodcuts. Crown 8vo. 7s. 6d.
  *** Questions on the above Work, 12mo. 2s.
———— HISTORY OF ROME; from the Earliest Times to the Establishment of the Empire. With the History of Literature and Art. By Dean Liddell. Woodcuts. Crown 8vo. 7s. 6d.
———— GIBBON; an Epitome of the Decline and Fall of the Roman Empire. Incorporating the Researches of Recent Commentators. Woodcuts. Post 8vo. 7s. 6d.
———— OLD TESTAMENT HISTORY; from the Creation to the Return of the Jews from Captivity. Maps and Woodcuts. Post 8vo. 7s. 6d.
———— NEW TESTAMENT HISTORY. With an Introduction connecting the History of the Old and New Testaments. Maps and Woodcuts. Post 8vo. 7s. 6d.
———— BLACKSTONE: a Systematic Abridgment of the Entire Commentaries. By R. Malcolm Kerr, LL.D. Post 8vo. 7s. 6d.
———— MANUAL OF ANCIENT GEOGRAPHY. By Rev. W. L. Bevan, M.A. Woodcuts. Post 8vo. 7s. 6d.
———— MODERN GEOGRAPHY. By Rev. W. L. Bevan. Woodcuts. Post 8vo. (In the Press.)
———— ECCLESIASTICAL HISTORY. Containing the History of the Christian Church from the Close of the New Testament Canon to the Reformation. Post 8vo. (In preparation.)
———— MORAL PHILOSOPHY. With Quotations and References. By William Fleming, D.D. Post 8vo. 7s. 6d.
———— ENGLISH LANGUAGE. By Geo. P. Marsh. Post 8vo. 7s. 6d.
———— ENGLISH LITERATURE. By T. B. Shaw, M.A. Post 8vo. 7s. 6d.
———— SPECIMENS OF ENGLISH LITERATURE. Selected from the Chief Writers. By Thomas B. Shaw, M.A. Post 8vo. 7s. 6d.

STANHOPE'S (EARL) History of England, from the Peace of Utrecht to the Peace of Versailles, 1713-83. *Library Edition.* 7 vols. 8vo. 93s. Or *Popular Edition.* 7 Vols. Post 8vo. 5s. each.

———————— British India, from its Origin till the Peace of 1783. Post 8vo. 3s. 6d.

———————— "Forty-Five;" a Narrative of the Rebellion in Scotland. Post 8vo. 3s.

———————— Spain under Charles the Second. Post 8vo. 6s. 6d.

———————— Historical and Critical Essays. Post 8vo. 3s. 6d.

———————— Life of Belisarius. Post 8vo. 10s. 6d.

———————— ———— Condé. Post 8vo. 3s. 6d.

———————— ———— William Pitt. With Extracts from his MS. Papers. Portraits. 4 Vols. Post 8vo. 24s.

———————— Miscellanies. Post 8vo. 5s. 6d.

———————— Story of Joan of Arc. Fcap. 8vo. 1s.

ST. JOHN'S (CHARLES) Wild Sports and Natural History of the Highlands. Post 8vo. 3s. 6d.

———————— (BAYLE) Adventures in the Libyan Desert and the Oasis of Jupiter Ammon. Woodcuts. Post 8vo. 2s.

STEPHENSONS' (GEORGE and ROBERT) Lives. By SAMUEL SMILES. With Portraits and 70 Illustrations. Medium 8vo. 21s. Or *Popular Edition* with Woodcuts. Post 8vo. 6s.

STOTHARD'S (THOS.) Life. With Personal Reminiscences. By Mrs. BRAY. With Portrait and 60 Woodcuts. 4to. 21s.

STREET'S (G. E.) Gothic Architecture in Spain. From Personal Observations during several journeys through that country. Illustrations. Medium 8vo. 50s.

SULLIVAN'S (SIR EDWARD) Princes, Warriors, and Statesmen of India; an Historical Narrative of the most important Events, from the Invasion of Mahmoud of Ghizni to that of Nadir Shah. 8vo. 12s.

SUMNER (GEORGE HENRY), M.A. Principles at Stake, being Essays on the Church Questions of the day. By various Writers. 8vo.
(*In the Press.*)

SWIFT'S (JONATHAN) Life, Letters, Journals, and Works. By JOHN FORSTER. 8vo. (*In Preparation.*)

SYBEL'S (VON) History of Europe during the French Revolution, 1789—1795. Translated from the German. By WALTER C. PERRY. Vols. 1 & 2. 8vo. 24s.

SYME'S (PROFESSOR) Principles of Surgery. *5th Edition.* 8vo. 12s.

TAIT'S (BISHOP) Dangers and Safeguards of Modern Theology, containing Suggestions to the Theological Student under Present Difficulties. 8vo. 9s.

TAYLOR'S (HENRY) Notes from Life—on Money, Humility and Independence, Wisdom, Choice in Marriage, Children, and Life Poetic. Fcap. 8vo. 2s.

THOMSON'S (ARCHBISHOP) Sermons, Preached at Lincoln's Inn. 8vo. 10s. 6d.

———————— Life in the Light of God's Word. Post 8vo. 6s.

THREE-LEAVED MANUAL OF FAMILY PRAYER; arranged so as to save the trouble of turning the Pages backwards and forwards. Royal 8vo. 2s.

TREMENHEERE (H. S.); The Franchise a Privilege and not a Right, proved by the Political Experience of the Ancients. Fcap. 8vo. 2s. 6d.

TRISTRAM'S (H. B.) Great Sahara, or Wanderings South of the Atlas Mountains. Map and Illustrations. Post 8vo. 15s.

TWISS' (HORACE) Life of Lord Chancellor Eldon, with Selections from his Correspondence. Portrait. *Third Edition.* 2 Vols. Post 8vo. 21s.

TYTLER'S (PATRICK FRASER) Memoirs. By REV. J. W. BURGON, M.A. 8vo. 9s.

VAMBERY'S (ARMINIUS) Travels in Central Asia, from Teheran across the Turkoman Desert on the Eastern Shore of the Caspian to Khiva, Bokhara, and Samarcand in 1863. Map and Illustrations. 8vo. 21s.

VAN LENNEP (HENRY J.) Missionary Travels in Little Known Parts of Asia Minor. With Map and Illustrations. 2 Vols. Post 8vo. *(In preparation.)*

VAUGHAN'S (REV. DR.) Sermons preached in Harrow School. 8vo. 10s. 6d.

WAAGEN'S (DR.) Treasures of Art in Great Britain. Being an Account of the Chief Collections of Paintings, Sculpture, Manuscripts, Miniatures, &c. &c., in this Country. Obtained from Personal Inspection during Visits to England. 4 Vols. 8vo.

WELLINGTON'S (THE DUKE OF) Despatches during his various Campaigns. 8 Vols. 8vo. 21s. each.
————————— Supplementary Despatches. Vols. I. to XII. 8vo. 20s. each.
————————— Civil and Political Correspondence. Vols. I. to III. 8vo. 20s. each.
————————— Selections from Despatches and General Orders. 8vo. 18s.
————————— Speeches in Parliament. 2 Vols. 8vo. 42s.

WHITE'S (HENRY) Massacre of St. Bartholomew. Preceded by a History of the Religious Wars in the Reign of Charles IX. Based on a Personal Examination of Documents in the Archives of France. With Illustrations. 8vo. 16s.

WHYMPER'S (FREDERICK) Travels and Adventures in Alaska and on the River Yukon, the Russian Territory, now ceded to the United States, and Visits to other parts of the North Pacific. With Illustrations. 8vo. *(In preparation.)*

WILKINSON'S (SIR J. G.) Popular Account of the Private Life, Manners, and Customs of the Ancient Egyptians. With 500 Woodcuts. 2 Vols. Post 8vo. 12s.

WILSON'S (BISHOP DANIEL) Life, Letters, and Journals. By Rev. JOSIAH BATEMAN. *Second Edition.* Illustrations. Post 8vo. 9s.
————————— (GENL. SIR ROBERT) Secret History of the French Invasion of Russia, and Retreat of the French Army, 1812. *Second Edition.* 8vo. 15s.
————————— Private Diary of Travels, Personal Services, and Public Events, during Missions and Employments in Spain, Sicily, Turkey, Russia, Poland, Germany, &c. 1812-14. 2 Vols. 8vo. 26s.
————————— Autobiographical Memoirs. Containing an Account of his Early Life down to the Peace of Tilsit. Portrait. 2 Vols. 8vo. 26s.

WOOD (SIR W. P.) On the Continuity of Scripture, as Declared by the Testimony of Our Lord and of the Evangelists and Apostles. *Second Edition.* Post 8vo. 6s.

WORDSWORTH'S (ARCHDEACON) Journal of a Tour in Athens and Attica. *Third Edition.* Plates. Post 8vo. 8s. 6d.
————————— Pictorial, Descriptive, and Historical Account of Greece. *New and Cheaper Edition.* With 600 Woodcuts. Royal 8vo.

BRADBURY, EVANS, AND CO., PRINTERS, WHITEFRIARS.